SEDUCED

Beth Ciotta

PRESS ®

Jewel Imprint: Ruby
Medallion Press, Inc.
Florida, USA

Dedication:

For my husband, Steve.
The true love of all my lives.

Published 2005 by Medallion Press, Inc.
225 Seabreeze Ave.
Palm Beach, FL 33480

The MEDALLION PRESS LOGO
is a registered tradmark of Medallion Press, Inc.

Printed in the United States of America

Library of Congress Cataloging-in-Publication Data

Ciotta, Beth.
  Seduced / Beth Ciotta..
    p. cm.
  ISBN 1-932815-23-6
  1. Government investigators--Fiction. 2. Burn out (Psychology)--Fiction.
3. Actresses--Fiction. I Title.
  PS3603.I58S43 2005
  813'.6--dc22

                                            2005000478

ACKNOWLEDGEMENTS:

My thanks to:

Mary Stella and Julia Templeton for critiquing my work and brightening my darkest days with your enthusiastic cheers of support. Cat Cody for her insight on martial arts. Donna Callaghan, DNSc, APRN, BC for her medical advise. Connie Perry for keeping me sane. Adam Mock for his dynamic cover art. Helen Rosburg and Leslie Burbank for their never ending support and guidance, and for believing in a cast of characters who will live forever in my heart.

CHAPTER ONE

Superstition Mountains: Arizona

Snake dead ahead."

"Rattlesnake. Just veer off and don't provoke."

"Do I *look* like a bonehead?"

Joseph Bogart peered over the rim of his UV shades at his adopted brother, Colin Murphy—former Marine/current protection specialist AKA major badass. The man not only veered off, but scaled a six-foot boulder in the rock-choked gully to bypass the basking serpent. Joe adjusted his own path, navigating a dense patch of desert chaparral and cactus, before delivering a good-natured rib. "Since when are you afraid of anything, let alone a snake?"

"Since a slithery bastard swam up my shorts in '97. Don't ask." Murphy quickened his pace, borrowed hiking boots eating up the challenging terrain of the Siphon Draw - Flat Iron Trail despite the steep loose slope. "And I'm not afraid, just cautious."

"Wuss."

Without turning, Murphy flipped him the bird.

Smiling, Joe snagged his water bottle from the side pocket of his lightweight backpack and drank. Some things, gratefully, never changed. Even though their chosen careers had kept them apart for extended periods over the last twenty-odd-years, they were still in best buddy sync. "Gotta say, I miss you, Murph."

"Easy fix." The Irish-born, Italian-reared man turned and bullied him with one of those I'm-six-months-older-than-you-hence-I-am-wiser brother gazes. "Come home."

Damn, Bogart. Set yourself up, why don't you? Just the thought of heading back to the east coast, dealing with family and ex-coworkers at the Bureau, bunched his neck muscles. He rolled his head to ease the kinks, pocketed the water bottle, and took the lead. "We've been through this."

"No, we haven't. I brought it up. You shut me down."

"Like I said."

"Paulie Falcone's behind bars. Since when are you afraid of anything . . . let alone a wiseguy?"

Smirking, Joe peered over his shoulder, happy for the company if not the topic of discussion. Murphy had flown from Atlantic City, New Jersey to Phoenix, Arizona for a meeting with a prospective client. Since he was in the area he'd tagged on two extra days to visit with his "brother turned recluse". Recluse, he'd assured Murph, the same as he'd assured his parents, and former boss in the organized crime section, was an exaggeration. "You're determined to discuss the hell out of my resignation, aren't you?"

"Rather than handling life, you're hiding from it. *That's* what I'm determined to discuss."

A pro at evasion, Joe turned his attention back to the trail. Up ahead, Flat Iron rose in four-hundred-foot sheer cliffs from the canyon head, a huge outcropping of volcanic rock jutting forth like the bow of a ship. His honed body buzzed with the familiar challenge. He made this strenuous trek into the Superstitions at least twice a week.

"Seven months ago you were a top fed kicking ass on organized crime," Murphy continued. "Now you're giving desert jeep tours to snowbird tourists. If you don't want to deal with government bullshit, come work for me."

"Babysitting paranoid dignitaries isn't my style."

"There's more to executive protection than stereotypical bodyguard duties, and you know it."

Yeah, he knew. He also knew Murphy wouldn't take the slight to heart, but he had hoped to derail the conversation. He latched onto an overhang and got a toehold. "Concentrating here."

"Wuss."

"Save your breath, hot shot. You're going to need it." Though the ascent up the slick, narrow wall didn't call for technical climbing skills, it did require concentration and careful hand and foot placement. Overall, the five-mile hike tested a person's strength and stamina. Even though his brother was in prime condition, Joe perversely hoped he'd feel the burn big time tomorrow. Payback for his pain-in-the-ass nagging. "Careful you don't stick your hand into any crevices out of your line of sight." He quirked a devilish grin. "Snakes."

"You know, when you put your heart in it, you can be a real bastard."

He heard the smile in Murphy's voice, knew the comment had been made in jest, but all the same his stomach cramped with familiar guilt. He'd slept with an insecure, substance abuser and conned her into believing that he loved her in order to crack down an international drug smuggling ring and a notorious Jersey crime family. To make matters worse, every time he'd bedded Julietta Marcella, niece of mobster Paulie Falcone, he'd fantasized about Sofia Marino, another jaded, confused soul. His sordid undercover antics, no matter the success of the case, pretty much qualified him as a bastard.

Murphy held silent as they ascended the steep, rocky slope. Joe focused on the climb, battled the guilt . . . the longing. Two women. Two mistakes. One he'd never have a chance to rectify.

Ninety lung-busting minutes later they reached the top of the large, flat plateau. Straight ahead, a 150-foot-high grouping of rounded boulders known as the 'hoodoos'. At 5,027 feet they marked the highest point on the western massif. Joe wiped his dusty hands on the seat of his loose-fitting jeans as he led Murphy to the tip of the Flat Iron, affording them a breathtaking view in every direction but east. Nearly three thousand feet below sprawled Gold Canyon, the small desert community he now called home. Five miles down the pike: Apache Junction, a quaint, but fast-growing town, while further west, forty-five minutes away via US Highway 60, shimmered the Valley of the Sun, specifically Phoenix and its surrounding boroughs.

Hands on hips, Murphy scanned the sprawling desert and chaotic jumble of distant hills. "Worth the climb."

Joe tossed his gear at his feet. "Always is." At the base of the trail vegetation had been typical of the Upper Sonoran Desert: mesquite, paloverde, jojoba, prickly pear, saguaro, and hedgehog cactus. The temperature climbed toward ninety. Not bad for early May. Up here the air was cooler, the vegetation sparse. Stark beauty and rugged calm. "I come up here to think."

"Yeah?" Murphy peered over the edge, a sheer drop-off to the lower plateaus, then farther to the desert floor. He glanced back, dark brows knitted with concern. "What do you think about?"

"I sure as hell don't think about jumping." Shaking his

head in disgust, he squatted and unzipped his backpack. "You're as bad as the Bureau's shrink. I'm not suicidal."

"But you do have issues."

"Who doesn't?" Relegating thoughts of Julietta to an inner crevice as deep and infested as the canyon, he pulled two southwestern grilled sandwiches from his bag, and tossed one to Murphy. "Light seven-grain bread, turkey breast, reduced-fat Monterey Jack, and salsa." He kissed his fingertips in a wholly Italian gesture. "*Delizioso.*"

"No doubt." Murphy sat on the ground next to Joe and unwrapped his lunch. "No one cooks like you. Except Mom." He cocked his head. "Speaking of. . ."

"I'll call her tonight. As soon as I get back from taking you to the airport. Speaking of cooking," he said, changing the subject before Murphy could heap more guilt onto his already heavy load. "How's Lulu coming along in the kitchen?" A children's storybook teller and jack-of-all-artistic-trades, Murphy's bubbly wife's creativity stopped short of cooking. After nearly burning down his house while trying to fry eggs, Joe was shocked Murphy even let her near the stove. Murph had a thing about fire. He had an even bigger thing for his wife.

"I've always thought given the willingness to learn, anything is possible."

Reading into that, Joe gave a sympathetic nod. "She's hopeless."

"Pretty much."

"From the smile on your face I'm guessing you don't give a damn." He bit into his sandwich thinking his brother practically buzzed with contentment. Must be nice.

"Kind of hard to worry about my stomach when my heart's overflowing."

Joe choked on his turkey, wiped toast crumbs from his chin, and gaped. "I can't believe that sentimental puke came out of your gutter mouth."

Murphy swigged from his water bottle then dragged his muscled forearm over his moist brow. "How's this? I'm so fucking in love, who cares if her gourmet best is P&J on wheat?"

He laughed. "Better. Sort of. Christ, don't scare me like that."

"Love warps a man." He bit into his sandwich, chewed, and studied Joe an uncomfortable minute. "Almost as much as stifled infatuation."

Joe lifted an eyebrow.

"Still keeping tabs on Sofia?"

"No."

"Liar."

Joe concentrated on his lunch, hoping his brother couldn't read the severity of his sweaty-palmed obsession. He knew exactly where Sofia Marino was, who she was seeing, and what she was doing. How could he not? Her exotic face and killer body had made the cover of more than one Hollyweird gossip rag over the last few months. He didn't buy the tabloids, didn't have to. They were at his fingertips every time he stood in a check-out line. Who could resist skimming? And okay, yes, he visited her fan site twice or twenty times a week, and watched her farfetched TV cable show, "Spy Girl", every Wednesday night. Again, he couldn't help it. It was like watching a train wreck. Morbid fascination. She'd gone from Broadway bomb to TV action star in less than a year, with a short stint in between as a skimpily-costumed casino greeter girl. Her costumes were still provocative, a cross between Emma Peel of the Avengers and that Tomb Raider chick, but now she had a hefty bank account and a league of fanatic fans. Mostly teenage girls and horny, techno-geek males.

Unlike those espionage-wannabes, *he* did not have a boner for Cherry Onatop—and what kind of lame, rip-off Bond girl name was *that*? No, he'd fallen in lust with Sofia Chiquita Marino, pre-Cherry, during Operation Candy Jar. He'd been seduced by a vulnerability he was certain no one other than her sister even knew existed. A vulnerability that would suck the strength and sense out of him if he allowed himself to explore their undeniable chemistry.

He didn't need or want the complication. Just now he needed to keep life simple.

"Rudy Gallow bought a bed and breakfast up in Vermont," Murphy said of a mutual acquaintance. "A group of us are heading up there for a week—Lulu and I, Jake and Afia, Jean-Pierre and Sofia—partly to relax, partly to give Gallow someone to practice on." He shrugged. "What the hell? It's gratis, Gallow's an excellent cook, and I hear the scenery's kick-ass. Company's not bad either. You should come."

Joe stuffed the empty sandwich bags into his backpack. "Let me put this in words you can understand. Not just no, but *hell* no."

"I know what the tabloids say, but Sofia's not seeing anyone. Lulu would know. Jean-Pierre would know. The guy's living with her, for chrissake. He would have told Rudy and Rudy would have told Afia."

"Who would've told Jake, and now since you two are tight again, Jake would've told you. Christ, Murph. Three couples, one of them gay, and two incompatible, but hot-for-each-other singles. You're asking me to fly to Bumfuck, Vermont to take part in a warped version of *The Big Chill*."

"Good movie. Better soundtrack. Percy Sledge. Marvin Gaye. Smokey Robinson."

"You're still hooked on Motown?" Joe smoothed his thick, shoulder-length hair off of his face, pulling it into a stubby ponytail. "Step out of the sixties, man."

"Look who's talking, Mr. Tie-dye-T-shirt. All you're missing is a joint and a peace sign. When are you going to cut your hair? What's with the goatee?"

Once a Marine, always a Marine. Murphy sported a buzz cut and a clean-shaven jaw. When he wasn't undercover,

Joe normally copped a similar look, topping it off with the classic dark suit, white shirt, and black tie. Stereotypical G-man right down to the dark shades. He'd kept the shades, protection against the Arizona sun, but chucked the suit in favor of T-shirts, jeans, and cargo shorts. The hair and the beard, well, hell, once a rebel always a rebel. He stroked his groomed facial hair, waggled his eyebrows. "Women dig this thing."

Murphy rose. "So you're not a total recluse then. You're actually *dating*?"

Joe pushed to his feet, and slung the pack over his shoulder. "Let's just say I'm not lonely."

"Anyone special? Because this thing with Sofia. . ."

"There is no *thing* with Sofia." He felt his calm slipping. A calm he'd fought hard for these last few months. There'd been a kiss. Two kisses. Two un-frickin'-believable kisses. But there was no *thing*. After utilizing a pressure point to knock her unconscious, he was relatively certain Sofia would just as soon spend a week with a baboon than with him. Which was fine, no *perfect*. "Stop trying to fix me up. Stop trying to fix my life. I'm fine. I'm happy."

"Bullshit."

"Fuck you." The calm exploded. Shards of guilt and anger pierced his toughened skin, making him edgy and restless. *Dammit*. He searched the vivid blue sky, summoning tranquility. Turkey vultures circled above, probably hoping for remnants of their lunch, but vultures,

Christ, wasn't *that* an ominous sign?

"You didn't kill that girl, Bogie."

"Yeah?" He eyed the precarious path beyond the hoo-doos, needing to burn off the anxiety. He turned his back on his brother, faced his past, and hit the trail. "I guess that depends on who you ask."

CHAPTER TWO

Sofia Marino woke up with a cell phone in one hand, a gun in the other, and the nauseating feeling that she'd done something wrong. Had she blown a stunt? The director insisted on using a stunt double for precision driving and high falls, but she always tried to take on as much as possible.

Especially hand-to-hand combat.

She'd been training in martial arts for almost nine months. The longest she'd stuck with schooling of any kind. "*You need to pay attention in class,*" Joseph Bogart had once said after easily besting her. Arrogant prick. Then again, his criticism had worked as excellent incentive. Her hard-earned skills had cinched her role on "Spy Girl". She wondered if he watched her show. She hated that she cared. The last thing she wanted to obsess on was the man who'd seduced and broken her heart with a single kiss.

Muscles aching, she shoved disheveled hair off of her clammy face and pushed to her feet. Her *bare* feet. Where were her shoes?

Moonlight streamed through a small window, illuminating what looked to be the inside of a tool shed. What scene was this? What episode? Damn, her head ached. Had she taken a hit?

Disoriented, she pushed open the aluminum door, expecting Dirk Brevin to yell, "Cut!" But all she heard was her own uneven breathing. All she saw was the back of a strange house and . . . was that a cactus? She inched closer to the house, wincing with each step. A motion detector light flooded the lawn. A landscaped lawn of desert flora and crushed stone. No wonder her feet hurt.

She stopped and frowned down at the phone. Her personal cell phone. Not Cherry Onatop's compact, secret gadget phone. She blinked at the gun. Not Cherry's gun. The villain's gun, maybe? Had she kicked it out of his hand? Had the actor retaliated and accidentally knocked her out? If this was a set, where were the cast and crew? Where were the lights and cameras?

She swallowed hard, focused on her surroundings. That was definitely a cactus. A cactus, a house she didn't recognize, and distant mountains. A hot, arid breeze ruffled her hair. She smelled sweat, fear. Her heart raced as she licked her dry lips and tried to think past the persistent pounding at the base of her skull.

Phoenix. She was in Phoenix, Arizona. That was it. Not Los Angeles, California. Phoenix. But why? The harder she tried to remember, the more the throbbing increased.

Phone. Gun. Phone. Gun. Her gaze dropped to her linen skirt. *Blood*.

The throbbing intensified. She staggered back toward the tool shed, pulse racing. Why was there blood on her skirt and legs? Wait. Don't panic. It had to be from a squib. A blood pack placed over a charge. Fake blood. Right? *Where is the stunt coordinator?*

She backed into the shed. Her pulse slowed. She felt safer here. Less panicked. How absurd. Safe from what? She placed the gun and phone on a work bench and groped in the dark, squinting—as if that somehow helped—to make out the contents of the moonlit shed. She located a flashlight, excellent, a pair of rubber flip-flops, and an ankle-length rain slicker. Okay, good. Protection for her feet. A coat to cover the blood. The *fake* blood.

This isn't real. This isn't happening. The words echoed in her fuzzy mind.

Head throbbing, Sofia stuffed the gun into the deep pocket of the yellow slicker—God save her from the fury of the prop master if she misplaced a piece of his personal stock—and forced herself to leave the sanctity of the shed.

Battling irrational panic, she rounded the sizable, upscale property and aimed the flashlight at a street sign. Lincoln Drive. She didn't recognize the name. The circular driveway was empty. The house was dark. Maybe the residents were away. No matter. No way was she knocking on the door. Her brain spun in rusty circles, but her gut compelled her to gravitate toward a public place.

Dazed, she meandered down the paved street toward a softly lit, rambling adobe resort. She squinted at the distant red neon sign. *The Camelback Inn.* Surely this place had a lounge. She needed to sit. She needed a drink.

The gun weighed down the left side of the plastic slicker. The phone burned a hole in her sweaty palm.

She needed help.

She hit speed dial, her eyes on the front steps of that inn, her thoughts on a shot of tequila.

"Murphy here."

Her lungs bloomed with relief at the sound of her brother-in-law's no-nonsense voice. A voice of reason in any crisis. She couldn't remember why she was in Phoenix. She was in possession of a gun and covered with blood. That qualified as a crisis, didn't it? *This isn't real. This isn't happening.* "It's Sofia." Her voice sounded weak and shaky to her ears.

Murphy heard it too. "What's wrong? Oh, hell, don't tell me you're canceling the trip to Vermont. Lulu hasn't seen you in months. . ."

"I think I'm in trouble."

"What kind of trouble?"

"I don't know. I . . . "

"Where are you?"

"Phoenix."

"What are you doing in Phoenix?"

"*I don't know.*" Her temples throbbed as she pushed through the front door and moved into the cool, swanky interior of the lobby.

"What do you mean . . . Damn. The plane's leaving the gate. I can't get off and they're going to make me disconnect. Where are you? Exactly."

"The Camelback Inn. Lincoln Drive." She ditched the flashlight and snatched a brochure from a rack on the wall, scanned the address. "Scottsdale." An upscale suburb of Phoenix. She massaged a fierce stabbing in her temple. *How did I get here?*

"Plant your ass in a chair and don't move. Someone will be there in twenty, give or take five."

A professional bodyguard, Murphy had contacts all over the states. Apparently he knew someone in Phoenix. Someone he'd trust with his sister-in-law's welfare. She ignored the curious once-over of the front desk clerk, snapped the slicker to her chin, and shuffled her stolen flip-flops toward quiet conversation and the acoustic strumming of a Spanish guitar. The urge to drink herself into oblivion was overwhelming. "I'll be in the bar."

She disconnected and pocketed the cell. She located a secluded table in a dimly lit corner of the lounge and planted her ass in a chair. She wanted a cigarette and a drink. Her cigarettes were in her purse along with her cash and credit cards. Her purse was MIA.

Like a portion of her memory.

She pressed the heel of her hand to her forehead and fought tears. She was not without resources. She glanced toward the bar. Plenty of men at the bar. Men who'd be willing to buy her a drink, or ten. Four Wall Street types were checking her out right now despite the klutzy shoes and chintzy raincoat. All she had to do was smile. Hell, a slight tilt of her head would do the trick. But then eventually one or all would come over, wanting to sit down. Then she'd be obligated to make small talk or to come up with a clever, unoffending reason as to why they couldn't join her. *I have a headache*, even though it was true, probably wouldn't fly. The last thing she wanted just now was the company of a randy man. And weren't they *all* randy?

"*You're even more beautiful in person.*" The garbled compliment poked through her hazy memory. Her stomach turned.

Instead of smiling at the Brooks Brothers barflies, she slipped into bitch mode, adjusting her expression and body language to telegraph a pointed thought: "*Leave me the hell alone.*"

The trolling businessmen quickly turned their attention

back to the bar.

What do you know? For once the ice princess had an effect. Where she was concerned, men were usually more persistent.

When the waitress appeared, Sofia purposely warmed. Switching character as easily as most people changed underwear, she affected her celebrity persona. She fluffed her processed, signature red hair and flashed a dazzling, mega-buck smile.

"Oh, my gosh," the young woman chirped. "You're Cherry Onatop. Wow. I . . . wow. I *love* your show. Are you on vacation? Shooting on location? Is that why you're dressed like that? Are you staying with us?"

Sofia opted to answer the last question. "Yes, I am." She leaned toward the girl, lowering her voice to a conspiratorial whisper. "Not something I'd like to get around . . . " she glanced at her name tag, "Lisa."

"Low profile. I get it." Lisa hugged her empty tray against her chest and winked. "Actually, lots of stars stay here, although they don't usually hang out in the lounge. Or so I've heard. This is my first night. You're my first VIP." She beamed at Sofia as if to say, *you're really cool for hanging like a normal person.* "So, would you like to run a tab?"

"That would be fabulous," Sofia said, feeling far from normal. *This isn't real. This isn't happening.* "Let's start with a pack of Salems, a Corona and two shots of Cuervo gold." With any luck by the time Murphy's friend arrived, she'd be numb.

CHAPTER THREE

Frank James was pissed. His nose throbbed like a mother. His stringy arm muscles burned from overuse. Instead of whizzing over the border to enjoy a windfall and some prime Mexican booty, he was driving around the outskirts of Phoenix, resisting the urge to strangle his paranoid brother, and wondering how he was going to deal with one crazy bitch.

"Where are we?" Jesse asked.

Frank washed down another painkiller with a swig of beer before glancing sideways. "Even if I knew I wouldn't say." His lanky body vibrated with frustration. "I'm not talking to you, you stupid moron."

"Sure you are. You just called me a stupid moron.

Which, by the way, is an *oxy*moron." The younger James brother wiggled the fingers of his broken hand, something the doctor had suggested to reduce swelling and stiffness. His pretty-boy features contorted in misery. "I hope to sweet Christ that doctor's needle was sterile. Was he even certified? We should've asked for credentials."

"You saw his credentials."

"That framed diploma?" Jesse grunted. "So what? Now days you can forge just about any document so long as you've got the right computer program." He used his forearm to tip back the brim of his Stetson. "At least he wore gloves. Although . . . I didn't actually see where he got them. What if they weren't new? You know, fresh? What if he wore them before and touched someone else's wound? If I hadn't been in such pain, I would've thought to ask." He licked his lips, blew out a breath. "I feel sick."

"Don't start." Wired, Frank tugged at the brim of his own Stetson and gunned their beat up Chrysler down the darkened highway. He had no sympathy. "If you weren't such a germ-a-phobe . . ."

"The clinical term is Verminophobia."

". . . we wouldn't be in the mess to begin with." Jesse's freakish injury had required a tetanus shot and a cast that extended from his knuckles to above the wrist. Broken bones, torn ligaments and cartilage, but it could've been worse. At least his injury was under wraps and wouldn't diminish his appeal with the ladies. Frank looked downright grotesque between his two black eyes and the cotton tubes the doc had stuffed up his swollen, fractured nose. How in the hell was he supposed to get laid when he looked like a fricking monster?

Using his good gloved hand, Jesse wiped down the dashboard with anti-bacterial spray for the second time in ten minutes. "Do you know how many diseases can be transmitted through a simple sneeze or cough?"

"Actually, yes. You list them fairly often."

"The man spit in my face."

"I know. I was there." Talk about a disaster. It's not like they hadn't done what they'd been hired to do. Just that they'd been sloppy about it. Once Frank had regained consciousness, they'd eliminated the evidence, but unfortunately there was a loose thread.

"I want my gun back," Jesse moped.

Breathing through his mouth, Frank envisioned the woman who'd marred his face and threatened the future of the James brothers. He tightened his murderous fingers around the steering wheel and squeezed. "I want more than that."

CHAPTER FOUR

You've got to be kidding. What kind of set up . . .?"

"It's not a set up and I don't have time to argue. I'll call you from the onboard mobile as soon as I'm able." *Chirp.*

Joe tossed his cell phone on the passenger seat. Murphy's voice rang in his ears like a knell. *"Sofia's in trouble. She sounds upset."*

And he was supposed to drop everything and race to her rescue.

Okay, so it's not like he had major plans for the evening. It's not like he'd even cleared the Valley of the Sun. All he had to do was make a U-turn and head back north into Scottsdale. Actually, Lincoln Drive was closer to Paradise

Valley, one of the many offshoots of Metropolitan Phoenix. If Scottsdale was the Beverly Hills of Phoenix, Paradise Valley rivaled Bel-Air. Posh. Almost exclusively residential. Lavish homes, many owned by celebrities. Given Sofia's recent notoriety, it made sense that she'd chosen accommodations in the star-studded area. But, *man*, the Camelback? She had to be raking in the dough.

He gritted his teeth and swung the jeep in the opposite direction. Just his luck she was in his neck of the woods. Or was it vice versa? Of all weekends for Murphy to be visiting. Of all nights to have to drive him to Sky Harbor International. "*It's not a set up.*" It sure as hell felt like one.

He gunned the accelerator, exited Highway 143, and peeled onto 44th Street. The sooner he handled whatever mess she'd gotten herself in, the sooner he could leave. A straight shot until he got to McDonald Drive, a short jog onto Tatum, and then a right onto Lincoln. "*Sofia's in trouble.*" It had to be a man. With Sofia it was always a man.

He spent the next few minutes steeling himself. She'd prick his anger, annihilate his last vestiges of inner calm. She'd piss him off worse than Murphy. She had a real talent for pissing him off. The last time he'd seen Sofia in person he'd gone ballistic. She'd put herself in danger in order to salvage a drug bust. As if that weren't enough, earlier that day she'd challenged a piece-of-shit, persistent ex-lover, and then buckled. She had more moxy than common sense. More sass than substance. In spite of her scorching, exotic beauty and confident, cocky demeanor, she was insecure as hell. And like three-quarters of the male population, he wanted to fill her needs.

With several inches of morning pride.

Oh, yeah. He was a bona fide bastard. Then again, she was a shallow seductress. Toss up as to who was worse for whom.

By the time he parked the jeep and pushed through the doors of The Camelback Inn he'd spun himself into an iron cocoon. She couldn't affect him if she couldn't get to him. He'd solve her problem and hit the road. He wouldn't feel a thing.

Then he saw her.

Who could miss her? Glossy red hair. Shiny yellow coat. She threw back a shot of liquor, and then pursed those enticing, full lips around a cigarette, somehow managing to turn a nasty habit into something erotic.

He was toast.

Jaw clenched, he tamed an untimely hard-on by reminding himself that her troubles probably revolved around a man. Someone she'd slept with in hopes of advancing her career. Someone who'd turned the tables and used her and dumped her, or used her and stuck around. He told himself that he preferred her natural sable hair color to the studio's Bing cherry red, and that she looked ridiculous in that shapeless, yellow rain slicker. He watched her slam back another shot and then polish off a half a bottle of beer. He noted her slouched posture and pegged her intoxicated. Watched her light up another cigarette, thinking if he kissed her right now, the way he was dying to—slow, deep—she'd taste like an ashtray. He mentally nit-picked and criticized Sofia Marino with every step in her direction.

By the time he dropped into the seat across from her he was thoroughly annoyed. It was a hell of a lot better than horny.

Cigarette poised between two slender fingers, she gaped at him through glassy eyes. "Christ."

"Nope." He summoned a smartass grin. "Although I have managed a miracle or two in my time."

Elbows on table, she dropped her forehead against the heels of her hands. "How could Murphy do this to me?"

"I hear you, babe." He nabbed the cigarette, crushed it out in the ashtray alongside several other stubs. He nodded toward the beer and two empty shot glasses. "How much have you had to drink?"

"Not enough." She straightened and tossed a sloppy wave toward the lone waitress in the room. A perky, young blonde who beamed at Sofia as though she were her hero. An obvious fan of "Spy Girl". Or rather Cherry Onatop, the classified operative who kicked evil-doer-ass. "Two more, Lisa," she called in a husky slur. There'd be no ass-kicking tonight. He doubted if she could find her own just now, let alone someone else's. After two tries, she crossed her arms over what he knew was an amazing chest—hard to appreciate her luscious breasts when they were concealed beneath a fisherman's slicker—and smirked at Joe. "Anything for you?"

"Pass." They glared at each other for several seconds. He silently cursed her smudged mascara, evidence that she'd been crying. Cursed the fact that her hand trembled as she fired up another cigarette. She cocked a defiant brow and blew out a stream of smoke. She was playing it cool, but man, she was stressed. He rolled back his shoulders, cocked his own damn brow. "Expecting an indoor monsoon?"

She glanced down at the rain slicker, momentarily flustered. "Oh. No. This isn't mine. I just . . . borrowed it. My clothes were ruined and I . . . " She looked up, registered his blatant appraisal. "Screw you."

I wish. She looked confused, disheveled, and too damned gorgeous to be real. An explosive combination of Jennifer Lopez and Sophia Loren. A hot-blooded, almond-eyed, wide-mouthed sex kitten. Mocha skin. Voluptuous curves.

Holy Jesus, he was scum. She was upset and he was fantasizing about what she did or didn't have on beneath that slicker. His agitation quadrupled. "What's the problem, Sofia?"

"No problem. You can leave."

"I'd like nothing better, but Murphy would have my ass." She glanced away. "I shouldn't have called him."

"But you did, and now he's worried."

She smiled at the waitress, "Thanks, Lis," and Joe found himself wishing she'd smile at him like that, all warm and fuzzy. Christ, he was pathetic.

Lisa set down two shots of amber liquid. She looked expectantly at Joe. "Are you sure I can't get you anything, Mr . . . "

"Special Agent Joseph Bogart. One of the good guys," Sofia supplied with a derisive snort, then downed a shot.

"Just Joe," he countered. "And just the tab, thanks. We're leaving."

"A fed. Wow. But not a real one, right? Because don't they have, like, short hair and wear dark suits and stuff? You're an actor, right? You're . . . " Lisa leaned closer, lowered her voice to an awestruck whisper. "Omagod! Johnny *Depp*?"

"Afraid not." He forced a smile. "Could we get the check, please?"

Lisa straightened. "Sure. And don't worry, Mr. Depp. Your secret's safe with me." She winked and slipped away.

He shook his head in wonder and reached for his wallet.

"I'm not ready to leave," Sofia said.

"Guess again."

She grabbed the beer bottle like a lifeline and reached for the second shot. "I'm not done."

He shanghaied the glass and tossed it back. *Tequila.* No salt. No lime. Plenty of disgust. He'd lost two days compliments of Jose Cuervo while undercover a lifetime ago in Tuscon. Suppressing a shudder, he slammed the glass to the table, chased it with the remnants of her beer. "I'll walk you to your room."

"I don't have a room."

"You're not staying at the Camelback?"

"Not that I know of."

What did that mean? He glared, waited.

She took a long, slow drag off that damned cigarette, her full lips caressing the filter, pursing seductively as she blew out a thick stream of smoke. Hypnotized, he had an explicit vision of her working another kind of magic with that mouth.

Whoa.

He jerked his mind out of the gutter, shifted in his seat. It's not like she was coming on to him. She just *oozed* sex. She could belch and he'd probably get a boner.

Her sable brown gaze bounced from the empty shot glass to the table's flickering candle. She looked frazzled and tired, and he had to fight like hell not to reach across the table and stroke his thumb across those million-dollar cheekbones. "I don't know where I'm staying," she finally said in a far-off voice. "I don't know why I'm in Phoenix, Scottsdale, whatever. I guess I'm shooting on location, but I lost the crew."

Great. Not just intoxicated, but totally whacked. As of last week, "Spy Girl" was on hiatus. Unless she was shooting a commercial. Cherry Onatop hawking an energy drink or some stupid shit.

"It's probably nothing. Probably a prank. My stunt double doesn't like me. She's pulled some mean spirited jokes, but . . . it has to be a prank." She bit her lower lip, shook her head. "This isn't real. This isn't happening."

He dragged a hand down his goatee, summoned the patience of a Zen master. "What's not happening?"

"I woke up with a gun, but it wasn't my gun. I mean, it wasn't Cherry's gun."

His senses buzzed as this meeting took on a heightened edge. He leaned in and lowered his voice. "Woke up where? What gun?"

"The shed." She motioned over her shoulder in a vague direction. "I woke up holding a prop gun."

She dipped into the pocket of the slicker, slid a pistol across the table.

Prop gun my ass. How about a freaking Beretta 92FS? Using his bandanna, he shifted the semi-automatic to his lap, checked the chamber—empty—and then the magazine. Twenty round 9mm ammo. The high capacity factory magazine had been banned from civilian use in '94. It was also down three rounds. Damn. "Where'd you get this?"

"I told you, I woke up and . . ."

"Here you go." Lisa placed a leather binder on the table between them, clearly unsure as to who was footing the bill.

Joe discreetly tripped the safety and slipped the Beretta in the jumbo pocket of his cargo shorts.

Sofia glanced apologetically at him. The first time since he'd sat down that she'd looked at him with anything other than hostility. "I, um, don't have my purse."

As if he'd allow a lady to pay. His dad, an old-world Italian, would've smacked him in the back of the head.

"We accept all major credit cards," Lisa said, flashing him a toothy smile.

He flipped open the binder, eyed the total. Holy shit. Any other woman would've been under the table by now. He didn't know whether to be impressed or concerned. He covered the bill with cash and a generous tip, tamping down his impatience when Lisa asked them both for their autograph. Wanting to make a quick getaway, he penned, *Love that smile, J.D.*

Lisa accepted their autographed cocktail napkins with a teary thank you, and graciously took her leave.

Joe pocketed his wallet and stood.

Sofia stared up at him with a funny look on her face.

"Yeah. I know. That was dishonest."

"Actually, it was really nice. You made her night."

The compliment made him uncomfortable. *Sofia* made him uncomfortable. He barely knew her and yet she'd monopolized his thoughts and dreams for nine solid months. He glanced away, not wanting her to see the frustration and longing in his eyes. *Fuck*.

"Joe?"

He blew out a tense breath, feigned interest in the solo guitarist. "Yeah?"

"I don't know how I got here precisely. I mean, I don't think I have a car. I don't know where my purse is. I don't have any money so I can't get a room. I can't remember . . ."

Her voice hitched. Yeah, boy, *that* got his attention. He glanced down and caught her rubbing her temples.

"I can't *remember*."

He touched her then. Like he had a choice. Like he hadn't been dying for an excuse to touch her since he'd walked into this ritzy bar. He grasped one of her hands and gave what he hoped was an impersonal, but comforting squeeze. "Come on. We'll find your car and purse tomorrow."

She looked up at him with watery eyes. "But I don't have . . ."

"You have me."

She burst into tears.

He'd seen her cry before. After her ex-boyfriend, ex-agent had tried to coerce her into her grandmother's house for a quick lay. But, Christ, this was the vulnerable Sofia. The one that scared the hell out of him.

So much for the iron cocoon.

He made some sort of dumbass comforting sound, then offered her his bandanna and shifted to shield her from the bar. The last thing he wanted was attention.

Especially when he had an illegal Beretta in his pocket and a plastered celebrity under his protection. Whether he liked it or not, thanks to Murphy, he was now responsible for this woman.

She mopped her tears with the kerchief, smearing more mascara, rubbing her nose red. Still gorgeous. *Man.* He brushed her hair from her face. "Come on. Let's get you out of here."

She managed a terse nod, pushed back from the table and shot up like a rocket. Off balance, she tripped, and fell into his arms.

"Damn flop flips," she blubbered.

He held her steady, trying not to think about how good she smelled—vanilla and musk? Trying to decipher her words. Then he glanced down at the cheap thong sandals she'd stumbled out of. *Flip-flops.* Somewhere in the vicinity of a size eleven. One of the first things he'd noticed about Sofia all those months ago, aside from her gorgeous face, mouthwatering yabos and shapely legs, was her penchant for wearing spike-heeled or funky-heeled, but always three-inch high-heeled shoes. Size seven. During their initial face-to-face meeting, she'd jammed one of those heels down hard on his foot, nearly breaking his toes and emblazoning her favored footwear in his memory. "Guess you borrowed those sandals too."

She leaned heavily against him, sighed. "My head hurts and my legs are numb."

"Nine shots and three beers will do that to you, kid." And she was a kid. Not even thirty. Which almost qualified him as a dirty old man. Now *there* was a depressing thought.

She clutched his T-shirt as her knees gave way. "I don't want to cause a scene," she said, slowly sliding down his body.

Too late. Ignoring the murmuring clientele, he swept her off her bare feet and headed for the lobby. Halfway to the front door, he nixed the idea of pouring her into his jeep and driving forty-five minutes to his place. He handed his credit card to the front desk clerk, thinking he was going to have to sign on for a couple of extra jeep tours before this night was over. Or, he could send the bill to Murphy. It would serve him right for disrupting Joe's peace. And he *had* been at peace. Well, relative peace. At least he'd started sleeping through the night. Nice while it lasted. He was definitely sending Murph the bill.

After securing a standard room—Christ almighty, *no*, he did not want a suite—he spirited away fast-fading Sofia who kept muttering something about reporters and a scandal. The front desk clerk had assured her they could count on the resort's discretion. Joe had slipped him a hefty tip as insurance. The fact that he was shacking up in a posh hotel with a plastered television star didn't faze him. The Beretta fazed him. He wanted to know why she was in possession of a pistol with an illegal mag. He wanted to know who owned the slicker and flip-

flops. He had a lot of questions, but he wouldn't be getting any coherent answers until tomorrow.

His cell phone vibrated just as he shouldered open the door of the guest room. He placed Sofia in the center of a King-sized bed. "Don't move." Like there was any chance of that. She was damn near comatose.

He turned on the desk lamp, answered his phone. "Hey, Murph."

"So?"

The clipped one-word-question brimmed with concern. "Relax. I've got her."

"Is she okay?"

"Depends on your definition." He glanced over and saw Sofia pushing herself up into a sitting position.

"It's hot in here," she complained.

"No, it's not," Joe said, away from the mouthpiece. "It's that slicker. Take it off."

"What's going on?" Murphy asked.

She shoved her bountiful, layered hair out of her red-rimmed eyes, swayed slightly as she fumbled with the top snaps of the coat. He imagined sliding his fingers through those decadent cherry locks. Imagined thumbing open the coat snaps one by one, peeling off layers of clothing and . . . He blew out a breath, wishing to hell she'd put him out of his misery and pass out. "She's trashed."

"Drunk?"

"Oh, yeah." He freed his hair from the elastic band, scratched his hand over his pounding head.

"I watched that woman put away a bottle and a half of champagne at our wedding. She wasn't even tipsy. I've seen her do shots of whiskey without batting an eye. Lulu said she's never seen her drunk."

Sofia wrestled with the snaps, cursed.

Joe massaged a dull ache in the center of his forehead. "Trust me on this."

"What about the trouble she mentioned?"

He studied the Beretta a moment before placing it in the desk drawer. "Not up to speed on that yet." No need to worry his brother, until he knew the score. "I'll let you know. In the meantime, have a safe trip and give that pretty wife of yours a hug for me."

"Fly to Vermont and hug her yourself."

At that moment he heard a succession of pops, snaps unsnapping and . . . "I have to go."

"I really appreciate this, Bogie."

"Don't worry." His mouth went dry at the sight of mocha-skinned Sofia in a white satin demi-bra and G-string. "You'll pay." He signed off and laid the phone on the desk.

She sighed as she shrugged out of the rain slicker. "That's better."

For her maybe. Personally, his temperature just shot to one-fifty. Joe palmed his forehead while gathering his wits. She'd gone from hostile, to weepy, to barely coherent. Asking her to make sense just now was probably futile, but he had to try. "Sofia. Sweetheart. Where are your clothes?"

"I told you. Ruined." Her speech was halted, softer, definitely slurred. "I know it was fake, but . . . couldn't stand it. Threw them out."

"Knew what was fake?"

"The blood."

A muscle jumped under his right eye. "There was blood on your clothes?"

"Fake blood."

Yeah. And she also thought the Beretta was a prop.

"And on my legs. But . . . " Heavy sigh. "I washed it off."

He glanced at her legs then. All two-hundred miles of them. Her knees and shins were covered with scrapes and welts. *Damn.* He squatted down and inspected the superficial wounds. "What happened?"

She shrugged. "Don't remember."

The running theme of the night. His mind exploded with a dozen ugly scenarios. Rape. Assault. Attempted murder. *Murder.* Something traumatic. Something she'd blocked out. Worried that she'd suffered other injuries, he examined her thighs, stomach, arms, back . . .

"Having fun?"

But there was no humor or real outrage in her words.

Just resignation. Christ. He sank down beside her on the bed, framed her face in his hands. "Try to focus. Do you hurt anywhere?"

"Only when I try to focus."

He registered the sad quirk of that sexy mouth, the confusion in her heavy-lidded eyes. "All right. Let it go. We'll talk tomorrow when you're sober." He dropped his hands, averted his gaze. "I should get you some water and aspirin. Salve for those scrapes." And some clothes. The only reason he wasn't turned on just now was because he'd fixated on the gun and blood. On the fact that someone may have harmed or threatened her. On the possibility that she'd maimed or killed in self-defense.

She leaned forward and grazed her fingers over his goatee, his mouth. "You're sexy when you're intense." She studied him with a mocking pout. "Which is most of the time."

"Mmm." He couldn't comment. Wouldn't comment. Had to be the liquor talking.

She smoothed his hair out of his face, her soft fingers caressing his forehead and cheeks. His skin burned and his cock stirred. She leaned closer and his heart slammed against his chest. "Why do you have to be such an arrogant prick?"

He laughed at that. "For the same reason, I imagine, that you're a consistent pain in the ass. Comes naturally."

She smiled, warm and fuzzy, at *him*, Christ almighty,

and moistened her lips. "You ruined me for other men, Joseph Bogart. I'll never forgive you."

With that bit of good news/bad news, his fondest obsession slumped forward and passed out in his arms, shooting any hope of a simple, peaceful life to hell.

CHAPTER FIVE

Rainbow Ridge, Vermont

Rudy Gallow's hopes for a relaxing, joyous reunion with friends and lovers blew sky-high when the electricity went off. And on. And off. For the third time that week.

"That settles it." He wiped his hands on a dishtowel, groped for his cordless phone and speed dialed his best friend while making his way to the utility room.

She picked up on the second ring. "Four days and counting! Oh, Rudy, I can't tell you how excited . . ."

"I need to reschedule."

"What do you mean *reschedule*? You're not serious.

Please, tell me you're not serious!"

He winced as Afia Leeds babbled into the phone, her normally mellow voice climbing to an ear-piercing level. His friend was definitely stressed. He knew the feeling. He needed a Valium, or four. He'd settle for a glass of wine, that's if Casper the meddlesome ghost hadn't hidden his bottle of cabernet. Household items had been disappearing and reappearing in the oddest places for three weeks now. At first, he'd attributed the frustrating occurrences to the typical chaos of moving into a new place. But then the problems had escalated. This evening he'd resigned himself to the notion that Hollyberry Inn, his newly purchased, quaint, but ancient, bed and breakfast resort, was indeed haunted.

"Do you know what I had to go through to get Jake to agree to this trip in the first place?" Afia continued in a strangled whisper. "He made me get a doctor's written note stating it was safe for me to fly!"

"I think the airlines require . . ."

"Then he *blackmailed* me. Said we'd fly up and spend the week in Vermont if I stopped visiting the HIV babies at the hospital!"

"I happen to know you're a mess every time you leave those poor kids, sweetie, and that Jake only asked you to take a break until . . ."

"He lays out my vitamins every morning and stands there watching until I wash them down with a glass of milk! What am I, five-years-old?"

He cradled the receiver between his shoulder and ear while tinkering with the breaker panel. *Sans* electricity his salmon soufflé teetered on ruination. "Honey, I know Jake's been a little controlling lately, but . . ."

"*Lately*? He's always controlling, Rudy. I've learned to handle that. *This* is much worse. This is a . . . a dictatorship! Yes, that's what it is. I'm living under the iron fist of Jake Leeds. Do this. Don't do that."

Rudy almost laughed. But then he risked Afia biting his head off or bursting into tears. Talk about hormonal. Poor Jake. Yeah, the alpha P.I. was a control freak, but he worshiped his wife, recent mood swings and all. "Well, you *are* eight months pregnant."

"So what? Women have babies all the time!"

"But this is your first. Jake's first." He grappled for patience, flicked more switches. "And there was that problem with his sister's first pregnancy. Joni pulled through with flying colors, thank God, and Kylie's a cutie. But it *was* touch and go for awhile. You can't blame Jake for being nervous. Cut the guy a break, honey."

"You're supposed to be *my* best friend."

"I am."

"But you're siding with Jake."

"I'm not siding with anyone." He heard the distant sound of his radio, turned, and saw the kitchen and dining room lights shining which meant the electric stove was back on. He glanced at his watch. Eight-minutes had passed. "Dammit, Casper."

"Who's Casper?"

Rudy flushed. "No one." No way was he confessing he had a ghost, poltergeist, whatever. His friends would declare him bonkers or say, "*I told you so.*" Jake had tried to talk him into investing in a newer property. He and Afia were constantly pouring money into their genuine Victorian home. Not that Afia couldn't afford it. She was an heiress. Jake, however, was old fashioned and insisted on handling renovations himself. Since his expertise was in private investigations, not plumbing and roofing, progress was slow. "*Save yourself the hassle and the money,*" he'd said.

But Rudy had wanted a place with history.

Well, Hollyberry Inn had history, all right. The realtor had shared several stories of happy honeymooners and vacationing families throughout the decades, but had failed to mention that in the early 1900s a lovesick, artistic youth had committed suicide in the Evergreen Suite. He'd learned *that* juicy tidbit through town gossip. "Listen, Afia, I'm serious. I don't want you and the gang to come up here yet. I'm not ready."

"But the grand opening is . . ."

"I'm going to postpone that too."

"But Jean-Pierre . . ."

"I'm calling him next." His stomach curdled with disappointment. He'd spent months getting his emotional cookies together, basing his recovery on an observation by his estranged lover, Jean-Pierre Legrand. He'd abandoned his self-help library in favor of seeking answers through meditation, hoping to embrace what he feared most: total commitment. As a result, he knew his heart inside out. He knew exactly what he wanted.

Unfortunately, Casper was screwing up his perfect scenario. With his luck he'd be on bended knee and the temperamental ghost would choose that exact moment to lob a candlestick at Jean-Pierre's head. Rumor had it, if Casper couldn't have the love of his life, no one could. First thing tomorrow he'd reactivate his Amazon.com account. This time he'd stock up on ghosthunting books.

"It's not that big a deal, sweetie," Rudy lied as he deserted the breaker panel and moved down the hall. "I just need three or four more weeks." *However long it takes to boot a pesky ghost into another dimension.* "I'll ask Jean-Pierre to pass the news on to Sofia. Will you do me a favor and call Lulu and Murphy? It's already late and I don't know how long I'll be on the phone with Jean-Pierre."

She groaned. "What am I supposed to tell them exactly?"

He was midway through the great room when the TV turned on by itself and the kitchen light went out. Rudy sighed. "Tell them that I've got a wiring problem."

Los Angeles, California

Hands on hips, Jean-Pierre stared at the note Sofia had taped to the refrigerator door amidst her shoe magnet collection. *Going to a spa. See you in Vermont.* The note didn't make any more sense now than it had this morning. What spa? He knew that she was planning to spend a week at Hollyberry Inn. And, *oui*, he was scheduled to fly in a few days ahead of her, allowing him private time with Rudy before the gang arrived. But why had she not mentioned this side trip to a spa? Why had she not left a contact number? He'd tried her cell twice today only to get her voice mail. He knew that she was a big girl; still, he worried. Sofia was not as tough as she pretended. After several months of rooming together, he figured he knew her better than anyone did, except perhaps her sister.

Sofia Marino, Hollywood's newest cable sitcom celebrity, the star of a bazillion straight men's wet dreams, was plagued with insecurities. Much like Rudy (the star of *his* wet dreams). And like Rudy, she needed to come around on her own. She needed to believe in herself, to find happiness within before she could find happiness with a life partner. These days Sofia found joy, albeit superficial joy as far as he was concerned, in her work. Wherever she was, whoever she was with, it had to do with "Spy Girl", or some other theatrical venture. He just hoped she kept her wits and "resolutions" about her and didn't do something she'd regret come Monday. A moment of stupidity could ruin a lifetime of happiness.

He should know. He and Rudy had almost wrecked their relationship over an isolated indiscretion. But after months of living on separate coasts, extended soul-searching, and Rudy's surprising decision to sell his limousine service to invest in an idea they'd once dreamed up over a bottle of sangria, it looked like they were going to reunite. Finally. Thank goodness. He was so over Los Angeles, and so not over the man he'd nicknamed Gym Bunny.

Rudy Gallow: tall, dark and buff. *Sigh*. He pictured that bodacious butch body decked out in his form-fitting black T-shirt and jeans and straddling the seat of his Harley. Then he imagined him straddling another kind of seat altogether and . . .

The phone rang, startling him out of an erotic daydream. He hurried toward the cordless, hoping it was Sofia, delighted that it was Rudy. "*Bon soir*, Bunny."

"Hi, honey. How was your day?"

"Long. Hard. Boring. And yours?"

"Long. Hard. Not so boring."

Blood flowed hot and south of his waistline. Jean-Pierre sank down on the sofa and palmed his bulge. "Let us focus on the long and hard." Since he could not pop over to Vermont for *un sexuel rendevous*, he'd have to make due with hot and heavy phone sex. Something they'd engaged in a lot lately.

His heart throbbed as mightily as his shaft. This separation was killing him. It wasn't just the lack of sex. It was the lack of intimate time. The cuddling, the talking, the laughing . . . Living with Rudy for those few months last summer had been the greatest turn-on, emotionally and physically, of his life.

There was a pause, some disturbing throat-clearing and then, "Not that I'm not up for polishing the rocket, but . . . "

"*Oui?*"

" . . . Houston, we have a problem."

Bracing for an anxiety attack—he'd been getting a lot of those lately—he massaged his chest as a flurry of awful scenarios pirouetted in his brain. "You fell off the ladder and broke something, *oui?* Your arm? Your leg? I told you to hire a professional to clean out those roof pipe thingies."

"Rain gutters. And I didn't fall, nor did I need to hire someone to scoop out a bunch of leaves and sticks. Mission accomplished. Ye have little faith in my manly skills."

"I have every faith in your manly skills. I will prove it Sunday night when I let you clean *my* pipes."

Normally that crude remark would've elicited a laugh, or at the very least an equally crude reply. Instead, Rudy sighed. "About your visit . . . "

Jean-Pierre's heart sank. There would be no phone sex tonight. By the end of this conversation, instead of breathing heavily, he'd be breathing into a paper bag and dialing the emergency number of his analyst. He summoned patience even as his pulse accelerated and his brow beaded with sweat. Even though he was a costume designer, living in LA he'd picked up a few acting skills purely by osmosis. He could get through this conversation without letting on that he was teetering on some sort of emotional breakdown.

As Rudy yammered on about faulty wiring or such nonsense, Jean-Pierre started wondering about his own internal wiring. Maybe Dr. Mitchell was right. Maybe it was time to move on. His obsession with Bunny was compromising his happiness.

Forcing a calm, "But of course, I understand," past the lump in his throat, he leaned forward and snatched the tissue box from the coffee table. In doing so, his teary gaze fell upon a quote he'd scribbled down recently from an unknown source. *The best relationship is the one in which your love for each other exceeds your need for each other.*

Ah, oui, he thought as Rudy essentially blew him off, *time to move on.*

CHAPTER SIX

Scottsdale, Arizona

Places! Camera!

An explosion popped in Sofia's head. She bolted upright, a scream lodged in her throat.

Action!

Disoriented, she scrambled to her feet. Something had hold of her ankles. She kicked out, lost her balance, and went down hard. She laid there for a second, trying to catch her breath, her bearings. Her heart and head pounded in sickening tandem.

She heard a graphic curse, forced open her heavy lids, just as two hands reached for her. "No!" She grabbed, pulled, kicked, and flipped. He too landed with a thud.

Before she could peel her leaden body from the floor, he recouped and pinned her down. Skin on skin. Hard muscles. Slick. Wet. *Blood.* She thrashed for her life.

"Sofia, it's me. Calm down." He palmed her forehead. "You're safe."

His deep, commanding voice registered, her vision cleared. *Joe.* A very naked Joe, but Joe. And, thank you Jesus, the wetness was water, not blood. Her heart hammered, and she had to remind herself to breathe as she struggled to collect her thoughts. "You're soaked." It was a stupid thing to say, but better than *your semi-hard dick is pressed against my stomach.*

"I was getting out of the shower when I heard you fall."

"That explains why *you're* naked. What's my excuse?" Her voice sounded scratchy and a full octave lower than usual. Was she coming down with a cold? What the hell was that god-awful taste in her mouth?

"You're not naked. You're wearing underwear." He flashed a coy smile. "If that's what you want to call those matching wisps of satin."

Her brain glitched as she stared up into his smoldering brown eyes. *Decadent as aged cognac.* Mischief and concern sparkled in his intoxicating gaze, and that wise-ass mouth of his looked as sexy as ever, a well-trimmed goatee intensifying his already sinful good looks. A hundred questions crossed her mind, but she was too distracted by the weight of his buff body to voice even one.

Except for the naked part, this reminded her of their first encounter when he'd snuck into her dressing room at the casino and pinned her against the wall. She'd assumed the worse and had defended herself by raking his shin and stomping hard on his foot. The struggle had ended like this. With her flat on her back, him sprawled on top.

"We've got to stop meeting like this," he quipped.

She didn't see the humor. "You can get off me now."

He didn't budge, except to shove a hank of wet hair off his chiseled cheekbones. He was even better looking than she remembered, putting every one of her male "Spy Girl" co-stars to shame. "Your strikes and counters have improved significantly."

She wasn't in the mood for compliments. She couldn't breathe. Worse, she couldn't form a thought that didn't have to do with sex. She remembered the feel of his mouth on hers all too well. He could seduce a nun into bed with one of his full-assault kisses. And his body . . . Jesus. Curiosity dared her to explore the texture and sinew of his bare back and to cup what had to be a stellar ass. Instead, she shoved at his muscular shoulders. "Get . . . *off.*" She closed her eyes, not wanting to get a full frontal view, even though she'd dreamed of such an opportunity several times. It's just not something she thought she could handle now. Although closing her eyes proved just as troubling.

The room spun.

Cool air drifted over her clammy, prickly skin as Joe eased away. Her throat burned with bile. Her head throbbed and her stomach turned. "Oh, God." She must've looked as sick as she felt, because, next thing she knew, he had her on her feet and in the bathroom.

She spent the next several minutes hurling into the toilet. It was painful and disgusting, and unbelievably humiliating because, damn him, he wouldn't go away. He held her hair back from her face as she threw up whatever she'd ingested the night before. He smoothed a damp, cool cloth over the back of her neck, and then over her sweaty face when she finally eased back and collapsed against the tiled wall.

She wanted to die. The way she felt just now, it was a definite possibility.

Joe was still naked, though she seemed to be the only one who was self-conscious. She snatched the wash cloth from his hand and pressed it over her eyes, otherwise, even though she was two steps from death's doors, she would've stared. The man was frickin' gorgeous. "Could you at least wrap a towel around your waist?"

For some reason he found her request funny. Either that, or he was laughing at her sorry-looking-ass. She didn't know. She didn't care. No way was she lowering that cloth from her eyes to find out.

His good humor was fleeting. She felt his hand on the top of her head, a comforting gesture that brought tears to her eyes. "Feel better?"

"I feel like shit."

"Hangover's are a bitch."

"I wouldn't know. I've never had one." She flashed back on a few beers and several shots of tequila. "Until now." What had possessed her to drink so much so fast? She tried to recall last night's events and was rewarded with a nauseating migraine. "My head is killing me."

"I'll have aspirin and black tea waiting in the other room."

His hand fell away, and she instantly mourned the loss of contact. Not that she let on. Hell, no.

"I ran down to the gift shop earlier," he continued. "Bought some essentials—toothpaste, toothbrushes, deodorant. They're on the counter. Help yourself. Oh, and I cleaned your scrapes with peroxide last night, but you might want to reapply that antibiotic ointment." He cleared his throat, stepped away. "I'm going to throw on some clothes. Take your time."

"I may not move for a week."

"The tea will be cold, but the aspirin and I will keep."

The gentle reassurance tweaked her unease. Why was he being so nice? In the past, he'd made it clear he considered her an impetuous bimbo. A woman of poor judgment and easy virtue. *Eye candy*.

She flashed back on the bed she'd tumbled out of, the rumpled sheets. Warm skin, entangled limbs. Oh, no.

Heart pounding, she lowered the cloth. Yep. A stellar ass. "Joe?"

Securing the towel around his waist, he paused on the threshold and glanced back. "Yeah?"

"Please tell me we didn't sleep together."

"Can't do that, babe." He was smiling when he shut the door, leaving her alone in her misery.

It was a toss up as to whether the coroner would attribute her death to mortification or a hangover.

Leading Sofia to believe that they'd had sex last night had been cruel, but damn, he'd been unable to resist. Twisted payback for the torture she'd inflicted in the middle of the night when she'd rolled into his arms, pressed that luscious, toned body against him, and clung. Man, had she clung. In return he'd lain awake with a stubborn hard-on. He was pretty certain he could've taken advantage and that she would've been a willing, though drunk, participant in a carnal slam. *"You're sexy when you're intense."* But even *he* wasn't that much of a bastard. He had, however, returned the embrace, smoothing his hands over her silky skin when she'd moaned and trembled from a nightmare. Physical contact purely for her benefit.

Yeah, right.

The shower blasted and Joe had to fight not to imagine

what Sofia looked like naked, water streaming over her hot *naked* body, the same body that clung to him in bed where she might as well have been *naked*, because damn, those skimpy Victoria's Secret undies barely covered her fine assets. Not imagining her in the shower wasn't working, he decided while stepping into his shorts. He had the boner to prove it.

You're in serious trouble, Bogart. Even watching her puke her guts up hadn't diminished the attraction. If anything it had only highlighted that vulnerability of hers that burrowed under his cynical, thick skin. He had to get a grip. Solve her problem and get out with his heart and sanity intact.

Room service arrived just as he finished dressing. The perfect distraction, along with the two local newspapers he'd purchased in the gift shop. He scoured the *Arizona Republic* and the *Phoenix New Times* while inhaling two cups of a hearty Brazilian roast. Neither newspaper featured an article describing an accident or a crime that Sofia may have been involved in. He poured a third cup of coffee, needing all the caffeine he could get after three lousy hours of sleep, and pondered a course of action. First order of business, pick Sofia's brain. With any luck she'd regained her memory with her sobriety. Otherwise, he'd have to call in a favor. He had a bad feeling about that Beretta.

Pipes groaned as she cut the shower. He gave her a

few minutes to towel off, another vision he resisted, and then knocked on the bathroom door. During his gift store shopping spree he'd snagged a grey, hooded jogging suit, white T-shirt, and black sports cap. The outfit, each item embroidered with the hotel logo, had been overpriced, but she needed something to wear and, what the hell, in the end Murphy would be the one to pay. Just the thought of handing his brother an itemized bill for sticking him with Sofia caused him to smile.

Of course, that's when she cracked open the door. "Forget it, Bogart. Just because it happened once, doesn't mean it will happen again. Hell will freeze over first."

It took him a minute to figure out what she was talking about. Then it registered and he didn't know whether to laugh or be insulted. "Damn, Marino. I was just messing with you."

Instead of dropping the towel in a flustered moment of outrage, she clutched it tighter, effectively concealing her magnificent breasts—much to his disappointment. She narrowed her bloodshot eyes. "You mean we *didn't* sleep together?"

He leaned against the jamb, one eyebrow cocked as moist steam swirled behind her, heating up the pulse-pounding scene. "Oh, we slept together, babe. You were all over me." He itched to needle her for the sheer hell of it, but her mortified expression had him bailing. "Relax. If I'd nailed you, trust me, you'd remember. Besides, I prefer my women sober."

She smirked. "Since when?"

Well, tou-fucking-ché and then some. But, hey, okay, this was good. Hard to be attracted to someone who'd just driven a spear through his heart. Jaw clenched, he passed her the clothes and returned to his coffee. "Get a move on. We've got work to do."

"Joe, I . . ."

"Forget it." The softness in her voice suggested she was about to apologize. Lulu had probably told her about Julietta's death. He didn't want to talk about it. Especially not with Sofia. "I struck. You struck back. You're a fighter. That's not a bad thing." He snatched up his cup and turned, his gaze sliding from her bruised forearms to her skinned knees. "In fact, it may have saved your life."

Sofia wanted to go home. Far from whatever mess she'd gotten herself into.

Far, far from Joe.

She could feel his frustration seeping through the bathroom door as she quickly dressed. Luckily, the clothes he'd provided her with were baggy so she didn't have to worry about under-things. Her G-string and bra were hand-washed, rinsed, and hanging over the towel rack to dry. Maybe she could ask him to make a lingerie run.

She'd bet her shoe collection Joseph Bogart was no stranger to buying sexy undergarments. Probably kept his girlfriends stocked in racy teddies. He certainly didn't strike her as an I-like-my-women-in-flannel kind of guy. While he was deliberating over a lacy thong or satin G-string, she could steal away.

But then what? She had no money. No ID.

Where the hell was her purse?

Maybe she'd been mugged. If she'd fought back as Joe had suggested, that would explain her scrapes and bruises. Thing was, she didn't remember an assault.

She braced her hands on the vanity and took a deep breath. She felt horrible. Not just because she had a fierce hangover, and a lapse of memory, but because she'd been unwittingly cruel. Yes, she hated that Joe had blatantly used a young woman as a means to an end. A woman who, by his own admission, had been insecure and dependent on drugs and alcohol. And, yes, she empathized with Julietta Marcella who'd fallen for a charming man's lies. Sofia had been down that road more times than she cared to remember. But as irresponsible as Joe had acted, in her estimation anyway, Julietta's death wasn't his fault. According to Lulu, who'd gotten it straight from Murphy, Joe believed otherwise. He blamed himself so much that he'd walked away from his job with the FBI.

She definitely regretted throwing Julietta in his face. But, *dammit*, he shouldn't have teased her about something as serious as lovemaking. She hadn't been physically intimate with anyone since her breakup last summer with Chaz Bradley. Her ex-agent had promised her a bright future, professionally and personally. He'd made her feel secure and cherished, *special*. But like every other man in her life, when he'd used the "L" word, he'd really meant "lust". For some reason she was never "the one", just "the one of the moment."

Then Joe had kissed her, two short months after her breakup with Chaz, and she'd felt herself falling . . . again. When she'd learned that the sexy special agent was sleeping with another woman, and worse, that he was <u>using</u> that poor girl, it had reinforced her opinion that men were pigs and not to be trusted. Jean-Pierre had taken great exception to her generalization, suggesting she merely needed appropriate time to heal.

To prove to herself that she wasn't a sexaholic or one of those women who only felt complete if they were involved in a relationship, she'd resolved to remain celibate until the one-year anniversary of her breakup with Chaz. When a man wined and dined her, the only thing he'd be getting a piece of was her *mind*. She was more than willing to share her thoughts, ideas, and opinions on a wide variety of subjects, but her body was off limits. She was more than just a pretty face, dammit.

"You're even more beautiful in person."

Sweat broke out on Sofia's forehead as a garbled voice

echoed in the recesses of her fuzzy mind. No face. No name. Just a vague recollection.

She stumbled out of the bathroom on the verge of hyperventilating as scant memories unfolded. "I had an appointment. I flew into Phoenix to meet someone. Someone important."

Joe pushed out of his chair and met her halfway across the room. "Who?"

"I don't know. I can't remember." She grabbed two fistfuls of her wet hair and tugged in frustration. "Why can't I remember?"

"Slow down." He grasped her upper arms and guided her into a chair. "Do you remember packing?"

"Yes. Yesterday morning. Very early. I remember packing for the weekend. I remember leaving Jean-Pierre a note saying that I'd see him in Vermont."

"Did you tell him where you'd be over the weekend?"

"I told him I'd be at a spa, but I didn't say where. I told my publicist and Lulu the same thing, but it was a lie. I didn't want them to know my real plans. It was a secret. Or, I wanted it to be a secret." She balled her fists in her lap so as not to rip her hair from the roots.

Joe poured her a cup of tea. "Sugar? Milk?"

"Black." She thanked him, cursing her trembling hands as she lifted the cup to her lips. *This isn't real. This isn't happening.* She sipped the bland brew, hoping it would calm her stomach. Swear to God she'd never touch another drop of tequila.

As if knowing her misery, he set a glass of water and the bottle of aspirin within her reach. "Visualize and walk me through yesterday. What were you wearing?"

"My pale blue linen suit—tailored jacket, mid-thigh skirt. Matching Prada shoes and handbag. I dressed to impress." She curled her fingernails into her palms, thought hard. "I took a taxi to LAX. I remember flying into Phoenix. I don't remember details, just fuzzy emotions. I was nervous, but excited."

"So you landed at Sky Harbor International sometime yesterday late morning, early afternoon. Then what? Did someone meet you? Did you rent a car? Take a shuttle?"

"Someone met me. A tall blond in a dark suit. A limo driver. Tom. I remember a lot of traffic. Beautiful houses. Expensive houses. Not so much traffic. I remember driving through a big gate, up a long drive. Nervous. God, I was nervous. Then Tom stopped the limo and the door opened."

"The limo door?"

"No, the house door and . . . "

"Go on."

Sofia swallowed as disjointed images blurred and faded. She closed her eyes, shuddering at the Picasso-like figure in her mind's eye.

"What do you see?" Joe's tone was gentle, persuasive. "Talk to me, Sofia."

"Pieces of a man. Hands. Shoulders. Feet. I can't look him in the eyes. He has no face."

"That doesn't make sense."

"I *know.*" She pressed the heels of her hands against her twitching eyelids. Her head was two seconds from exploding.

"Move inside the house. Tell me what you see."

Her stomach lurched. "I can't. I don't remember anything beyond getting out of the limo and Tom driving away." Unnerved, she opened her eyes and chased three aspirin with a glass of water. "The next thing I remember is waking up in the shed with the prop gun and . . ." She palmed her forehead. "I can't believe I threw away my suit. It was just stage blood, colored gel. How hard could it be to clean?"

"About that." Joe stroked his goatee and studied her with unnerving patience. "You do know "Spy Girl" is on hiatus."

She smirked. "How could I not know the schedule of my own show? Oh, wait." She drummed her fingers on the table. "I mentioned my stunt double, didn't I? I don't know why I did that. I just, I had a sense that I screwed up an action scene. I'm certain my being here is work related. It must have been another kind of shoot."

"The gun's real, Sofia."

Her skin prickled. "Real?"

"You said you threw away your suit. Where?"

The gun was *real*? "The ladies room down the hall from the lounge. I vaguely remember stripping in the stall and shoving the suit in the garbage pail." She looked away, embarrassed. "I'd had a few drinks by then."

He pushed a bowl of oatmeal and a plate of dry toast in her direction. "Eat something. You'll feel better."

"I'd rather have a cigarette."

He reached into his shorts' pocket, offered her a stick of gum, Wrigley's Spearmint. She remembered he'd tasted like spearmint when he'd kissed her all those months ago. She resisted the memory and his offer.

Emotionless, he pocketed the gum, and moved toward the desk.

Goosebumps rose on her arms when he opened the drawer and removed the handgun in question. "If that's a real gun, then the blood on my skirt could have been real."

"Your legs and feet are pretty banged up. Could have been your blood."

She wanted to believe that. She clasped her hands in her lap, fidgeted. "What if I did something wrong? What if I hurt someone and . . ."

"Don't jump to conclusions." He snatched up his cell phone. "Eat so we can get out of here. We've got a mystery to solve."

She envisioned all sorts of bizarre tabloid headlines. *An overnight success ruined overnight.* She thought about her sister and Murphy. How they wanted to adopt a child.

Would an agency reject them based on a relative's mistakes? "I can't afford a scandal."

He frowned as he placed a call. "Then we'll do our best to avoid one."

She heard him ask for Special Agent in Charge, Creed. "But . . ."

"Trust me."

He may as well have asked her for the moon.

CHAPTER SEVEN

A nything?"

"Zip." Frank tossed the newspaper aside. He'd read three local rag sheets cover to cover. No mention of last night's debacle. It seemed too good to be true. Why hadn't the Marino dame run to the cops? Unless, she didn't want the world to know where she'd been, or more precisely who'd she'd been with. Maybe her career couldn't withstand the scandal. Maybe she was going to pretend like it never happened. Or maybe, just maybe the crazy bitch planned on blackmailing them as soon as she regrouped and figured out how to establish contact. The world was full of greedy people who worked all sorts of angles.

He cracked open a warm beer and swallowed his first

painkiller of the day. Bottom line, her silence afforded him and Jesse the upper hand. Career thieves, this was their first and last professional hit, the payoff big enough to fund an early retirement. He refused to spend the rest of his life looking over his shoulder like their Wild West namesakes.

No loose ends.

Frank rose from the economy motel's sagging twin mattress and crossed to the bathroom. He winced when he caught sight of his battered face in the bureau mirror. Disgusted, he adjusted the angle of his Stetson hoping to shadow the swelling. He'd never been a handsome man, never known women to drool over him the way they did his little brother. Jesse had the face and body of an angel, according to the ladies. He could easily get laid seven days a week, fifty-two weeks a year. Thing was, being a germ-o-phobe, Jesse wasn't all that interested in swapping bodily fluids with a woman. Where was the fairness in that? Frank wondered. Not that wondering would change anything. Wasted energy, his mamma would say. He had bigger problems.

Like keeping the James brothers out of prison.

Jesse stood at the chipped enamel sink washing his left hand with anti-bacterial soap. Not surprising. He'd been on the phone, and even though he'd disinfected the receiver, his fears wouldn't subside until he'd ridded his skin of germs, real or imagined. For a smart man, the kid was a real head case. Frank didn't bother to ask if his broken hand was paining him for fear of setting him off on a tangent. Best to keep his mind on business. "How'd you make out?"

"I must've called twenty hotels. No Sofia Marino." Jesse used his elbow to shut off the faucet, and a clean towel to dry his hand. "Crapped out with the car rental agencies too. Not that I expected different. We've got her purse, Frank. Her airline ticket and her wallet. She's got no ID, no cash or credit. I say she's still in the area. Shacked up with another friend, maybe."

Frank's gut said different, and his gut was almost never wrong. "I say she found a way home. If I were her, I'd dig out my passport, deplete my bank account, and disappear. Then again, there's a chance she has bolder plans. Either way she needs ID, money, and maybe the help of a close friend." He reached into his pocket and plucked out the photo strip he'd found in the woman's purse. A result of squeezing into one of those arcade-type photo booths. Frowning, he studied the four black-and-white snapshots of the dark beauty kissing and mugging with a shaggy-haired white boy. On the back she'd written *Me and JP, two stars on the rise*.

"Think that's her boyfriend?" Jesse asked.

"I'm thinking it's possible, seeing they live at the same address. Found a Jean-Pierre Legrand listed in her little address book. Same home address as the one listed on her driver's license."

Jesse nodded, confirming he caught Frank's drift. "So, we're driving to LA."

"Can't spare the time. We'll fly." He hated to fly, but unlike his brother, he wasn't ruled by his fears.

Jesse quirked a wicked smile while maneuvering the fingers of his busted hand. "California, here we come."

CHAPTER EIGHT

Los Angeles, California

Jean-Pierre was ticked. No, he was pissed with a capital P. Instead of giving Rudy hell last night, he'd placated him with a string of reassurances and sugar words.

"But of course, I understand, Bunny. Plumbing and wiring issues," he mimicked, while hurling underwear and socks into his suitcase. "Repairmen traipsing in and out. No privacy. Not a good time. Ah, *oui*, sweetie, we can reschedule. No problem."

Except, there was a problem. Jean-Pierre was tired of walking on egg shells while the man he loved worked through some insane life crisis. He was tired of being the strong one. Tired of waiting. He was just plain *tired*. He'd been struggling with his own personal and career crisis for months. Suffering with insomnia for weeks. Last night he'd tossed and turned, imagining tasty-cake handymen taking turns cleaning Rudy's pipes and electrifying his nights. Not a good sign. It meant that Rudy's one indiscretion still preyed on his mind. Deep down, he questioned the one time King of Quickie's ability to remain faithful.

He'd forgiven the slip months ago. Everyone makes mistakes. But apparently he had a lingering issue with trust. Otherwise, his mind wouldn't be spinning these lascivious images. Dr. Mitchell was right. He needed to confront Rudy about that night. Face to face.

"Wiring issues, my pansy tush." Furious, Jean-Pierre shoved random shirts and pants into the suitcase. He didn't fuss with coordinates, didn't bother folding properly to prevent wrinkles. He just crammed articles of clothing into the case and slammed it shut.

He grabbed the handle and stormed out of the bedroom, his pulse accelerating in anticipation of the upcoming row. Sweat beaded his upper lip as he battled an anxiety attack, focusing instead on the trip he'd rescheduled a mere two hours before.

He knew he was forgetting something but, for the life of him, could not think what. Currently, he was in between jobs, master of his own schedule. So, flying to

Vermont today instead of tomorrow, or instead of next month as he'd stupidly agreed to last night, would pose a problem to no one.

Except Rudy.

Just the thought of walking in on his lover and a handyman comparing their *tools*, had him sprinting toward the kitchen for a paper bag.

But then there was a knock on the door.

Had to be the cab driver. Better early than late. Bracing himself, he tightened the grip on the suitcase and steamrolled towards the door. There'd be plenty of time to hyperventilate *after* he faced his demons.

Gold Canyon, Arizona

"I think someone drugged me." Sofia tightened her seatbelt as Joe shifted gears and swerved the jeep off the highway, onto a bumpy dirt road. They'd held silent during the bumper-to-bumper drive from Phoenix to Apache Junction, each simmering in their own thoughts. She'd had twenty additional, nerve-racking minutes to ponder her predicament when Joe had refused to let her accompany him into the local Wal-Mart. He was determined to keep her low-profile. Like anyone would recognize her in the soccer mom get-up—*sans* make-up, hair divided into pigtails—but he'd been adamant.

So, she'd waited. And pondered. "There has to be a logical explanation for this memory gap." She couldn't blame it on the alcohol, as she'd blacked out before her asinine drinking binge. "I could've been at a party. Someone could've spiked my drink. Maybe they lured me into their car with nefarious intentions. Maybe I threw myself from a moving vehicle to escape their evil clutches. Maybe," she drawled, rolling with the dramatic scenario, "I slid down a rocky slope, ultimately sustaining a conk on the head that affected my short term memory."

Joe dipped his chin and glanced at her over the rims of his Ray Bans. "*That's* your logical explanation?"

She gave a righteous sniff. "It would explain my injuries."

"Don't muddy the waters by mixing fiction with fact."

"Meaning?"

He focused back on the road. "You just described an episode of 'Spy Girl'."

Specifically episode three: *Dr. Fleshpot's Revenge.* Her cheeks flushed with pride. "You watch 'Spy Girl'?"

He flexed and tightened his fingers on the steering wheel. "Read the synopsis in TV Guide."

"Oh." Disappointment sang through her blood. She'd secretly hoped that he'd tuned in, out of curiosity if nothing else. True, they weren't what she would call friends, but they were family. Wasn't he the least bit interested in his sister-in-law's accomplishments? Her ascent from "starving actress" to "celebrity icon" had been fast and furious, even by Hollywood standards.

Okay, so she was more of a cult fave than a respected artist, but as far as she was concerned the espionage cable show was merely a stepping stone. Regardless of the far-fetched premise and limited production budget, she was still proud of her work. Joe's apathy hit a raw nerve. Damn him. Damn *her*. The sudden rush of inadequacy intimated she was seeking self-worth in his eyes and transported her to a place she thought she'd left behind.

Striving to keep the bitterness from her tone, she tugged the brim of her cap lower, effectively shielding her bloodshot eyes. "So, what's *your* take on my memory loss?"

He cocked his head. "Could be psychological rather than a physiological. Could be dissociative amnesia."

"Which is?"

"Memory loss restricted to a period of time, such as the duration of a traumatic episode, possibly a violent crime."

Her stomach gurgled with remnants of tequila and newfound angst. "You said not to jump to conclusions."

"I'm not jumping. I'm working with what we know."

"Which isn't much." She swigged from her Evian water bottle to counteract the rising bile. "You think I shot someone."

"Didn't say that. It's possible an assault of some kind occurred. Probable it was ugly."

"Great."

His cell phone rang. He slipped on a headset and took the call, momentarily absorbed in a conversation with someone about a jeep tour.

Sofia studied the prickly, barren landscape, wondering why anyone would want to live in the godforsaken desert. Especially a man who'd, according to Lulu who'd heard it from Murphy, graduated college specializing in psychology and foreign languages. Federal agents also had to be versed in law and weaponry. She knew first hand that Joe excelled in martial arts. Given his extensive and varied training, why was he tooling snowbirds around in a jeep? Why was he living in the boonies as opposed to a city thriving with cultural and professional opportunities? She understood wanting to put the past behind you, wanting to start over, but damn, in purgatory?

Then she remembered something else her sister had said. "Colin's worried Bogie's never going to rejoin the living." Sofia hadn't given it much thought at the time, mainly because she didn't want to think about Joe Bogart period. Now, she was curious as hell.

She eavesdropped as the man bullshitted his boss, bailing last minute on two scheduled tours and, if his expression and tone were any indication, coming out of the lie smelling like a rose. Her publicist would be green with envy. He was *that* good. Add master manipulator to his list of special skills. Probably why he'd been such an effective undercover agent.

He'd sure snowed Julietta Marcella.

Sofia fidgeted in her seat. Just thinking about that poor woman made her skin itch. Maybe that's why Joe relocated to the desert, hot as hell and populated by venomous creatures. Maybe this was a form of punishment. Penance for what he perceived as an unforgivable act. Pretty harsh, considering he hadn't been directly responsible for her death. Was it possible that he'd actually been in love with Julietta? The thought had never occurred.

Uncomfortable with the idea, Sofia focused on the clump of mountains looming ahead, rough-edged and mysterious, like Joe. He signed off with his boss and fell into thoughtful silence. She soaked in the blazing sun and foreign sights, feeling as though she'd driven onto the rehearsal lot of a classic thriller.

Be careful what you wish for.

She used to wish she'd been born earlier so she could've starred in an Alfred Hitchcock film. A brilliant director, he'd seen beyond the radiant beauty of Ingrid Bergman, Grace Kelly, and Kim Novak, tapping into their smoldering sensuality and cool charm to illicit performances of a lifetime. Apparently, the spiritual powers-that-be had decided to award Sofia a role in a reality show version of a Hitchcock tale, the main components nail-biting suspense and twisted attraction. She could almost imagine the Master of Suspense sitting in his celestial director's chair chortling at her anxiety.

Joe's Wrangler Jeep raced and bounced over the rock and hole infested excuse for a road, leaving civilization in the dust, and heightening Sofia's trepidation. She clasped her hands in her lap rather than gnawing at her expensive French manicure. She struggled not to obsess on this morning's fruitless investigation as they zoomed closer to his desert home.

Still, her mind percolated.

Either housekeeping had beat them to the public restroom, carting off last night's garbage pre-dawn, or Sofia had imagined shoving her soiled suit in the gleaming trash receptacle.

Although she had managed to lead Joe back to the shed, they'd found no evidence that she'd ever been there. The owners weren't home, and the house itself was not the residence she'd been dropped at by the limo driver. Unfortunately, she could neither remember the address, nor could she offer a clear description of that mystery house. After two hours of driving around the ritzy neighborhoods of Scottsdale and Paradise Valley, she worried that she'd imagined that too. She seemed to be missing four to five hours of her life. What memories she did have were enigmatic, like the dream sequence designed by Salvador Dalí in Hitchcock's *Spellbound*. Only *her* distorted recollections more closely resembled the work of Picasso. It made no sense. The possibility that she'd experienced something horrific, as Joe had suggested, coiled her already taut nerves into a painful knot.

"There is no terror in the bang, only in the anticipation of it," she grumbled in a husky imitation of the cinematic genius.

"Quoting Hitchcock?"

Impressed and surprised, Sofia slid him a glance. "You're a fan?"

Joe smiled for the first time in hours. "The man was a genius."

Well, damn.

He instantly sobered, grasped the gear stick, and down shifted. "What?"

Realizing he must have sensed her awe, she focused on the rugged mountains, and curbed her tongue. She didn't want to tell him that he'd just echoed her thoughts. Didn't want to address the fact that they had something in common. She didn't want to *like* Joe Bogart. Bad enough she lusted after the cynical bastard.

Twisted attraction.

He swung the jeep into a driveway, thumbing a remote to open the garage door. The house, a small rancher in a classic southwestern design, looked pristine and welcoming against the daunting mountains he'd called the Superstitions.

Sofia folded her arms over her bra-less chest and burrowed deeper into the cloth, high-backed seat. Her body buzzed with sexual awareness and dread. "I'm not crazy about staying at your place."

He killed the engine. "I'm not crazy about it either."

Another thing in common, although—*ouch*. Had she also imagined the zing between them this morning during the naked wrestling match? Since leaving the Camelback Inn he'd been Mr. Cool. Mr. Professional. Throughout the morning, he'd maintained his distance, careful not to touch her in any way. She should be grateful. Touching led to kissing. Kissing Joe was a very bad idea. Just now she ached to be bad. *Not good.* "Why can't I stay at a hotel?"

He snagged three shopping bags and shouldered open the driver's door. "Because you're family." He hopped out of the jeep, adding, "Until I hear back from Creed, we're connected at the hip."

Earl Creed. The Special Agent in Charge of the FBI's Phoenix Field Office. The man Joe had entrusted with the Beretta. According to Joe, Creed owed him a favor and had promised to initiate some tests on the QT. He hadn't told his friend where he'd gotten the gun, and if Joe was to be believed, Creed hadn't asked. Again, he'd said something about trust. Again, Sofia had balked. Every time she trusted a man, she got burned.

Her door swung open, and there stood Joe—six-foot-one, dark, dangerous and devastatingly handsome. He'd been opening doors and providing for her, in one way or another, all morning long. Considerate and polite. Kind yet professional. "Stop doing that."

"Stop being a gentleman?"

"It's annoying."

"I'll keep that in mind."

They stared at each other five charged seconds before he stepped away and moved into the house via a side door. She followed. What else could she do? She had no money. No ID. No personal belongings, except for her cell phone and whatever Joe had just purchased at Wal-Mart, God help her. As her publicist would say, she needed to put a spin on this situation.

This isn't real. This isn't happening.

Denial. Yeah, that would put her in the comfort zone. Only, there was no denying her scrapes and bruises. Or the missing hours. So, instead she opted for the drugged-at-a-celebrity-party scenario. Believing she'd ended up the butt of a bungled practical joke was a hell of a lot easier on the nerves than thinking she'd participated in a violent crime. What she needed was to occupy her mind. She needed to focus on something other than her dilemma and Joe's stellar ass. "So," she said, dragging her gaze from his excellent butt to scan what had to be the tidiest home ever. "Do you get Internet access out here in cactus-ville, or what?"

CHAPTER NINE

Rainbow Ridge, Vermont

There were definite disadvantages to living in the middle of nowhere. Like, having to rely on a satellite dish to view television instead of basic, ordinary cable. Not that Rudy wasn't impressed with the endless and varied programming—a classic movie buff's dream—but, damn, dealing with proper dish placement, two receivers, and all the rest of the particulars had been a major pain in the ass. Finding the azimuth (which, by the way he'd had to look up in the dictionary to even know what an azimuth *was*), mounting the dish (mounting Jean-Pierre would've been more fun), setting the elevation, making sure his mast was absolutely vertical (uh-huh), and lastly fine-tuning the system. It had been a two-day project for someone who was somewhat technically-challenged. Casper had wrecked his efforts in the space of minutes.

Hands on hips, Rudy squinted up at the misaligned dish, his temper simmering towards boil. "If you weren't already dead, Casper Montegue, I'd strangle you." He meant it. He was *that* bent. He had little to no sympathy for the lovelorn ghost who'd put a kink in *his* love life.

Last night's phone discussion with Jean-Pierre had sucked. The usually good-humored man's disappointment rang clear, even though he'd claimed to understand when Rudy had listed his reasons for delaying the visit. Sadness, frustration, and dammit, *suspicion* had buzzed through the phone line giving Rudy a disconcerting zap. He'd spent a sleepless night regretting the stupid lie. *Wiring problem*. He should've confided in Jean-Pierre. Should've told him about Casper. Jean-Pierre might have questioned his sanity, but at least his integrity would've been intact.

"Damn!" Every fiber of his body ached to call Afia to lament his most current mistake, but their previous conversation had been bristly as well, and if he called, she'd no doubt start in again about wanting to stick to the gang's original vacation plans. He wasn't up for an argument. He wasn't up for company. Just now, Casper was handful enough.

Growling, Rudy turned and schlepped toward the

barn to get the ladder. First, he'd realign the satellite dish. Then, he'd boot up his computer and do some ghosthunting research on the Internet. That's if his unwanted houseguest hadn't screwed with the phone line. Then, he'd call Jean-Pierre and try to right his most recent wrong.

"I can't get through."

"Me either."

Afia watched as Jake and Murphy powered off their individual cells and pocketed their phones, a bad feeling swirling in her enormous belly. She glanced sideways at Lulu, a petite, golden-haired free spirit who'd once faced down a mob boss and his minions. In comparison, enduring the foul moods of two take-charge husbands was probably a cake walk. Forcing a meek smile, Afia reached into her Gucci handbag for her own cell. "Maybe I'll have better luck."

"Forget it, baby. If I can't get a signal, you can't." Jake kicked the rental car's flat tire in frustration. Just her luck the spare was also soft. He pushed his mirrored aviators up the bridge of his nose and surveyed the vast wooded area with a frown. "We're in the middle of . . . " He looked at Murphy. "Where the hell are we?"

"Off the beaten track." The protection specialist, who reminded Afia of a lean-mean George Clooney, raised a brow at his wife and then consulted the road map he'd spread out on the hood of the mid-sized four-door.

Lulu tossed the bag of chips she'd been devouring through the lowered window and onto the back seat. She brushed crumbs from her hands and shoved her wind-blown curls out of narrowed nut-brown eyes. "You fell asleep. Someone had to navigate."

"I fell asleep because, after arriving home from a long flight from Arizona, *someone* kept me up to all hours be-tween her night-owl raids of the fridge and trying to talk me into hopping an early plane to Vermont. The reason for flying in three days early still as clear as mud, I might add."

Unfazed by his sarcasm, Lulu rocked back on the heels of her pink high-top sneakers. "Rudy needs us."

"So you said."

Afia refused to believe that Murphy's grumpiness was due to lack of sleep. Given his past and current career, she'd bet her diamond stud earrings he could operate easily on sporadic powernaps. No, something else preyed on his mind. He'd been distracted all morning and he'd frequently checked his phone messages. Probably a case. Probably nothing. Still, she hated that she'd stoked his fire by involving Lulu in her ruse. Per Rudy's instructions, she'd called her new friend to cancel the trip, and had in-stead talked her into arriving ahead of schedule.

Fighting a flash of guilt, she tucked her stick-straight, waist-length hair behind her ears and frowned at Murphy.

"Don't blame Lulu. A short cut seemed like a good idea. The sooner we get to Rudy's, the better." Last night's conversation with her friend had left her edgy and perplexed. They'd been planning this get-together for weeks. After her initial disappointment had subsided, she'd replayed their conversation in her mind. Who the heck was Casper? And why in the world would Rudy allow wiring problems to interfere with his romantic reunion with Jean-Pierre? Something was rotten in Vermont.

"I'm not blaming Lulu. She wasn't at the wheel." Murphy glared over his shoulder at Jake, who was pacing. "Why did you let the girls talk you into veering off the main highway?"

"Because Afia's had a tiring day and the sooner I can get her settled the better."

Afia rolled her eyes. "Here we go."

"She looks fine to me," Lulu said.

"More than fine," Murphy said. "She's glowing. And she sure as hell has more energy than me. Leave off, for chrissake. You've been fussing over her all morning." He turned to Afia. "How do you take it? I would've decked him by now."

She snickered.

Jake glowered. These two men had a like-loathe relationship that she'd yet to figure out. "Just pinpoint our location on the map, and point me in the direction of the nearest town," he told Murphy. "You stay with the women.

I'll start walking."

Afia immediately sobered and touched Jake's arm. "I don't like the idea of you wandering around in the wilderness. What if you get lost? What if a bear wanders out of the woods?"

Murphy's head snapped up. "Oh, no. Don't . . ."

"What if the bear's rabid, or hungry?" Lulu added, eyes wide. "Or just plain mean?"

". . .start with the 'what ifs'," Murphy finished. "My wife can 'what if' any situation . . ."

"What if a car rounds the corner too fast and . . ."

"Luciana. Hon." Murphy's voice was gentle yet firm.

The children's storyteller, renowned for her creativity, glanced at her husband, then at Afia who now had a death grip on Jake. She thunked her hand to her forehead. "Ignore me, Afia. My imagination gets the best of me sometimes."

"I'm fine," Afia lied. She didn't want Lulu to feel bad. She didn't want Jake and Murphy to worry. But in reality, she felt ill. Born on Friday the thirteenth, she'd lived somewhat of a jinxed life, losing two previous husbands to freak accidents. Although she'd cared deeply for Randy and Frank, she hadn't been in love. If anything ever happened to Jake . . . Blinking back tears, she looked up at the father of her baby, the man she loved heart and soul. "I think we should stick together. Someone will drive by at some point and we can ask them to send back a tow truck."

"What if no one drives by?" Lulu asked, then winced. "Crap."

Murphy gently tugged his wife to his side.

Jake flashed Afia a one-dimpled smile. "Nothing bad is going to happen," he assured her as he'd done time and again over the past year. He believed in the power of positive thinking, much like Rudy. Well, before Rudy had experienced his life crisis.

"You stay," Murphy said. "I'll go."

Lulu nabbed his hand. "I'll come with you."

"Oh, for chrissake." He kissed her forehead. "*What if* you have a little faith in my survival skills?"

Jake laughed. "Murph's faced down enemy troops. I'm sure he can handle one cranky bear."

"Not funny," Afia pouted.

"Very funny." Jake bumped up the brim of his baseball cap and glanced a kiss across her mouth. "But regardless, we'll wait here, all of us, together. A car has to drive by at some point, and if not," he teased, "caretaker that he is, Rudy will send out a search party when we don't arrive on time."

Blushing head to toe, Afia traded a guilty look with Lulu.

Lulu dipped her chin and twirled a golden curl around her finger.

"Ah, hell," Murphy said, locking gazes with Jake. "We've been had."

Jake swiped off his glasses and glared at Afia. "Rudy's not expecting us, is he?"

She cleared her throat. "Um, well, no. He sort of cancelled on us."

"Sort of?"

She balled her fists at her side and stood her ground. "He called last night and asked us not to come. Said he was having wiring problems. But something's wrong, Jake. I just know Rudy needs us. So, I talked Lulu into coming up here early. I'm sure once Rudy sees us he'll be glad we ignored his wishes. I know you're mad, and I'm sorry I lied, but I'm not sorry we're here."

Jake glanced at Murphy and sighed. "And to think she used to have a problem sticking up for herself."

CHAPTER TEN

Gold Canyon, Arizona

It wasn't the best script she'd ever read. It wasn't the worst. The clichéd romantic comedy certainly didn't merit four consecutive read-throughs.

But it did give Sofia a reason to stay holed up in Joe's study.

As long as she didn't have to interact with her host, she didn't have to combat the need to take refuge in his arms. Or his bed. The easier it was to fool herself into thinking she was actually on holiday and not hiding from the law. The notion that she'd hurt someone still niggled at the back of her brain.

Needing to redirect her thoughts, she'd used Joe's computer to check her email. Since the battery on her cell phone had died, she hadn't been able to check voice messages. Most of her business associates were computer junkies and usually backed up calls with emails. Sure enough, she'd logged on to hear those magical words, "You've got mail."

She had two emails from her agent. One note informing her that the studio was pressuring him about her contract—had she made up her mind yet? Another note asking her to read and consider the attached screenplay, citing it as a guaranteed cash-cow. He didn't seem to care which project she took on as long as he got his commission. Typical. Another post was from her publicist, feeling her out about an interview and a pictorial layout for *Playboy*. The last post, and most disconcerting as she hadn't actually given him her email address, was from her former agent/lover, Chaz Bradley. *Coming to LA on business, baby. Let's hook up.*

Fuck you, she'd replied.

Her response to her publicist's request had been more delicate. Yes, she knew what that kind of *exposure* could do for her career. No, she wasn't interested.

Aside from her own pride, she had the sensibilities of future nieces and nephews to consider. Bad enough she was the sexpot poster girl of several Cherry Onatop fan sites. She could only hope that if she committed to additional seasons, these devoted viewers would focus less on her skimpy-ass costumes and more on her kick-ass acting when the new head writer came on board.

Sofia fingered the screenplay entitled, *From Venice With Love*, and sighed. Maybe she should audition. Playing a buttoned-up history major was a vast departure from her "Spy Girls" balls-to-the-wall alter-ego. At least it would show some range.

She'd done enough research on characterization and archetypes to know that her need to excel boiled down to validation. She came from a long line of actors, dancers, and variety artists. She wanted to do honor to the Marino name. She wanted to be acknowledged for her brains and talent, not her tits and ass.

She glanced down at her baggy sweats and bargain running shoes. No risk of being ogled in this getup. Joe certainly hadn't spared her a second glance. A good thing, she told herself, as she tossed the script on the spotless desk. She didn't want him, of all people, to ogle. Well, okay. If she were honest, a little attention might be nice. She'd been shut up in his pristine study—who knew a man could be so anally tidy—for three hours and he hadn't checked in once.

Did he find her that unappealing? That easy to ignore? Just because she wasn't wearing her usual form-fitting clothes and sexy heels? Again, his disinterest tweaked a nerve. Repulsed by her insecurities, she pushed to her feet. She was better than this. Stronger than this. She was more than a pretty face. And by God, she could seduce the pants off of Joe Bogart even if she was bald, fifteen pounds heavier, and chafing with eczema.

That's, if she wanted to. Which she didn't.

At least, that's what she told herself as she snatched up the script for a fifth read.

Being cooped up with a woman who made his eyeballs sweat wasn't Joe's idea of fun. The trick was in maintaining the physical aloofness he'd adopted earlier today. As long as he didn't touch Sofia, he could refrain from jumping her bones. Didn't mean he didn't *think* about it. He was only human. But he wouldn't act. Human, yes. Stupid, no.

Consummating the attraction would be a messy mistake.

Never mind his personal issues. Sofia Marino was a tangle of contradictions. Tough yet sensitive. Intelligent yet impulsive. Her priorities were so freaking screwed up it made his head spin. She'd suffered an assault of some kind and all she could think about was avoiding a scandal. God forbid jeopardizing her fame and fortune. Even now, she was poring over a script she'd downloaded from the Internet. He supposed he should be grateful since it saved him from having to make inane conversation.

It had also allowed him to speak to Earl Creed in private when he'd called to report on the Beretta. Verifying ownership had been a bust as the gun wasn't registered. The only fingerprints, aside from a partial smudged print of Joe's, belonged to one Sofia Chiquita Marino. The report had been far from helpful in establishing her dilemma. He'd finessed Creed into personally holding on to the gun, while tap dancing around his friend's curiosity concerning the Hollywood spy-babe.

That had been an hour ago. Joe's biggest fear was that the owner of the mysterious house was going to turn up dead, compliments of a 9mm slug, in which case Sofia would be the number one suspect. She'd flown in from LA to spend the weekend with someone. Someone who'd sent a limousine to pick her up at the airport. Someone who lived in an affluent area. Joe's money was on a wealthy industry professional. A man who could advance her career. With Sofia, it was always about her career.

Sometimes he wished he hadn't done an extensive background search on the woman. But at the time, he'd still been working for the Bureau, and as Lulu had been unwittingly connected to his undercover op, he'd had an excuse to dig into her sister's past.

Orphaned at an early age, Sofia had grown up with her grandmother and older sister. They'd apparently failed to instill the notion of commitment. The twenty-eight-year-old woman formed and abandoned relationships with men as frequently as she dropped jobs and classes. In his estimation, her hunger for stardom was a veiled need for attention. If she really wanted to be the next Meryl Streep, she would've pursued her dramatic studies. But instead of perfecting her craft and paying her dues, she opted to skip to the head of the class via men in power.

No doubt about it, the man in question was a man in power.

Even though Joe despised the thought of her sleeping her way to the top, he couldn't shed the primitive desire to shelter her from harm. And though he lacked proof, his gut insisted she was indeed at risk. In order to help her, he needed a full account of last night. The bitch of it was amnesia served as a safety mechanism. If he forced her to remember before she was emotionally ready, he could send her over the edge.

A hike into the Superstitions might ease the way—the ancient, hallowed ground did wonders to heal his body and spirit—but she'd yet to emerge from his study. Apparently, that script was riveting. He'd peeked in to offer her a cup of herbal tea—God knew he was familiar with the lingering effects of a tequila bender—but had backed out when he'd remembered she'd asked him to cut the thoughtful crap.

Talk about irritating.

What? So she couldn't deal with a little simple consideration? Was she so used to men treating her like shit that she didn't know how to handle kindness?

Agitated, Joe lifted the lid off of the pot and stirred the simmering marinara sauce. He'd no doubt catch hell for cooking her supper. But, screw it, the woman had to eat. Not that she'd agree. Five-o-clock in the evening and all she'd had today was a slice of dry toast, a banana, and four bottles of water. Normally, he'd attribute her lack of appetite to the hangover. But he knew for a fact her eating habits sucked. He knew from Murphy who'd heard it from Lulu. For some crackpot reason she thought she was overweight. It couldn't help that she'd immersed herself in an industry obsessed with unrealistic ideals. He preferred the curvaceous bombshells of yesterday to the anorexic *Stepford* actresses of today. Intelligence and a healthy dose of self-confidence didn't hurt, either. Brains and beauty were a powerful combination.

Speaking of powerful combinations . . . Joe inhaled the mouthwatering aromas of onions, garlic, basil, oregano, and thyme, wondering when Sofia last had a home-cooked meal. And he wasn't talking a blender-generated smoothie.

"Smells delicious."

The clipped observation sounded more like a gripe than a compliment. Probably pissed her off that she was actually tempted to eat. He kept his back to her and quirked a smug grin. No one could resist his *Nona* Maria's marinara sauce.

"You forgot the cigarettes."

He glanced over his shoulder at her—speaking of delicious—frowning as she rooted through the Wal-Mart shopping bags. Frankly, he was surprised it had taken her this long to seek a nicotine fix. "I didn't forget."

She searched the bags a second time. "I don't see them."

"That's because I didn't buy them." He turned back to his cooking, amazed and annoyed. How was it possible for a woman sporting no make-up, hillbilly pigtails, and ill-fitting clothes to look so frickin' sexy?

"Is this your subtle way of telling me smoking's bad for my health?"

He ignored her sarcasm, tasted the sauce. "Let me guess," he said, while adding a pinch of sugar. "You smoke to suppress your appetite."

"That's one reason."

"What's the other reason?"

"Calms my nerves."

"There are healthier ways to alleviate stress." Now, why in the hell had he said that?

"Name one."

Against his better judgment, he ditched the spoon and turned, facing the exotic beauty head-on. "Hiking. Running. Rock climbing." *Mind-blowing sex.*

"That's three. But I get the idea." She frowned as she inspected the two additional sweat suits he'd purchased for her, along with denim overalls, two pairs of baggy

Bermuda shorts, and five oversized T-shirts. "Strenuous physical activity."

Sex. "Cardio exercise."

Her gaze flicked from the sportswear to him. *Oomph!* Those sultry eyes packed a powerful punch. She arched one perfectly-tweezed eyebrow. "What about sex?"

Yes, thank you. I'd love to have sex. With you. Now. On the kitchen table. On the floor. Against the fridge. Pick your poison. "What about it?"

"Does that count as cardio exercise?"

"Only if you do it right." He held her gaze, sort of a double dog dare. If she thought she could best him in a game of innuendo, she was mistaken.

But instead of flinging a comeback, she broke eye contact and pulled more loot from the bag. "Who are these for?"

"You said you needed fresh delicates."

"But, they're granny underwear."

Exactly. On the off chance that he was subjected to another drunken strip show, she'd be easier to resist in high-rise cotton briefs and an old-fashioned Cross-Your-Heart bra.

He hoped.

He gave a disinterested shrug. "They're functional."

She scowled. "Like these sweats and T-shirts? Which, by the way, are two sizes too big."

"Better to hide that figure than flaunt it." Those

dangerous curves would turn heads even if she were dressed in a potato sack. From the pained look on her face, he surmised she thrived on the very attention he strived to avoid. Christ. He was trying to lay low while they sorted out this mess, and she was worried about her wardrobe? Could she be anymore shallow? Disgusted with himself for being so damned attracted to her, he turned back to the bubbling sauce.

Ten seconds of silent tension. Ten seconds of anticipation. He felt the shift in mood. Felt her moving in for the kill. Whatever had possessed him to invite this potent creature into his sanctuary?

"That's not jar sauce."

Her warm breath caressed his ear, sending a rush of blood to his groin. Or, maybe it was the brush of her full breasts against his arm as she leaned in and peered over his shoulder. Freaking A. "Bite your tongue. *Nona* would roll over in her grave." He set aside the wooden spoon and moved swiftly to the refrigerator in search of something, anything. The act afforded him distance and a blast of cold air.

"Lulu said Murphy's an incredible cook. Says he's almost as talented in the kitchen as he is in the . . . well, I probably shouldn't go there."

"Probably not." Maybe if he stuck his dick in the freezer . . .

"So, do you two have anything else in common?

Hobbies?" She came up behind him, her voice tinged with blatant suggestion. "Size of your shoes?"

He mentally banged his head against the top shelf.

"I'm partial to Italian sausage."

His shaft throbbed in answer to her husky declaration.

"Some people like it sweet, but I say the spicier the better. How about you?"

His rising temperature burned away vital brain cells. He glanced over his shoulder, his gaze lingering on her stunning face. Suddenly, he was transported back to the time in Atlantic City when he'd kissed her out of frustration. He licked his lower lip, remembering the taste of her, the feel of that luscious body when she'd succumbed to his will. "What do you think?"

She arched a sassy brow, intimating she'd hopped the same memory-train. "I think you like it hot."

His skin tingled as her arm snaked around his waist and grabbed his sausage—recently purchased at the local butcher shop.

She withdrew the cellophane-wrapped package from the shelf, read the label. "I was right. Hot."

Bitch. And he thought that with the utmost respect. She was damned good with the innuendoes. He braced himself for a smug grin. Instead, her expression was one of pure innocence. Yeah, right. He'd seen that look before. "Spy Girl". Episode Six: *The Hunt.*

Sofia was playing him. But why? He wasn't connected to

Hollywood or New York. He couldn't do jack for her art.

"This *is* what you were looking for, right?" she asked sweetly. "Meat for the sauce?"

He calmly shut the fridge door, claimed the sausage, and moved back to the stove, mindful that his pole was still at half-mast. "Do you want spaghetti or linguini?"

"I'm not hungry."

"I'm not surprised." He wasn't in the mood to discuss the evils of carbs and starch. "Spaghetti or linguini?"

"Maybe I need to work up an appetite." She gently scraped her tigress claws along his forearm.

He probably imagined the seductive purr. Regardless, he'd had enough of this game. Like he needed her to turn up the heat on his personal hell. "Maybe you do."

Her lush mouth curved into a cat-ate-the-mouse smile. "Got any ideas?"

He clicked the burner off and nabbed Sofia's hot little paw. "One or two."

CHAPTER ELEVEN

Rainbow Ridge, Vermont

Rudy narrowed his choices down to three and then placed his order at Amazon.com. Access to the Internet had been iffy all afternoon. He'd been knocked off-line several times while perusing books on parapsychology. He didn't know whether to blame Casper, his Internet server, or the phone company. Not that it mattered. The result was the same. A wasted afternoon and threadbare nerves.

For a moment he lamented purchasing a bed and breakfast twenty minutes from civilization in any direction. DSL and cable had yet to come to Rainbow Ridge.

Then again, he'd been drawn to Hollyberry Inn because it *was* so isolated. He'd discovered serenity in wooded hillsides and endless sky. No casinos. No malls. No alternative dance clubs to tempt him back to his old trolling ways. His closest neighbors: two competing B and B's and a popular roadside tavern. The proprietors, according to his gaydar, June-and-Ward-Cleaver straight.

It's not that he had any inclination to stray. He'd learned his lesson on that score. Seeking satisfaction, emotionally or physically, through casual sex was a quick fix. A cop out. He was stronger than that. Better than that. Self-help books and affirmations had steered him down the right path—*I am open and ready for a serious, long-term relationship*—but it had taken a major misstep to drive the concept home. A misstep he regretted to this day. A misstep he and Jean-Pierre had yet to openly discuss.

Jean-Pierre maintained details were insignificant.

Rudy had been so desperate to put the ugliness behind them, that he'd welcomed the man's blind forgiveness. Now, he deliberated the wisdom of that decision. Mostly because his betrayal wasn't as tawdry as what he knew Jean-Pierre assumed. What if that misassumption had been festering all these months? What if the details *did* matter? How could he propose a lifetime commitment when the possibility loomed they'd be building a future on shaky ground?

Rudy tapped his fingers on the mouse pad and stared

at the empty inbox of his AOL account. More than ever he longed to clear the air. In the past four hours, he'd sent the man two emails and, between his cell and home phone, had left five voicemails. Jean-Pierre had yet to return a single message.

Rudy didn't know whether to be worried or irritated. Either JP was more pissed about the postponed reunion than he'd admitted last night, or he *couldn't* return the calls. Meanwhile, Rudy's brain cranked out a dozen catastrophes that could have befallen his lover, including such goodies as a drive-by shooting or freak household accident.

Ironically, he'd put Jean-Pierre through this same hell the night of his betrayal. He'd driven around in a daze, avoiding confrontation rather than placing a simple phone call to let his lover know he was alive and well.

Rudy was getting a taste of his own medicine and it tasted like shit on a Ritz. Aggravated, he abandoned the computer and his tiny office in favor of the kitchen and a cup of apple-cinnamon tea. He'd prefer a glass of wine, but Casper had confiscated his stash. He could steal away to Pearl and Earl's Tavern, but he didn't want to risk missing a call from Jean-Pierre. The cell phone reception in this area was spotty. He'd have to settle for a cup of tea and an hour of meditation on the front porch swing.

Five minutes later, steaming cup in hand, Rudy stepped outside and settled on the traditional red cedar swing. The unfinished wood creaked beneath his weight. He relaxed against the sloped backrest, sipped his aromatic tea, and focused on positive thoughts. At least he didn't have to worry about putting on a happy face and playing Martha Stewart to an inn full of guests.

Again, the wood creaked. The comfort springs twanged. A ripple of dread shot up his spine a split second before one of the hanging chains snapped and the left side of the bench seat collided with the porch. Rudy hit hard and careened sideways. Hot tea splattered. His ass smarted and his thighs burned. He pushed himself up, cursing Casper to hell.

He swore he heard laughter.

Rather than ramming his fist through one of the four porch posts, he muttered the sentiment he'd shared with Afia last summer when her life had taken a downward spiral. "No matter how bad it seems, it could always be worse."

A beat later, the sentiment proved true when car tires crunched over pea rock.

"He doesn't look happy to see us," Murphy said.

"Nope." Jake killed the motor. "Looks pretty pissed." He took off his sunglasses and slid Afia a scolding look. "Then again, he did ask us not to come."

Afia massaged her wrist, a nervous habit from her past. She didn't regret coming, but she did regret tricking her husband and Murphy. They'd made their displeasure evident while awaiting roadside aid. Jake had been against her flying to begin with. To know she'd arranged a trip against Rudy's wishes really burned his butt. She'd almost kissed the tow truck driver when he'd arrived with a new tire as he'd saved her from yet another lecture on her "delicate condition".

Murphy's reaction was to the opposite extreme. He'd fallen into tension-filled silence. She didn't know how Lulu stood it. At least Jake got his anger out and over with. Mostly.

"Rudy doesn't know this car. He doesn't know it's us," Lulu volunteered. "He'll perk up. You'll see." She didn't wait for Murphy to come around and help her out. She pushed open the back seat door and sprang out, that adorable pink poodle purse looped over her arm.

Afia tried to follow suit, but her big belly and a spasm in her right calf made it impossible to move with the same pep and speed as Lulu. Hard to believe the golden-haired sprite was almost five years her senior. Afia wholly admired the professional storyteller's childlike aura. Oh, to be that confident and carefree. Self-confidence had long been an issue for Afia. She'd mostly conquered her insecurities, but now and again they reared. Like now.

Suddenly Jake was there, his strong arms easily shifting her from the car to the gravel driveway. "He sees it's us," he grumbled in her ear. "Still looks pissed."

That's what had her insecurities flaring. Had Rudy's moving hundreds of miles away taken a toll on their friendship? The notion shook her to the wedge heels of her Via Spiga mules. True friendship, something she'd experienced little of in her sheltered life, was far more precious to her than her inherited fortune. Long ago, she'd bought Rudy a limousine to help him launch his own chauffer business. It seemed only fitting that he'd recently sold that car to help finance his new dream. It never occurred to her that *she* wouldn't somehow fit into his new life.

Gritting her teeth against the calf spasm, Afia waddled toward the Inn. Pictures hadn't done the rambling two-story lodge justice. Rich wood exterior. White paned windows flanked by hunter green shutters. Two cobblestone chimneys. The overall classic design echoed a bygone era. Elegant in its simplicity, Hollyberry Inn looked warm and welcoming.

More than she could say for its owner.

Closing in, she noted the broken swing, fractured mug, and Rudy's wet lap. Maybe the mishap, and not their arrival, was the source of his foul mood. One could hope.

She climbed the steps, with Jake's help, and moved forward to hug her old friend. The tension in his normally loving arms was unsettling. She backed away, eyed the swing, then the chauffer turned resort owner. "Are you all right?"

His troubled gaze shifted from her swollen belly to the

broken swing. "I don't want you here, Afia. Dammit, I told you I needed to postpone. It's not safe."

Through the years, this man had accepted her on any terms, unconditional love. He'd stood beside her even when rumors circulated that she'd offed two husbands to inherit their fortunes. Aside from Jake, Rudy Gallow was her most cherished friend, and now he was pushing her away. She fought hard to stem welling tears. If she cried, Jake would give Rudy the riot act. Normally, her bulked-up friend could easily defend himself, but there was nothing normal about this moment. "Why? Just because of some faulty wiring and a broken swing? Jake can fix the swing." She looked up at her husband, a man she thought capable of snatching stars from the sky if he put his mind to it. "Right?"

Jake interlaced his fingers with hers and lovingly squeezed, letting her know that he understood her distress. He peered up at the broken hook and chain dangling from the ceiling. "How hard could it be?" He eyed Rudy. "As for your wiring problems, Murphy's a whiz with all things electronic."

"On it." Murphy moved in beside them with Lulu in tow. "Just tell me what you need, Gallow."

Lulu rushed forward and threw her arms around Rudy, telegraphing her sincere fondness for the man. It spoke well of Murphy that he didn't even raise a brow. Obviously, he was confident in their relationship. "It's a beautiful property," she said, kissing Rudy on the cheek and then stepping back with a bright smile. "Jean-Pierre's going to love it."

Cheeks flushing, Rudy averted his troubled blue gaze.

His strange behavior verified something was amiss. Knowing the boys had experienced a few rocky months, Afia shifted uncomfortably, worrying that Rudy had broken off with Jean-Pierre. Or vice versa. It would be just like him to withhold bad news for fear of upsetting her. He and Jake had sheltered her from the truth more than once. She sighed heavily, weary of their overprotective tendencies. For once she wished someone would lean on *her*.

Misreading her discomfort, Jake raised a brow at Rudy. "Are you going to invite us in, dude? Afia needs to get off her feet."

"No, I don't. I've been sitting in the car for hours." She smiled up at Rudy with all the love in her heart. *Lean on me.* "I need to stretch my legs. How about a tour of the grounds?"

"I'll get the luggage." Murphy nudged Jake and pointed to the ladder leaning against the corner of the house. "You get started on the swing."

Jake kissed Afia's temple. "Don't overdue it, baby." He rapped Rudy on the shoulder. "Take good care of my girl." Then he readjusted his ball cap and set off to play repairman.

Lulu had already located a broom and was sweeping up the broken mug.

It was then that Afia knew her husband and new friends sensed the same trouble she did. They were pulling together and digging in. Now that they were here, there'd be no getting rid of them until Rudy's problems were solved. A caretaker at heart, he'd played Cupid and the voice of reason in their lives. It was time to return the favor.

Squaring her shoulders, Afia grasped Rudy's big hand and tugged him toward a clump of leafy trees. "So. Who's Casper?"

CHAPTER TWELVE

Los Angeles, California

"We're jinxed."

"Aren't you being a little paranoid, Frank?"

"Ain't that the pot calling the kettle black?" Frank resisted an eye roll as Jesse used a sanitized towellette to disinfect the tabletop the waitress had just wiped down. "We should've been halfway there by now." He snatched up a handful of airport lounge peanuts, jiggled them in his palm like a pair of hot dice. If it weren't for circumstances, he'd be sitting in a Mexican casino just now shooting craps and flirting with a brown-eyed, hot-tamale cocktail server. Talk about a freaking run of bad luck. "That's the second time our flight's been delayed."

Jesse shrugged. "That's not jinxed. That's unfortunate."

"Same difference."

"As for gay-boy . . ."

"I don't want to talk about it."

"How was I supposed to know he'd be so squeamish? All I did was threaten to cut off his wanker. He took one look at the carving knife I swiped from the kitchen and fainted. *Fainted*, for chrissake."

"I know. I was there," Frank said dryly. He popped a cashew, chewed.

"Right. So you know it wasn't my fault."

"Whatever. Result's the same. The polesmoker's dead."

"So what?" Jesse disposed of the anti-bacterial wipe and leaned closer to Frank, careful not to touch the table. "The cops will label it an accident," he said in a low voice. "The pansy-ass fucker was drunk. He tripped or passed out, bashed his head on the table, and bled to death. Case closed."

Frank agreed. Otherwise, he would've disposed of the body. Still, his gut warned trouble. The sooner they tied off that loose thread and crossed over to Mexico, the better. "Where in the hell's that waitress with our drinks?"

"You've been downing pain pills and shots of whiskey on and off all day. Keep it up and by the time we get on the plane, you'll be comatose."

"That's the plan." The only thing he hated more than

a botched job was flying.

"At least we've got the goods to trap the bitch," Jesse said, applying lotion to the reddened skin around his cast. Fearful of an infection, so far he'd followed the doc's instructions with anal precision.

Frank patted the journal tucked in the inside pocket of his denim jacket, smiling when the waitress served him a double shot of Wild Turkey. His ego smarted when the bitch frowned at him and beamed at Jesse. Then again, he looked like the friggin' Elephant Man, thanks to Sofia Marino. He adjusted his Stetson and shrugged off the waitress's disgust. He had bigger fish to catch, and the bait was in his pocket.

He and Jesse's visit to Marino's apartment hadn't been a total bust. The note they'd snagged off of the fridge tipped them off to Vermont. The journal they'd found in her bedside drawer named specifics and the means to lure her to Hollyberry Inn, if she wasn't already there.

Jesse inspected his cola glass for tell-tale lipstick or finger smudges, then pulled a twenty out of the wallet they'd lifted off gay-boy.

Frank's mood lightened significantly as he sipped the whiskey and watched his brother try to pay the tab without physically touching the waitress. He couldn't count on much in life, but he could count on his brother's freaky phobia. Most times Jesse's quirks got on his nerves, but sometimes, like now, he found them damned amusing.

One thing was for sure and certain; Jesse was blood and thereby his first priority. He wondered if Sofia harbored the same devotion toward her sister?

Hell, he was banking on it.

CHAPTER THIRTEEN

Gold Canyon, Arizona

Sofia's leg muscles screamed. Her lungs burned.

Joe had the stamina of an Olympic athlete.

He palmed her ass and she froze. She absorbed the strength of his touch, warning bells clanging in her head as heat registered between her thighs.

"Just trying to help," he said, misunderstanding her panicked expression. "Jesus, woman. Give me your hand." When she didn't comply, he captured her fingers with a curse. "Grab this and . . ."

"I don't need instruction." She yanked her hand from his grasp and swiped at her moist brow. "I've done this before."

"Could've fooled me."

She ignored his sarcasm and put her back into it.

His brow creased with discomfort. "Want me to slow down?"

"Why, are you tired?" Somehow she managed the sarcastic reply in an even tone. Why was she so winded? Obsessed with maintaining a svelte figure, she worked out with a personal trainer four times a week. In addition, Tae Kwon Do kept her conditioned and limber. Then again her lack of energy could be due to lack of food, and although she was by no means a novice where *cardio exercise* was concerned, she was used to a more controlled environment.

"Almost there," Joe said.

They crested at the same time.

He let out a grunt of satisfaction.

She collapsed, her body vibrating from head to toe. "Not for anything, Bogart, but where's that big payoff you promised me?"

"Open your eyes."

She'd rather sleep for an hour, but her screaming thigh muscles demanded satisfaction. Reluctantly, she forced open her lids and was rewarded with a breathtaking view.

Joe started to comment. She cut him off. "Don't ruin the moment."

"I was just going to say they don't have sunsets like this in New Jersey."

"No, they don't. Now shut up." She swiped off her

sport's cap, crossed her legs at the ankles, and settled back against the rock wall, enthralled. She'd been so focused on what he'd described as a moderate hike into the mountains that she'd failed to notice the deepening and shifting colors of the evening sky. Stark, bright blue had given way to a subtle blend of orange, red, and purple. The sheer vastness caused her lungs to bloom with wonder. No skyscrapers. No smog. Just spectacular summits and canyons, and miles of endless sky. All right, so maybe there was one perk to living in the godforsaken desert. Kick-ass sunsets.

"That's Weavers Needle," Joe said, pointing to one particularly remarkable rock spire. "Some say it's the finger of God, pointing up to the sky. Others claim it's a symbolic tombstone for all the treasure seekers who've died there. Ever heard of the legend of the Lost Dutchman's Gold Mine?"

Sofia affected the accent of a salty prospector. "You mean there's gold in them thar hills?"

Joe laughed. "Rumor has it."

The uncharacteristic show of mirth tweaked the heat he'd incited when he'd given her the boost up and over the last boulder. She squeezed her thighs together, suppressing a sensual tingle when he raked his hands through his shaggy hair, securing the top half in a ponytail. The man's profile was as chiseled and hypnotic as the legendary rock spire.

She focused back on the sunset. Why torture herself

by drooling over a guy who'd made his disinterest blatantly clear? She'd made a fool of herself, coming on to him in the kitchen. But when he'd made that derogatory comment about her figure, she'd felt compelled to assert her feminine wiles. A quickie ego boost. She didn't plan to follow through—no way was she breaking her no-sex-until-the-anniversary-of-her-break-up-with-Chaz resolution—but she'd certainly expected him to pounce on the invitation. Any other man would have. "I suppose you know the particulars of this Lost Dutchman legend?"

"I know the particulars of several legends. The Superstition Wilderness is steeped in myth."

"Why?"

"Why, what?

"Why are you familiar with all of the legends?"

"A. Interesting stuff. B. Useful in my job."

"The jeep tour thing?"

"Yeah, the jeep tour thing."

She didn't get it. Against her better judgment, Sofia tore her eyes from the heart-stopping vista and regarded Joe—also heart-stopping—with renewed interest.

They'd hiked for ninety minutes, sidestepping precarious rocks and various forms of cactus, eventually veering off Peralta Trail altogether. In his obsession to keep her out of the public eye, he'd chosen a less traveled route to Fremont Saddle. His rugged shortcut had proven a real heart-pumper, but Joe wasn't even breathing hard. In fact, he looked relaxed, more relaxed than she'd ever seen him. And recently she'd seen more of Joseph Bogart than any woman who'd been celibate for eight months and counting should see.

She surreptitiously admired the cut, sun-bronzed muscles of his arms and legs, struggling not to reflect on their early morning wrestling match. Specifically, his naked body. The man was in prime condition. He looked oddly erotic in his ratty brown T-shirt and baggy khaki shorts. Normally, she panted after more cultured men, like her ex-agent, ex-lover Chaz, who suited up daily in Armani. Men in pursuit of prestige and wealth. Joe had abandoned a vital, intense job to play tour guide. Aside from the shallow physical aspect, she didn't get her attraction. She didn't get *him*. "So you drive tourists around, show them the sights, regale them with a few folk tales."

"Basically."

"And you find that fulfilling?"

"Do you find pretending to be someone else fulfilling?"

Her cheeks flushed. "Excuse me?" What the hell did that mean? Was he calling her a fake? A liar?

He lifted a brow. "Acting."

The clarification only fueled her impatience. "Do you have a problem with entertainers?" She instantly regretted the question. It smacked of insecurity. She didn't give a damn what he thought. She didn't need his approval.

"I have a problem with an industry that crams youth

and physical perfection down the public's throat."

She wanted to argue the point, but couldn't. Meaty roles for actresses over forty were rare. Just shy of thirty, Sofia was already feeling the pressure. As for physical perfection, although she'd been blessed with her parents' exotic good looks, she'd always been too fleshy, by most directors' standards. Even after securing her role on "Spy Girl", she'd still been at the mercy of an unforgiving camera. The day after filming the first episode, the director had shown up on her doorstep, offering her a packet of white powder. What she'd feared was cocaine turned out to be a laxative. *"You looked a little puffy in the rushes,"* he'd said. She'd thanked the man (arguing would've been career suicide), flushed the laxative down the toilet, and intensified her diet and time at the gym.

Even though Joe's criticism had merit, she felt compelled to defend her profession. From Vaudeville to Broadway musicals to Hollywood films, the Marinos had been in entertainment for generations. Attacking the industry was like attacking a member of her family. "Believe it or not, talent does factor in."

He glanced sideways at her. "Sometimes."

Was that a *but-not-in-your-case* sometimes? Or, a *like-in-your-case* sometimes? Or, was it simply a blanket comment? After all, he'd never seen her perform. Unless he'd lied about not watching "Spy Girl". "Granted," she said, drawing her knees to her chest and hugging them to hide the agitated rise and fall of her chest, "sometimes it's not about what you know, but who you know." Even as she said it, her head began to throb.

"*I can give you the recognition you deserve.*"

Sofia closed her eyes, tried to envision a face to go with the masculine voice invading her head with the menace of an enemy army. Her heartbeat raged as she broke out in a nauseous sweat. No face. Just arms and legs. A nose. A shoe. Colors. Red seeping into orange and white. Blue splattered with red.

Blood.

Run!

Disoriented, Sofia pushed to her feet so fast she lost her balance and staggered forward, her dazed vision fixed on the adjacent rocky slope.

Falling . . .

Her knees buckled just as someone hooked her by the waist and hauled her against a strong, unyielding body.

Joe.

Shaken, she dropped her head to his shoulder, conscious that she was trembling, but unable to rule her actions or dark, anxious thoughts. Her lungs ached. Her fingers tingled. Heel to bone. Spike through flesh. <u>Pain</u>! "This isn't real. This isn't happening."

"Let the memories come, Sofia." He tightened his embrace, cupped the back of her head as he spoke calmly in her ear. "I'm here. You're safe."

She gasped for air. "Not safe."

"Why?"

"Can't breathe. Can't . . ." She massaged a fierce pain in her chest. "Oh, Jesus. I think I'm having a heart attack."

He lowered them both to the ground, pulled her onto his lap. "You're not having a heart attack. Stop thinking about last night. Focus on something else. Something that makes you happy. Something special."

"Lulu."

"Your sister." He laughed softly, his tone full of admiration. "She's special, all right." He smoothed his hand over her back, massaged her shoulders while she continued to clutch her chest and gulp for air. "Relax. Focus on Lulu. Imagine her in the kitchen cooking dinner for my brother."

She imagined comical chaos. Nervous laughter squeezed past her constricted throat.

"Uh-huh." He continued his relaxing ministrations, his hands comforting and sure. "Did she tell you about the night she made Chili Con Carne for him and his security team?"

She nodded, unclenching her fists as the tightness eased in her chest and the queasiness began to subside. "She said all five of them lapsed into coughing fits."

"Murph said he and Gordo washed theirs down with beer. Moose and Davis swallowed theirs dry like the Neanderthals they are, but Bulls-eye . . ."

". . . spit ground beef across the table hitting Gordo in

the chest," Sofia finished with a quirk of her trembling lips.

"Bulls-eye's a wuss. A superior marksman, but a wuss." Smiling, Joe pulled a bandanna from his shorts' pockets. "Murphy said she must've used half a jar of chili pepper and Tabasco."

"She asked them if it was too hot," Sofia said in defense of Lulu. "They answered no, and cleaned their bowls."

He smoothed his kerchief over her clammy face. "Eating the chili was safer than dealing with Murphy if they'd hurt her feelings. They picked their poison. No offense to your sister."

"None taken." She'd been a victim of Lulu's cooking on more than one occasion. Unsettled by Joe's tender care, Sofia nabbed his wrist and stilled his fussing. She felt his pulse thrumming beneath her fingers, met his gaze, and experienced an intense rush of sexual awareness.

No mistaking. No misinterpreting. His decadent whiskey-eyes swirled with raw desire. He worked his jaw. "Feeling better?"

"I feel like an idiot." Her voice came out a strangled croak. "What just happened?"

"Panic attack."

She trusted his diagnosis. A man trained in psychology would know the difference between hyperventilating and a coronary. She licked her dry lips. "A hangover, and then a panic attack. You're not exactly seeing me at my best."

His intoxicating gaze slid to her mouth. "I wouldn't

say that."

More lethal than tequila, his warring gentle and dangerous aura struck her woozy with lust. "I thought you weren't interested."

"I'm not."

"Me either." They were both lying. Thing was, she wasn't going to make a fool of herself twice in one day. He had to make the first move. *Move*, dammit.

Joe's body sizzled as he registered the challenge in Sofia's eyes. *Don't do it*, he told himself. *Show some restraint, asshole*. A light breeze ruffled her hair, wafting the scent of generic hotel shampoo. He envisioned her in her demi-bra and G-string, all that mocha flesh, and he snapped. Fuck restraint, he was all over her, and she was all for it.

They segued into a heated blur of groping hands and sloppy, open-mouthed kisses. Eager fingers raked through each other's hair, snaked beneath shirts to explore bare skin. Lips, teeth, tongue. She tasted better than he remembered. How was that possible? He framed that gorgeous face within his hands and devoured, savored, his brain cells burning away as she bested his enthusiasm.

In an erotic haze, she shifted and straddled him, wrapping her long legs around his waist, grinding against what seemed like a year-long hard-on. This was better than his dreams. Better than his daily fantasies. He was hot and hard, starving and feasting. He was sitting atop a mountain with his lap and heart full of Sofia Marino. The setting sun burned into his back while Sofia deepened the kiss and seared his soul.

He was on fire.

He wanted more. Sweet Christ, he wanted to rule her body, to rock her with endless orgasms. He wanted her to know the gentle, skilled hand of a respectful lover.

But not on a dusty, rocky trail. Not when she'd just suffered a memory that sent her into a tailspin. No matter how badly he ached to make love to Sofia, he refused to take advantage.

So why the hell did he have his hands down her pants, his palms full of her bodacious ass?

Because she was in his blood. Because he had a weakness for beautiful, vulnerable women.

Because he was a bastard.

His cell phone vibrated against his thigh, a life saver, because, fuck, she was working his goddamned zipper. If she got her hands on his dick, he'd lose it and nail her for sure. He was only a man. An obsessed one at that.

His insides twisted with disappointment as he redirected her eager hands to his shoulders and severed the kiss. "I'm vibrating."

"Me too," she rasped in a breathless voice. "So, why are we stopping?"

Free of those Fanny-farmer pigtails, her hair was a sexy, just-rolled-out-of-bed mess, her full lips puffy and red from his assault. Oh, man. He glanced away before he lost control . . . again, reached in his pocket and fumbled.

"I would've done that for you," she teased in a husky drawl.

Jaw clenched, he jerked out his phone, thumbed the talk button. "Yeah?"

Sofia looked at him as though he'd gone insane. Maybe he had.

"Lulu wants to know what you're doing with her sister?" Murphy asked.

Joe felt like he'd just been caught feeling up Sofia in the back seat of a car. He resisted the ridiculous urge to scan the jagged slopes for a hidden camera and focused on his "date". She looked more than a little pissed that he'd interrupted their lustful frenzy to take a phone call. His ego roared, *yes*, even as his conscience yelled, *bastard*. "I thought you weren't going to alert Lulu until I got back to you with details."

Hearing her older sister's name, Sofia scrambled off Joe's lap and righted her clothes, her expression morphing from pissed to embarrassed.

"I didn't tell her anything. She saw it on one of those entertainment news shows."

"What?"

"Someone took a picture of you and Sofia coming out of the Camelback Inn. She looked frumpy and hung over. You had your arm around her. The newscaster claimed you two spent the night engaged in a, quote: drunken love-fest."

"Hell."

Sofia tucked her hair behind her ears, tugged on her sports cap. "What?"

Joe waved her off.

"The media ID'd you, Bogie." Murphy lowered his voice. "It's only a matter of time before they track your address and a camera crew turns up on your front lawn."

"I hear you."

"Any reason why you haven't called me with particulars on whatever panicked Sofia last night?"

"A: I don't have particulars. B: I tried your cell three times. No service. Tried you at home, got the answering machine. Didn't figure you'd want me to leave a message. Where are you?"

"Bumfuck, Vermont."

Joe started down the trail, motioned Sofia to follow. "I thought you weren't due at the inn for a few more days."

"Yeah, well, things aren't exactly going as planned."

He hung back and watched Sofia scale a boulder. "I'll say." He salivated as the thin cotton jogging pants stretched and molded to her thighs and backside. A minute ago he'd had his hands on that goddess-like ass.

"Has Sofia heard from Jean-Pierre?"

"I don't see how. Her cell phone's dead. Wait." He caught up to her and squeezed her shoulder. "When you checked your email, was there anything from Jean-Pierre?"

"No." She knuckled up the brim of her cap. "Why?"

"She hasn't talked to him since yesterday," Joe told Murphy. "Why?"

"According to Gallow, he and Jean-Pierre had a fight last night. He hasn't been able to reach him all day. He's worried."

"Gallow confided in *you*?" Joe snorted. "Exploring your sensitive side, Murph?" His amusement died when Sofia pressed her luscious body up against him, trying to hear whatever Murphy had to say.

"Screw you, dickhead," Murphy quipped. "He told Afia who told Jake . . ."

"Who told you. Got it."

Sofia tried to grab the phone. Joe nudged her away. Her sexy scent made him insane. "We'll give it an hour, and then give him a try."

"I'll keep trying too," Murphy said. "Probably nothing. Sofia recovered from that hangover yet?"

"Almost." Joe winked at her in an effort to cool her rising agitation. They didn't have time for another panic attack.

"She didn't look so hot on the news," Murphy said. "Getting back to that, if Sofia's in trouble, you better haul ass."

He'd made that last statement in Italian, which told Joe that Lulu had just walked in and Murph didn't want her to know her sister was at risk.

Joe prodded Sofia back into motion while continuing his conversation with Murphy. "So, what did you tell your wife when she asked about us?"

"That you're exploring a mutual attraction."

Joe frowned at the humor in his brother's voice. "*Cazzone*. I'll call you with a report when we get situated." He powered off, pocketed the cell, and hurried Sofia along.

"How does Lulu know we're together?" she asked. "Where are we going? And why did you call Murphy a prick?"

He glanced sideways at her as they navigated the rocky descent. "Been brushing up on your Italian?" Last summer she'd butchered the insults she'd hurled at him in their parents' native tongue.

She shrugged. "So, what's going on?"

"We made the news."

She stopped in her tracks.

"*Entertainment This Millisecond*, or some shit. Must've been that front desk clerk at the Camelback," he explained. "He's the only one who knew we shared a room last night. He saw how trashed you were. Probably assumed we were an item. At least, that's what he told the media when he sent in the picture that he snapped of us this morning when we were leaving the hotel. To think I tipped the jerk to keep his mouth shut."

"He probably made a fortune off of that photo." Sofia blew out a tense breath. "Give me your phone."

"Not now." He grasped her elbow and urged her forward. "We have to get back, pack, and relocate before the media tracks down my address."

She jerked away. "Give me your phone, Joe. I mean it. I want to check on Jean-Pierre and then I have to call my publicist. I have to tell her something, anything. She can't protect my reputation and career if she's in the dark. I can't afford a scandal, dammit."

"So you keep saying." He bit the inside of his cheek, swallowed his opinion on her *career*. He handed her the phone. "Don't tell her about your memory loss. About the gun. Tell her . . ."

"Yeah, yeah." She waved him off, while her call connected. "I'm getting an automated message on JP's cell. Let me try home." She punched in more numbers. Waited. "Answering machine." She disconnected, pursed her luscious lips. "Maybe he's at Luc's."

He rolled his eyes heavenward, begging patience. Instead, he was rewarded with the ominous sight of a vulture circling high above Sofia. His neck muscles bunched. "We don't have time for this, babe."

She shot him a look, dialed more numbers, and set off walking. "Laura? Hi. Yes, it's me. I know. I heard. How bad did I look?"

Joe shook his head. Unbelievable.

"What do you mean, I have worse troubles?"

Dread bolted through his system as he watched her

falter and pale.

"No, I didn't get the message. My cell phone died and . . ." She blinked back tears. "That can't be right, Laura. The police must be mistaken, I . . . Okay. Okay. Yes. I'll handle it. I'll let you know. Thanks for the damage control." She disconnected, tossed him the phone, and took off toward the canyon at a dangerous pace.

What the hell? Did she even remember the way? He raced after her, easily navigating the rocky descent, but he made these treks several times a week. She was a novice. "Where do you think you're going?"

The glance she spared him resonated with pain and grief. "LA."

CHAPTER FOURTEEN

It took Joe three phone calls and fifteen minutes to verify the identity of the body.

It took him far longer to convince Sofia that the Frenchman who'd died earlier that evening was not Jean-Pierre Legrand, but his friend, Luc Dupris.

According to his contact at the LAPD, the man Sofia's eighty-five-year-old neighbor had found bleeding to death in the apartment adjacent to hers resembled Jean-Pierre in coloring and build. She must not have gotten a close or clear look at the man's bloodied face. She'd just seen the shaggy brown hair, pink corduroy trousers and floral shirt, and had assumed it was her twinkle-toes neighbor.

A paramedic and a uniformed cop supported her

theory by reporting that the victim had mumbled his final words in French. No identification had been found on his person. Nothing to suggest Mrs. Liddy was mistaken in her identification. No evidence to suggest foul play. When asked about his next of kin, Mrs. Liddy named Sofia. Unable to reach the TV star, LAPD reached out to her publicist—typical Hollyweird thinking. The publicist had explained Sofia was out-of-state. She would inform her of the tragedy and have her get in touch.

In the meantime, another mutual friend had braved the morgue to identify the corpse as screenwriter, Luc Dupris. The preliminary autopsy report confirmed that the man was intoxicated and had died of loss of blood from a head injury. The verdict: accidental death.

"It doesn't make sense," Sofia said, as she crammed her script, phone, and bargain wardrobe into the backpack Joe had supplied. "Why was Luc in our apartment alone? I mean, he could've let himself in. He knows where we keep the spare key. But where's Jean-Pierre?"

"You skipped town early. Who says Jean-Pierre didn't do the same? Don't borrow trouble." He brushed past her, re-entering the kitchen to stow away the pots and utensils she'd washed while he'd transferred the marinara sauce from the fridge to the freezer. If reporters or photographers managed to breach his security system, they'd find a spotless house devoid of any sensitive materials. No family photo albums, address books, or personal correspondences to leak to the public. He'd spent the last several months laying low, riding out a death threat issued by Julietta's uncle, mobster Paulie Falcone. Not that he'd been particularly concerned. Operation Candy Jar had dealt a crippling blow to the Falcone organization. Paulie's energies were divided, his power restricted. Still, there were plenty of other scumbags in Joe's past who might jump at the chance to attack his soft spot. Meaning his family, which now included Lulu and, God help him, Sofia. His sister-in-law. The woman he lusted after in his heart and dreams and occasionally, in the light of day and a moment of insanity.

"That doesn't explain why Jean-Pierre's not answering his phone messages or emails," Sofia said, refusing to let the matter rest.

"Murphy said he had a fight with Gallow. Maybe he decided to slip away, someplace other than Vermont. Maybe he's genuinely pissed and needs some down time." He sponged off the memo board, erasing his Aunt Tessa's new phone number and her recipe for biscotti.

"No. Something's wrong." Her voice shook with frustration. "Would you please stop with the housekeeping crap? A man's been killed, another's missing. Time's ticking."

Jaw clenched, he placed the sponge in the sink and turned, hands on hips. He kept expecting her to fall apart. Instead, she was pumped and motivated. As soon as they'd blown into the house, she'd changed into a fresh

T-shirt and the baggy denim overalls. After taming her thick, blazing red hair into a low ponytail, she'd commandeered his Diamondbacks baseball cap and denim jacket to complete her transformation into her version of a redneck local.

Maybe it was him, but she still looked gorgeous. Exhausted, but gorgeous. "This disguise isn't going to work," he said, gesturing to her clothes. "People are going to recognize you."

"I'm not *that* famous."

"Famous enough." And drop-dead beautiful. They might not recognize her as Cherry Onatop. But they'd sure as hell notice those striking cheekbones and sultry eyes.

"People aren't going to recognize me," she assured him in a confident tone. She zipped her bag and met his gaze, her body emanating a tangible nervous energy. "You, on the other hand . . ."

He'd changed into vintage denim bellbottoms and a baggy, long-sleeved thermal, but other than that he looked exactly as he had when that front desk clerk had snapped their picture. "Don't worry about me, sweetheart. I've spent years dodging attention."

"And months dodging life," she muttered while stooping to tighten the laces of her shoes.

Joe stared down at the top of her capped head. What the hell was that? A comment on his resignation from the Bureau? She sounded like his brother. Since when was reevaluating and reprioritizing *dodging*? "What I meant to say," he managed in a calm tone, "is that I'm trained in deception."

"That makes two of us." She stood, hefted her bulging backpack, and shifted anxiously on the generic running shoes he'd bought her. She looked all of eighteen and ready to backpack across Europe. "Ready?" she asked.

And willing.

"Almost." He cursed his lustful thoughts—*pull it together, Bogart*—and ran a mental check list. He'd packed a suit and essentials into a rolling garment bag. His laptop was secured inside a leather case along with his genuine passport, and two sets of false ID—just in case. As Murphy was fond of saying, expect the unexpected.

He didn't like what they were about to do, but knew she'd find her way to Los Angeles with or without him. Since he didn't aim on letting her out of his sight, and since they had to relocate anyway, he'd set the wheels in motion. After a couple of pit stops, they'd be on a plane headed for LA.

Joe gave the home he'd come to think of as his sanctuary a last visual sweep. The thought of the paparazzi closing in, encroaching on his solitude and privacy, torched his blood. "How do you put up with it?" he wondered aloud as he lowered the living room blinds.

"How do I put up with what?" Sofia asked.

What he really wanted to know was not how, but why.

Her professional aspirations were no doubt rooted in her childhood. He knew his were. "Never mind." Understanding Sofia would only solidify an emotional bond. Bad enough the physical aspect of their relationship was spinning out of control. He tripped the security system, his body buzzing with sexual awareness as he cupped her elbow and ushered her out the door. "Let's roll."

Rainbow Ridge, Vermont

"I'm exhausted."

"You're actually admitting that?"

Afia tipped up her face and kissed Jake on his cocky jaw. "You don't look so spry either, Mr. Fix-it."

Jake just smiled.

Rudy started to thank him again—he'd not only fixed the swing, he'd helped Murphy reposition the satellite dish—but a case of the fuzzies clogged his throat. He relaxed deeper into his recliner, the one piece of furniture that he'd brought from his old townhouse, and watched his two closest friends in the world snuggle on the antique chaise. Cocooned in her husband's arms, Afia glowed with contentment and love. The same love radiated from Jake along with a fierce protective streak. Next month this cozy couple would expand to a family of three. A boy or a girl, he didn't know as they'd opted to be surprised.

Jake smoothed his hand over Afia's rounded belly and kissed the top of her head as the commercial segued back into the movie and she focused on the television. Sunshine cracked through the gloom that had dogged Rudy since daybreak. *This* was what he'd hoped for, the creative visualization that had cinched his decision to buy Hollyberry Inn. Aside from wanting a home and business that he could share with Jean-Pierre, he'd wanted a resort where loving couples, straight or gay, could cuddle and talk, and rediscover why they'd fallen in love in the first place.

He glanced over at Lulu and Murphy sitting together on the great room's velvet sofa, a little less cozy, but no less in love. That blurb on *Hollywood Highlights* had been a kick in the gut to everyone.

Especially Lulu.

Presently, she was munching on popcorn and watching Cary Grant and Grace Kelly's *To Catch a Thief*, the only movie they'd all been able to agree on. But Rudy wasn't fooled. He knew she was thinking about that gossip feature and trying to make sense of it. Admittedly, he'd been equally surprised to learn that Sofia and Joe Bogart were an item.

Sure. There'd been some chemistry between those two over the fall during that FBI sting, but no one expected anything to come of it. Sofia sought approval and fame, while Bogie, as Murphy called him, craved justice

and anonymity. Both headstrong and blind in their dedi-
cation, they clashed on several levels. Then again, Afia
and Jake were as different as the sun and moon yet, somehow *they* made sense. As did Lulu and Murphy. And, yes
dammit, he and Jean-Pierre.

What didn't make sense was him sitting in the great
room of the Hollyberry Inn, the place he'd purchased as a
show of love, without the man he loved.

Sweat beaded his brow as catastrophic thoughts returned full force. During their walk, Afia had assured him
nothing bad had happened to Jean-Pierre. *"He's just angry,"*
she'd said. *"He'll get over it."* Well, as soon as he "got over
it" and called, Rudy would beg him to hop the first plane
east. They'd de-ghost Hollyberry Inn together. Screw his
earlier concerns. It wasn't like JP was a wimp, far from it.
If Casper lobbed a candlestick, he'd duck and curse the
bitter ghost in French. Too bad he hadn't been thinking
this clearly last night. Yet again, he'd made things worse
by underestimating the younger man.

Jake glanced away from the screen, rubbed the heel of
his hand over his brow. "Is it hot in here, or is it me?"

"It's not you." Murphy shoved up the long sleeves of
his crewneck pullover.

Afia yawned loudly. "It's making me sleepy."

"Well, I'm not tired," Lulu said in her little girl voice.
"I'm jazzed. I hope that satellite thingee doesn't go out
again, because I plan on surfing the channels after you

guys go to bed. Maybe there'll be an update on Sofie and Joe." She glanced sideways at her husband, scowled. "I have to get my information *somewhere*."

Murphy didn't flinch. "There's nothing to tell. They're together. They're fine."

"Then, why won't she answer her cell phone?"

"I told you, hon, the battery's drained. And before you ask again, no, I'm not giving you Bogie's cell number. Give them some privacy."

The last part sounded like an order to Rudy. Then again, Murphy was former military and current leader of a protective specialist team. He routinely barked orders. Lulu routinely blew over his concerns. She had a mind of her own, and even though she taxed his patience, Murphy was powerless to combat her whimsical charm.

Rudy smothered a smile. The hard-assed bodyguard was a veritable mush when it came to his wife. He'd scoured every toy store in Atlantic County for a pink poodle purse when hers had been torched in a fire. He probably wasn't angry with Lulu just now as much as concerned that, if he didn't nip it in the bud, she'd work herself into a red-hazed fury and, as she called it, wig-out. She'd approached the red zone earlier tonight during dinner when she'd obsessed on that unflattering news piece. *What had possessed Sofie to drink so much? How could Joe take advantage of her in that state, and why were they together anyway?*

Everyone had reminded her that *Hollywood Highlights*

was a gossip program. Drunken love-fest was probably an exaggeration. Unfortunately, there was no taming her imagination. She had it in her head that Sofia was in trouble, and that was that.

"I'm sure your sister would have called you if anything was wrong," Afia gently said.

"You don't know Sofie. She doesn't confide in me if she thinks it will upset me."

Afia looked from Jake to Rudy. "Sounds familiar."

Rudy refrained from raising his hand and admitting, "*Guilty as charged.*" He simply slid Jake a glance that said, "*Thanks a lot.*" He wished he'd stop letting the man manipulate him into shielding Afia from the occasional painful truth. Like when he and Jean-Pierre separated after the indiscretion. Not wanting to upset Afia at a critical time in her pregnancy, Jake had convinced them to downplay their troubles.

It had taken Afia all of three weeks to deduce the real score. His ears still smarted from her lecture on friendship and honesty. Thing was, sheltering a sensitive soul like Afia came as second nature for a caretaker like Rudy. This afternoon he'd lied about Casper, saying he was an obnoxious stray cat that sometimes got underfoot. It was better than risking the truth and spooking her. Born on Friday the thirteenth, his sweet-natured friend had old issues with bad mojo. If she overreacted and went into early labor, he'd never forgive himself.

Just then the TV reception skewed. Warped images. Static.

"Nuts!" Lulu set aside the bowl of popcorn and sighed. "How am I supposed to get an update on Sofie?"

"We're going to miss the end of the movie," Afia pouted.

Jake eyed Murphy. "I thought you tweaked the position of the dish antenna for the strongest signal."

"I did. I fine-tuned the hell out of the system."

The lights flickered.

Rudy grit his teeth. There hadn't been a paranormal incident since the porch swing debacle. He'd hoped Casper was shy, that the gang had scared him into hiding. He should've known the ghost's silence was too good to last.

"Maybe there's a storm coming." Lulu hugged herself against an imagined chill.

She couldn't possibly be cold. Rudy's shirt was sticking to his skin. It occurred to him that it wasn't just warm in this room, but abnormally hot. No wonder everyone was cranky. Ghostly fingers must've tapped the thermostat. "Dammit, Casper."

The roof creaked. Metal whined. An eerie yowl infiltrated the walls.

Afia sat up straight, eyes wide. "That doesn't sound like a cat to me."

Jake and Murphy bolted to their feet. "Stay put," they ordered their wives while exiting the room as a team.

Rudy followed. Typically these two carried guns.

The last thing he wanted was a shootout at Hollyberry Inn. That kind of press would definitely put a damper on business. Then he remembered that they'd flown on a commercial flight which probably meant they'd left their weapons at home. And what was he thinking anyway? How could they shoot what they couldn't see?

Unless the intruder wasn't Casper, but a living breathing burglar trying to break in. He didn't know which was worse.

"You take the front," Murphy said to Jake. "I've got the back."

The lights flickered off, on, off, and stayed off. Moonbeams shone through the gauzy curtains. Shadows danced on the walls. "What about me?" Rudy whispered.

"Stay with the women," Murphy said, before disappearing toward the back door.

Rudy bristled. "It's my property. If someone's trespassing, I'll deal with it."

"We're trained to track and detain." A silent *you're not* hung in the air. Jake squeezed his shoulder. "Stay with Afia and Lulu. Protect your home. Protect the women."

The former Jersey cop didn't wait for an answer. He blew out the front door and left Rudy standing in the pitch-black foyer. His senses buzzed with heightened clarity. Every creak, ping and tick seemed amplified by the darkness and silence. He'd been living in the middle of nowhere for two months now. He'd never been bothered by the silence or seclusion. Then again, he'd never suspected an intruder. Well, aside from Casper. But he didn't count. He was dead.

Protect the women. Yeah. Okay. He could do that. He'd earned a blue belt in Tae Kwon Do. And thanks to his dad, if push came to shove he knew how to fight dirty. Early on Barney Gallow had suspected his son, a Broadway show tune fanatic, might need to defend himself against bullies AKA homophobes.

He felt his way from the foyer through the living room, destination: the great room and the girls.

Except the girls weren't in the great room.

He whispered their names. He called their names. He stood there for a moment, anxious and slightly disoriented.

He heard a metallic creak and distant pops.

The TV and the great room lights blared in tandem with two feminine shrieks.

Rudy flew toward the sound of hysteria. Oh, Jesus. Sweet Jesus. He whizzed around the corner of the dining room too fast and banged his hip on the solid mahogany china cabinet. Eyes crossed in pain, he rushed forward and collided with a misplaced side chair. He and the chair tumbled over the threshold into the darkened kitchen just as Murphy exploded through the back door. The protection specialist tripped over Rudy's body and plowed into Jake who'd sailed in on Rudy's heels. A collage of blasphemous curses polluted the air as Murphy pushed out of

Jake's arms and Rudy untangled his arms from the chair's carved legs.

The kitchen light flicked on.

Rudy's head snapped up.

"Holy smoke," Lulu said on a breathless giggle. "The Three Stooges live."

"What happened?" Afia asked.

Rudy blinked. The wide-eyed women stood side-by-side, safe and sound. Relief struck him speechless.

Not so Murphy. "What do you mean, what happened?" he railed. "You screamed."

"Are you all right?" Jake scanned the women head to toe as he massaged his right shoulder. Murphy must've clocked him good, aggravating an old injury.

"We're fine," Afia said.

"Then why the hell did you scream?" Murphy reached down and offered Rudy a hand up.

Lulu frowned. "You don't have to yell, Colin."

"I'm not yelling!"

"You're yelling," Jake countered. "Why did you scream?" he repeated just as loudly.

"There was a big honking spider on the breaker panel door," Lulu said.

Afia shuddered. "I hate spiders."

Rudy shifted his weight and winced. His hip and ankle smarted like the dickens. "What were you doing in the utility room?"

"Tripping the breakers," Lulu said. "Easier to catch someone creeping about if you can see him."

Jake looked over his shoulder at Rudy. "Where were you?"

"Looking for them." He eyed the side chair, ready to damn Casper for tripping him up and making him look like Curly or Moe, or whoever the third idiot was. He could never remember. Not that it mattered. A stooge was a stooge.

Afia winced. "Sorry about that. We put the chair in the doorway, thinking if someone followed us, they'd trip and the noise would alert us."

Jake kissed her forehead and smiled. "Smart girl."

"What part of 'stay put' didn't you understand, princess?" Murphy asked Lulu. He scraped a hand over his buzz cut, blew out a frustrated breath. "Every time you pull a stunt like this you take five years off my life."

Rudy was certain he'd sprouted twenty gray hairs in the last five minutes.

Lulu smiled apologetically and moved in to hug Murphy. "So, what did you find outside? Did you see anyone?"

"Not a soul. Whoever it was moved fast. All we found was a mangled rain gutter on the south side of the inn." He wrapped his arms around her, a loving, protective embrace that summoned an envious lump in Rudy's throat. He could use a hug himself just now. Specifically, from Jean-Pierre.

"Someone tampered with the satellite dish," Jake said, steering Afia into a kitchen chair. "Guessing here, but since I didn't see a ladder, I'd say someone climbed that big oak and scaled a branch to get to the dish. Probably slipped and grabbed on to the rain gutter, only the gutter gave and the prankster fell and landed hard on the ground."

"Hence the howl," Afia surmised. She shivered. "Sounded like something out of a horror movie."

Rudy's mind raced, rehashing information he'd read on *bust-a-poltergeist.com* Paranormal activity included things such as moaning, shrieking, electrical glitches, and moving objects. It would've been easier to suspect a burglar or vandalizing teen if he hadn't suffered similar occurrences already. *And* if the satellite dish wasn't near the Evergreen Suite.

"I hate scary movies." Lulu snuggled closer against Murphy. "Vampires and werewolves. Flesh eating zombies intent on revenge."

Jake laughed. "Jesus."

Murphy rolled his eyes.

"What about disgruntled ghosts," Rudy muttered.

Lulu groaned. "They're the worst. Oh, my gosh," she said, pushing out of Murphy's arms to sit next to Afia. "Did you see *Poltergeist*?"

Wide-eyed, Afia shook her head no. "Dead people and demons creep me out. I'd rather face a spider than a ghost."

Great. Rudy limped toward the fridge. "I need a beer. Anyone else?"

"Hit me," Jake said.

Murphy nodded.

"Nothing for me, thank you," Lulu said.

Afia passed as well. "If you hate scary movies," she said to Lulu, "how did you make it through *Poltergeist*?"

"I closed my eyes a lot. But Sofie filled me in. Oh, wow," she said, just as Rudy shut the fridge and turned, hands full. "This place is really old, right? What if it's built on an ancient burial ground? What if the inn's haunted?"

Rudy fumbled the longneck bottles.

Jake moved fast, catching the one that slipped his grip.

Murphy relieved him of another, saying to Lulu, "You might want to curb that imagination, hon."

Jake sat next to Afia, twisted off the bottle cap. "Relax, baby. The inn's not haunted. No such things as ghosts."

Rudy swigged his beer.

"Whoever it was is long gone." Murphy took a pull off the longneck, then eyed Rudy. "Had any trouble like this before?"

Like he was supposed to fess up now? "No." He made the mistake of making eye contact with Afia.

Her sable eyes sparked with suspicion. "You would tell us, wouldn't you?"

Oh, boy. If he glanced away, she'd know he was withholding. If he lied, she'd know that too. "Busted." He drank more beer, tempered his expression. Maybe if he acted like it was no big deal. "The inn's haunted."

He expected a barrage of questions, a unified gasp, something. No one reacted. Not even a flinch.

Finally, Lulu snorted. "Yeah, right."

Afia sighed. "I give up."

Jake's lip twitched. "A simple I-don't-want-to-talk-about-it would've sufficed, Gallow."

Incredulous laughter bubbled in Rudy's throat. They didn't believe him. Rather than launching into the legend of Casper Montegue, he casually tipped his beer to his lips and expanded on the absurd. "No, seriously, I've got a ghost with a grudge."

Afia rolled her big brown eyes. "A grudge against Cary Grant movies? Or TV in general?"

"Speaking of," Lulu said to Murphy, "I don't suppose you'd consider going back outside and realigning that dish."

"No, I don't suppose I would. Not tonight. I'm beat. I'm going to bed."

She glanced at her Cinderella watch. "It's only ten-thirty."

Murphy nabbed her hand and gently tugged her to her feet. "We've been up since five this morning, princess."

"Us too." Jake set his beer bottle on the counter and helped Afia to her feet.

They exchanged goodnights while Rudy deposited the

empty bottles in a recycle bin. He couldn't believe his good fortune. He'd told the truth—no lectures on honesty coming his way—and they'd mistaken the truth for sarcasm, therefore no one was spooked or accusing him of going off the deep end. They were all hitting the sack, meaning he was free to surf the Internet for instant ghost-busting tips. While he was at it he'd shoot off another email to Jean-Pierre. With any luck, come morning, he and his soulmate would be back on track. With any luck, come morning, the mangled gutter and mysterious howl would be forgotten and he'd be off the hook.

Just before crossing the threshold, the two couples turned as one. "We'll talk about this tomorrow."

So much for being off the hook.

CHAPTER FIFTEEN

Phoenix, Arizona

"When you said you knew a guy, I assumed you meant Special Agent Creed," Sofia muttered under her breath as they exited the retro basement apartment of a computer whiz with an Austin Powers complex. Talk about weird. Her theory that she was an unwitting participant in a reality show version of a Hitchcock tale escalated with each ticking minute.

"Best to pick and choose what favors I ask of Creed." Joe cupped her elbow and escorted her up the stairs.

"I thought you trusted him."

"I do. And so can you."

"Excuse me if I take a wait-and-see attitude."

Joe spoke close to her ear. "You're a cynical one."

His breath heated her neck, inciting a vision of him leaning closer and kissing the sensitive patch of skin just below her ear. She suppressed an elaboration on that fantasy and focused on his words. "Your brother made the same comment when we first met."

"We're observant like that. I'll do one better." He squeezed her elbow, his touch burning through layers of fabric. "I'll ask, why?"

"Why am I so cynical?" *Because I've been betrayed by all of the men in my life.* She thought about the way Joe had duped Julietta into believing he'd loved her. Then, she thought about the way he'd kissed her earlier this evening, as if he couldn't get enough of her, as if he burned for her and her alone. "None of your business." She broke free and pushed through the outer door, desperate for a breath of fresh air. Sex. He'd been attracted to her sexually, period. A moment of heated lunacy. Love had nothing to do with it. In her case, it never did.

It was dark now. Her thoughts shifted and her body tensed at the sight of a silhouetted cactus and a small utility shed. Less than twenty-four hours ago, she'd awoken with a gun in her hand. She blocked the fragmented images, the fear. She couldn't think about that now. Her troubles paled in comparison to Luc's. At least she was alive. She prayed she could say the same for Jean-Pierre. She hugged herself against a cool breeze and dark thoughts. If it weren't for the street lights and Joe's company, she'd be paralyzed, or worse, hyperventilating.

The former FBI agent finger-combed his recently cropped hair as he strode to the Jeep. She was still adjusting to his new look. Midway between Apache Junction and Phoenix, they'd stopped at a strip mall. Again, Joe had ordered her to stay in the car while he'd disappeared inside the complex. Fifteen-minutes later, he'd emerged clean-shaven, sporting a short haircut and stylish sideburns. He'd completed the transformation from grungy handsome to *Esquire* gorgeous after they'd arrived at Lovejoy's apartment, exchanging his hippy duds for a chic indigo suit. This moment he looked nothing like the jeep tour guide who'd escorted her out of the Camelback this morning. This moment he looked every inch her dream man.

When they reached the jeep, he shrugged out of his three-button jacket, giving Sofia an unobstructed view of his narrow waist and tight ass. Those tailored slacks left little to the imagination. Not that she needed to use her imagination. She'd seen him in his birthday suit, and, *yeah, baby, yeah*, Joe Bogart's sculptured butt was worthy of worship.

Although she welcomed the distraction, there was something decidedly obscene about admiring one man's hot bod while another laid cold in a morgue. *Twisted attraction*. Disgusted with herself, she squinted at her computer generated documents. "This can't be legal."

Joe opened the passenger door. "Do you care?"

"Not really." She climbed in, fastened her seatbelt. They'd wasted enough time. Luc was dead. Jean-Pierre was missing. Her stomach ached with grief and worry. Her blood burned with purpose. She wanted to be in Los Angeles. She wanted to find Jean-Pierre alive and well, to assuage her, and his lover's, concerns.

Even though she'd moved to Los Angeles on JP's coattails, she felt responsible for the sensitive man. Jean-Pierre, though book smart, was far from street savvy. Of the two, Rudy was the more adventurous and experienced. How ironic that he was piddling around in a bed and breakfast resort in serene Rainbow Ridge while the poor, tender-hearted costume designer toughed it out in dog-eat-dog LA.

At any rate, her intentions were dead in the water without proper identification. Nigel Lovejoy, like that was his *real* name, had falsified a driver's license and two passports in an astonishingly short time. The horn-rimmed spectacled, shaggy-haired man was a genius. He was also a fan of "Spy Girl", and had recognized Sofia as Cherry Onatop the moment she'd taken off the baseball cap. "*Groovy baby*." Good for her ego. Bad, since she was striving for anonymity. Lovejoy had offered a solution via his rebel sister's vanity and closet. Eccentricity, it seemed, ran in family. Sofia recognized the brilliance in his thinking and didn't hesitate.

Joe remained skeptical.

"I can't get over what you did to your hair," he said, as he buckled up and keyed the ignition.

Ditto, she thought. The fact that he looked like her dream man wasn't sitting all that well. Dream men religiously broke her heart. She missed his grunge clothes, hippy hair, and that devilish goatee. Regardless, his new look wasn't bad, just different. His stern tone and frown indicated he was less accepting of her makeover. "That's the third time you've said that, Bogart. It's just hair. Get over it."

"It's just that it's so purple and . . . radical."

Not that radical. She'd just hacked off a couple of inches and given it a choppier, head-banger look with some rubbery hair pomade. Her hair grew fast and the dye was temporary. She'd be back to normal by the time they started shooting the new season of "Spy Girl". No harm done. "It was necessary. You were right. If I didn't do something drastic, the possibility existed that someone, like geek-boy Lovejoy, would recognize me. Since I don't know what I'm up against, I needed to take precautions."

She'd gone to the extreme. She'd dyed her chopped hair "vivid violet". She'd copped a gothic, black velvet mini-dress with a laced bodice and scalloped hem, purple and black striped tights, and platform Mary Janes. By applying a fake pentagram tattoo to the swell of her right breast and makeup to the max—thick kohl eyeliner, electric-blue glam false eyelashes, vixen-purple lipstick—she'd effectively obliterated her classy, exotic appeal. She'd topped the somber ensemble with a floor-length Victorian coat. Now, she resembled a Goth poetess at best; devil worshiper at worst.

Ninety-five percent of the population would avoid her like a Hare Krishna disciple. Guaranteed no one would recognize them as the couple featured on that entertainment news show. Or, as a couple period. Death-girl and businessman did not compute.

"When we get to the airport, let me do the talking," Joe said as he peeled onto the street. "Don't make eye contact. Try to look sullen and withdrawn. Goth's are typically non-violent pacifists prone to introversion when in public."

"I'm familiar with the Gothic subculture," Sofia said, inspecting her black nail polish and imagining the tsk-tsking of her manicurist. "I don't need instruction from you. As soon as we hit the airport parking garage, I'll shift into character."

Joe shifted gears and accelerated onto the highway. "You must be a director's nightmare."

Her insecurities and temper flared, causing her to shoot him a deadly glare. "Listen. Regardless of what you think, I'm not a hack."

"That wasn't a comment on your acting abilities. It was a comment on your inability to take direction."

"I take direction just fine when the person issuing said direction knows something I don't, and when it's in my best interest."

"Like last fall when I asked you to steer clear of Oz, and specifically Anthony Rivelli?" His fingers tightened on the wheel while his razor-sharp tone sliced and diced her nerves. "I knew a helluva lot more than you, and you better believe it was in your best interest to avoid Rivelli and the Falcones."

Fists clenched in her lap, Sofia resisted the urge to punch the chauvinistic ape as he navigated traffic with the skill and speed of a NASCAR driver. "Do you really want to revisit that night?" After dragging her out of the dance rave and into an alley, he'd kissed her stupid, and then rendered her unconscious. Knowing that he'd seduced her merely to distract and manipulate her still stung. She'd spent many a restless night dreaming about that atomic kiss. And now, on top of that, she had to live with the memory of this evening's lustful grope.

"I'm not going to apologize for putting you in protective custody, Sofia."

"I'm not going to apologize for seeking Anthony Rivelli's help."

"You put yourself in harm's way."

"To protect my sister and Rudy!" She threw up her

hands in frustration. "I don't know why we're arguing about this. It's ancient history."

"Not so ancient and you're doing it again."

"What?" she shouted.

"Disregarding my advice. Acting impulsively, irrationally."

She gawked at the man. *She* was acting irrationally? "Is this about my hair? I can't believe you're actually bent because I cut and dyed my hair." She flashed on the time a stylist had cut five inches off her waist-length hair and Chaz had thrown a fit. "Well, excuse me if it makes me less fuckable in your eyes."

Joe braked and swerved onto the bank of the highway so fast Sofia had to brace her hands on the dash to avoid whiplash. Her heart lurched when he reached across the darkened car and grabbed her by the shoulders. "I don't ever want to hear you belittle yourself like that again. Ever." He gave her a shake. "Understand?"

She nodded. His body vibrated with a restrained intensity that struck her breathless. She braced herself for a longwinded lecture or a punishing kiss. Instead, he released her and squealed the jeep back onto the highway.

No lecture. Not even a disgusted curse. Hands trembling, Sofia tucked her vivid violet hair behind her ears and settled back against the seat, processing an unspoken acknowledgment.

Joe Bogart regarded her as more than an exotic sex

object.

Somehow, someway, she'd won this man's respect.

Los Angeles, California

By the time they landed at LAX, Joe had a tension headache and a bad case of heartburn. Damned airplane food. Damned woman. Sofia's "Gothic Girl" persona had afforded her the luxury of giving him the silent treatment during the ninety-minute flight from Phoenix to LA. Either she was pissed at him for manhandling her earlier, or obsessing on Jean-Pierre and Luc. Probably a little of both.

He was good with that. Her sullen silence allowed him to brood in peace. He regretted losing his temper, but when she'd intimated that his interest in her was purely sexual, he'd blown. Partly because he *was* so fiercely hot for her body, but mostly because she didn't know, or wouldn't acknowledge, her real potential or worth. He'd once told Murphy she didn't use the brains she was born with, hence his impatience. In reality, she was more complex and intriguing than he'd ever imagined.

Damn.

Lusting after this woman was one thing. Liking her was unexpected and unnerving. He'd tangled with numerous unscrupulous dirt-bags in his years as an undercover fed. He'd been caught in more than one dicey situation. Very little rattled him.

Sofia Chiquita Marino shook his back teeth loose.

He battled for professionalism, struggled not to touch her as they moved quickly and anonymously through the crowded airport in search of ground transportation. If he touched her now, he'd combust. His gut, mind, and heart were at freaking war.

Months ago he'd labeled her as a classic, sensation seeking personality. Melodramatic, needy, and self-involved. Suffering from poor self-esteem, she used sex to get attention and to get ahead. A promiscuous manipulator. Typical artistic types often became overwhelmed and unable to function when confronted with intense situations, so the panic attack she'd experienced at Fremont Saddle hadn't surprised him.

The fact that she'd altered her appearance so drastically, and not for the better, blew him away. Granted, he hadn't been crazy about her red hair, but at least it had been a color found in nature. The style, a sexy cut reminiscent of Farrah Fawcett in her Charlie's Angel days, had been very attractive. This new cut and color, hell, it was hideous. The make-up was garish, the tattoo trashy, and the clothes suited a ghoulish clown.

All traces of vanity, gone.

The overt sexuality, gone.

Her overdramatic tendencies and penchant to argue
. . . gone.

The moment she'd learned a friend had died, and another had gone missing, she'd transformed into a clever,
composed woman. True to her word, she'd become Abby
Geyser, gothic poetess the moment they'd hit Sky Harbor
International.

He'd prepped her in the car, amazed when she didn't
interrupt or challenge his instruction. The plan was
straightforward. Easier not to get tripped up when you
kept things simple. He'd pose as a private investigator
hired to track and escort a depressed runaway home to
her family. The Goth persona shaved a good ten years off
of Sofia's twenty-eight, so it was believable. *If* she didn't
freeze or overact.

As it happened, they made the perfect team. She was
good. Better than good. She excelled in the art of deception. Utilizing the costume and specific, dead-on body
language, she sold her role with nonverbal clarity. Her
talents were definitely wasted on "Spy Girl".

Her compassion and intelligence, Joe thought as they
climbed into the back seat of a taxi, had been wasted on
every man who'd ever taken her to bed. Behind the glam-
our and blatant sexuality lurked a woman in search of love
and affection. He'd recognized the same vulnerability in
Julietta. But he'd never felt this insane pull.

Sofia was wrong. That hideous hairstyle didn't make

her less fuckable. It made her more lovable.

He was so screwed.

She dictated the address of her apartment building to the driver.

In dire need of antacid, Joe unbuttoned his jacket, loosened his tie, and settled in for the ride.

"Can I borrow your cell?" she asked in a hushed, somber voice. "I want to try Jean-Pierre again."

He passed her his mobile without comment, marveled as she left a calm, succinct voice mail on both her home phone and Jean-Pierre's cell. Even though she was upset about Luc and worried about her roommate, outwardly she appeared composed. Again, he was impressed with her acting skills. Only an astute few would peg her demeanor as contrived.

She passed him back the phone. "Thank you." She shivered beneath that Dickens-cum-Dracula crushed velvet coat.

He didn't think it was because she was cold. The temperature was moderate and she had Jersey-girl blood. More likely she was scared. He had to admit he was beginning to get a bad feeling himself. Last he'd checked with Murphy, Rudy still hadn't heard from Jean-Pierre. Everyone wanted to believe that the Frenchman was off on a power sulk. Even Sofia had said something about him being depressed lately. Still, she wouldn't rest easy until she laid eyes on the man. Hopefully, he was at their apartment, and just not answering the phone. Then again, that would be too easy.

Nothing about this case was easy.

"The next block," Sofia said to the cab driver. "You can let us off at the corner." Her nerves were stretched tighter than Jean-Pierre's bikini briefs. What she wouldn't give to walk through her front door to find her roommate flitting about in his Lycra underwear, trying to decide which pants didn't make him look fat. Lately, he'd been obsessing on the couple of pounds he'd put on since moving to California. It drove Sofia crazy. The man was an avid runner with a dream metabolism. Just now, however, she'd happily listen to him whine or philosophize on any subject from fashion forecasts to urban politics. Just as long as he was present and in good health.

Just then Joe reached over, grasped her hand, and squeezed. "We'll find him."

Her skin tingled. Her senses buzzed. His touch conjured a cyclone of emotions—hopeful, sexual, bittersweet. She pushed them all aside and took comfort in his confidence. She welcomed his expertise and calm. She also appreciated that he hadn't forced conversation on her during the tension filled flight and subsequent cab ride. It was all she could do to contain her anxiety. She couldn't slay the fear that she was somehow responsible for Luc's death and JP's disappearance, couldn't temper the dread and guilt scraping at her insides like a Brillo pad.

The cabbie pulled curbside. If Joe hadn't detained her with another gentle squeeze, she would've bolted from the car. She waited while he paid the driver, cautioned herself to stay in character at least until she was inside her apartment and behind closed doors. Who knew if the paparazzi lurked?

Please let JP be home.

While she mentally prepared, Joe exited, nabbed their bags, and rounded the cab. He opened the door and handed her out. Her legs felt like lead pipes—unbending, heavy. Were they even working? It seemed as though she glided, rather than walked, toward the entrance of the apartment building. She and Jean-Pierre had found artsy, two-bedroom digs in a conservative, moderate-income neighborhood. Given the late hour, most residents had settled in for the evening. All was quiet on Bleaker Street. All was quiet in the renovated halls of Whitley Manor.

Sofia slowed as they neared Mrs. Liddy's door. Poor woman. If she weren't so considerate and kind, she would have been spared the awfulness of finding Luc's body. According to the police, she'd noticed a UPS package sitting outside of Sofia's apartment. Afraid that someone might filch the box, she'd knocked on the door. When no one answered she used a spare key to let herself in. She'd set the package indoors and when she'd straightened, her gaze fell upon Luc.

"Maybe I should check in with Mrs. Liddy. Make sure she's okay."

Joe urged her to keep moving, his voice low and tight. "You're not checking in with anyone. *You're* not here. If you're concerned . . ."

"I'm concerned."

"Then I'll call her after we get inside."

She didn't argue. She understood his logic. The whole point of the excessive Goth-girl disguise was to keep Sofia Marino out of the public eye until interest dwindled on the "drunken love-fest" fiasco. On top of that, this afternoon a man had died in her apartment. Her publicist was currently spinning and wrangling to circumvent a negative impact on Sofia's reputation. Avoiding Mrs. Liddy was definitely smart. Besides, the way she looked just now, she'd probably give the old woman a heart attack.

They stopped in front of her apartment. Sofia's pulse spiked. Yellow police tape marked her doorway, driving home the reality of this visit.

"Standard procedure," Joe said, propping the luggage against the wall. "Secured crime scene."

Her heart sank with the knowledge that, since the tape was unbroken, JP most probably wasn't home. "But, there wasn't a crime."

He reached into the inner pocket of his jacket and

produced a small black leather case. "Even if it looked like
an accident, until the investigating officers had sufficient
proof, like the results of a preliminary autopsy, they'd
treat the incident as suspicious." He opened the flap, slid
out a skinny, silver tool.

"What are you doing?"

He squatted and concentrated on the door knob.
"What's it look like?"

Figures he'd know how to pick a lock. As her keys had
disappeared with her purse, it made sense, and there was
an odd fascination in watching him perform a task she'd
only ever feigned in episodes of "Spy Girl". She could learn
something here. But she was eager to find Jean-Pierre, and
the longer they stood in the hall the greater the chance
someone would come along and question their presence.
"Put your toys away, special agent man."

He glanced up as she retrieved a spare key from behind
the art deco wall sconce. "Unbelievable." He took the key,
unlocked the door, and after tearing away tape, shifted the
luggage inside and flicked on a wall lamp. "Didn't you
learn anything from your sister's run-in with that stalker?"
he asked as she followed him in and shut the door.

She knew he was referring to the fact that she and
Lulu used to keep a spare key hidden beneath the welcome
mat of their Jersey home. But, a sarcastic retort lodged
in her throat when she zeroed in on the place where Luc
had taken his last breath. Her gaze bounced from a near

empty bottle of merlot, to a soul wine glass, to the blood soaked carpet.

Her temples throbbed.

Joe's voice pierced through the white noise blaring in her ears. "Generally, the police don't double as a cleaning crew." He gently grasped her forearm. "I should have warned you."

Her throat constricted. Her fingers tingled. "I'm fine." *Liar.* Warped images attacked her mind with blinding speed. Red seeping into orange and white. Blue splattered with red.

Blood.

A body. A nose. A hand.

Grim images of assault and pain hammered at her conscience, inflicting terror and remorse. Unable to catch her breath, she loosened the laces of her bodice with trembling hands.

Joe wrapped one arm around her waist. "Look away. Focus on something else."

He tried to move her into the kitchen, but she resisted. "I don't want to focus on something else. This is important." She conjured the peaceful image of her martial arts teacher. *Center yourself,* she heard her Master Chai instruct. *Breathe deep. In and out. In and out.* "Can't panic," she said to Joe. "Have to deal."

"Then deal." He tightened his grip, held her steady. "The blood's triggering memories. Don't stifle the images.

Talk it out."

Heart pounding, she stared at the stained carpet. Blood. Panic. *Run!* "They're chasing me."

"Who?"

"The cowboys." Heel to bone. Spike through flesh. *Pain!* "I fought back. I hurt them. One's howling in agony. The other's . . . down. Silent."

"Unconscious?"

"Maybe. Or dead. I don't know. I ran. With the gun." She pressed a hand to her queasy stomach. It felt like someone was jamming knitting needles into her brain. She turned away from the blood, into Joe's arms. "I remember aiming and shooting. I remember hearing a gunshot. What if I hit him? What if he's dead?"

"You said they were chasing you. Why?"

"They were angry."

"Why?"

"I don't know." She pushed out of his embrace, palmed her clammy forehead. "I can't remember."

He grasped her shoulders, urged her to meet his gaze. "Did you know them?"

"No."

"Are you sure?"

She wasn't sure of anything. The night was a jumbled blur. She massaged her throbbing temples, tried to focus.

"You knew them enough to classify them as cowboys," Joe pointed out, his voice grim.

She shook her head. "Cowboy hats. They wore cowboy hats. I can't remember their faces, but I remember those hats. One black. One brown." A hand. A nose. Heel to bone. She glanced down at her foot, remembered Master Chai's advice on thwarting an attacker. "I think I broke the tall one's nose. The one in black."

Joe disregarded her comment, as if breaking a man's nose was no big deal. "Were they guests of your boyfriend?"

Her stomach bumped up to her throat. *"You're even more beautiful in person."* She pushed back the seductive voice, blinked at her stern-faced companion. *So intense.* "What are you talking about?"

"The man you went to visit. The man with no face. Were they friends of his?"

"No." She wasn't sure how she knew that, but she was certain they weren't on friendly terms. She narrowed her eyes. "And he wasn't my boyfriend."

He didn't comment, but she could tell he didn't believe her. She wanted to curse him, to defend her virtue. She was not an impetuous bimbo! But her skin flushed at a fuzzy memory of a man plying her with wine and promises. Guilt struck her speechless.

Joe worked his jaw, glanced around the apartment. "We need to clear out of here. If there's anything you want or need, grab it now. I'll take a look around, see if I can find a clue that will lead us to Jean-Pierre."

Sofia moistened her lips. "What do you know that

you're not telling me?"

Joe hitched back his suit jacket, slid his hands in his pockets, and studied her as if assessing her mental stability.

She resisted the urge to tame her purple head-banger spikes. So what if he didn't like her hair? She refused to care. "I'm not going to fall apart, Bogart. I appreciate your concern, but I resent being kept in the dark. Give it up."

He nodded. "All right. The police chalked up Luc's last words as drunken rambling, and it probably was, but he did mumble an American name amid indecipherable French."

Dread coursed down her spine. "What was the name?"

"John Wayne."

"The actor?"

"Maybe he was watching one of the Duke's old westerns just before he passed out. He was a screenwriter, right? Maybe he'd been researching the guy for a documentary and simply had him on the brain."

"If you really thought that, you wouldn't look so concerned." John Wayne. Westerns. *Cowboy.* The conclusion was instantaneous. The urge to retch swiftly followed. Aware that Joe was watching her, she schooled her expression and gestures. He'd shut her out if he thought she couldn't handle the ugliness and danger. He'd done it before.

So she suppressed her anxiety, her fear. She glanced down at her purple and black striped stockings and

platform Mary Janes.   She channeled Abby Geyser's
morbid calm.   "Luc was trying to identify his attacker.
But, he was drunk and delirious from the head wound. A
head wound inflicted by the cowboys."

Joe shook his head.   "There's no evidence to support a
break-in or foul play.   Nothing's out of place.   The police
dusted for prints and, aside from Luc's, only came up with
yours and Jean-Pierre's.   I asked."

"They were here.   I know it.   And you suspect it.
They were looking for me."   And instead they found Luc.
Guilt cramped her stomach.   *Deal, Sofia, deal.*   She slowly
turned and headed for her bedroom.   "They must have my
purse.   One mystery solved anyway."   Her voice sounded
foreign to her ears, distant, monotone.   She opened her
top dresser drawer, took out a fresh pack of cigarettes.
Abby would smoke.   It would totally be within character
to light up.   Good thing.   She'd never needed a calming
hit of nicotine as badly as she did now.   She glanced at
Joe, who stood on the threshold, daring him to recite the
Surgeon General's warning.

He said nothing.

She lit up.

"My address is on my driver's license.   My keys were
in the zippered compartment along with my wallet."   She
cocked a hip against the dresser, inhaled smoke and a
heady dose of tranquility.   The tranquility part was no
doubt psychosomatic.   But her senses definitely cleared as

she contemplated the scenario. "They let themselves in. I don't know where Jean-Pierre was . . . is, but thank God he wasn't here. He couldn't have been. He wouldn't have let Luc polish off three-quarters of a bottle of wine."

"Pretty early in the day to tie one on," Joe said.

Sofia crossed to her closet, fished out a small suitcase, and tossed it on her bed. "Luc's career is . . . was . . . in a slump, and his love life was a shambles. He drank to cope. He also leaned on Jean-Pierre. More than he should have." Her hands shook as she searched out essentials—underwear, shoes, fresh clothes, phone charger—and stuffed them into the open suitcase. She craved a stiff shot of whiskey, her *Nona* Viv's cure-all, but Abby would probably drink beer. She wondered if she had a Corona in the fridge, took another calming drag of the cigarette. "Jean-Pierre didn't confide in me much where Luc was concerned, but I'm pretty sure their friendship was on the skids."

"The reason Jean-Pierre was depressed?"

"Not the main reason, but it certainly didn't help." She glanced back and caught Joe staring at her and massaging his chest. He looked uncomfortable, but then he too schooled his expression. The man sizzled with repressed emotions. "You okay?"

"Heartburn." He adjusted his tie, stifled whatever he was feeling. Still, the air was charged with something potent and dangerous.

"I have some antacid tablets in the medicine cabinet.

I'll grab them and pack a few essentials. Don't worry, I'll hurry." She tried to ease past him but he blocked her way. She made the mistake of looking in his eyes. His dark gaze swirled with heart-stirring tenderness. His unspoken compassion roused tears of grief and anger. She blinked them back. *Please, don't touch me.* If he touched her, she'd crumble.

"Even if your cowboy scenario proves true, Luc's death isn't your fault."

She forced herself to hold his gaze. "Logically, I know that. But surely, you of all people understand why I feel somewhat responsible."

He worked his jaw, nodded, and then stepped back into the hall. "Which way to Jean-Pierre's room?"

She wondered if he'd ever spoken to anyone about Julietta, but now wasn't the time to ask. They had to get out of here. They had to find Jean-Pierre. She pointed to the door to his left, and then headed for the bathroom. "I'll get your antacids and meet you in a minute."

They couldn't get away from each other fast enough.

Sofia closed the bathroom door, allowing her the privacy to collect herself. *Keep moving.* If she stopped, she'd think and feel. Emotions were plentiful, some confusing, all turbulent. She flushed her cigarette down the toilet, but stalled at the vanity mirror. The girl staring back at her was a stranger. Toss up as to which was most bizarre; the electric-blue false eyelashes, the vixen lipstick, or her hair. On second hard look, Joe was right. Her hair was pretty radical and really, *really* purple. She looked like hell, or more pointedly something *from* hell. And yet, she didn't regret the disguise. As long as she was someone else, anyone else, she wouldn't have to deal with Sofia Chiquita Marino's internal chaos.

She acknowledged Abby Geyser with a curt nod and flung open the medicine cabinet. She nabbed the jumbo bottle of Rolaids, her toothpaste, deodorant, soap, face crème and cleanser, and packed them into her travel organizer case, along with cosmetics, a box of semi-permanent hair color, a razor, and her toothbrush. When she reached back for dental floss, her gaze fell on the pills she'd bought Jean-Pierre to help him with his insomnia and anxiety. Considering the stress-reducing drug a Godsend, she washed down three capsules with a Dixie cup of tap water, and tossed the bottle in her bag.

Fifteen-minutes. She should be feeling the effect in fifteen-minutes. Relief. Non-addicting relief. Unfortunately, Jean-Pierre had snubbed the natural supplement in favor of Valium.

Jean-Pierre's medication.

She searched the shelves. Gone. His toiletries were also missing. He'd packed up his toiletries! Maybe Joe was right. Maybe he'd slipped away for some down time!

She rushed into the hall and collided with her dark-suited companion. "His toiletries are missing. You're right, Joe. He went somewhere!"

He held up a piece of paper boasting Jean-Pierre's handwriting, and smiled. "Vermont."

CHAPTER SIXTEEN

Rainbow Ridge, Vermont

We need to talk."

Rudy jumped a good two inches at the sound of Jake's voice. "Jesus, don't sneak up on me like that, Leeds." He minimized the article he'd been reading on poltergeists, swiveled his chair away from his computer monitor, and focused on the two men standing on the threshold of his office. He wasn't sure which surprised him more, the late-night visit, or their state of undress. They'd obviously rolled out of bed for this tête-à-tête. Jake, who according to Afia slept in the raw, had slipped on a pair of sweat pants but hadn't bothered with a shirt.

Murphy wore a rumpled-T-shirt, but no pants, just his boxers. At one time he would've appreciated the beefcake on display, Jake had a fierce six-pack, but just now Rudy's mind and heart were full of Jean-Pierre. He assumed the men hadn't dressed for fear of waking their wives, but couldn't imagine why this couldn't wait until morning. "If this is about the prowlers . . ."

"It's about Jean-Pierre," Jake said.

"He's fine," Murphy added, before Rudy could think the worst. "In fact, he's on his way."

Rudy furrowed his brow. "Here?

"Seems Afia and Lulu weren't the only two intent on arriving early," Jake said as he moved into the room and sat on the edge of the brown leather club chair.

"The reason you haven't been able to reach Legrand is because he's been in transit to Vermont." Murphy shut the office door and then crossed and settled on the matching ottoman. "Between three connecting flights and layovers, traveling time amounted to eleven and a half hours. Once he landed in Burlington, I assume he rented a car."

"Provided he doesn't take any wrong turns," Jake said, "he should be here shortly."

Rudy leaned back in his desk chair assimilating the news. What a relief! "How did you learn this? When?"

"Bogie called me a few minutes ago," Murphy said. "He found a scribbled note in Legrand's bedroom relaying his new itinerary."

"What was your brother doing in JP's apartment?" Rudy asked. "I thought he and Sofia were in Arizona."

The stone-faced protection specialist rested his forearms on his knees, clasped his hands, and leaned forward. "There was an incident." He glanced at Jake.

The P.I. ran a hand over his face and eyeballed Rudy. "Luc's dead."

Rudy sat in shock while Murphy stated specifics as relayed to him by Bogie. Luc Dupris, a former lover of Jean-Pierre's, the man who'd invited him to LA thereby tweaking Rudy's insecurities and tempting him to stray in a moment of jealous insanity, was dead. As he didn't personally know the man, he didn't experience true grief. He did however, regret that the man had suffered. Bleeding to death from a head wound. What a way to go. He blew out a tense breath. "So, Jean-Pierre doesn't know?"

Jake shook his head no. "Listen. I know this Luc was a sore spot with you and JP. Maybe it would be better if I broke the news."

"No. Thanks, Jake, but it should come from me." He palmed his forehead. Wow. Talk about a helluva bomb.

"There's a slim chance that it could be worse," Murphy said.

Rudy and Jake spoke as one. "Worse?"

"I told you that the police declared Dupris's death accidental. Bogie's not so sure." He went on to explain Sofia's supposed run-in with two hostile cowboys and

Luc's last words.

Rudy traded looks with Jake, a bad feeling settling in his bones. "So, Bogie thinks the same men who tangled with Sofia killed Luc?"

Murphy shrugged. "No, that's Sofia's take. Bogie doesn't know what to think. So far he hasn't been able to nail down one piece of hard evidence to support any of Sofia's theories. All he has is her word and his gut feeling that she's in danger."

"That's good enough for me," Rudy said. Thank God Jean-Pierre hadn't been home. Nausea—acid sharp—roiled in his stomach and dank sweat beaded on his brow. The man he loved could have been lying in the morgue tonight. He shifted in his seat. "Your brother should bring Sofia here so we can keep her safe."

"Bogie will protect her," Murphy said.

"That's if she truly needs protection," Jake added.

Rudy's head spun as he swiveled around and signed off the Internet. Casper was the least of his troubles. "Sofia can't remember when, where or why she tangled with those . . . cowboys?"

Murphy grunted. "Apparently, she blocked it out."

"Selective amnesia," the blond P.I. surmised. He glanced at Murphy. "You don't want Lulu to know?"

"Until I have concrete information, I'd prefer that we kept this between ourselves."

Rudy groaned. "Keeping secrets from loved ones, even

when we only mean to protect them, usually backfires." He shot Jake a meaningful glance. "Right?"

"Sorry. I tend to agree with Murphy on this. Why upset Lulu if this is simply an exaggeration of some kind on Sofia's part?"

"I'm not saying nothing happened," Murphy put in. "But whatever caused the amnesia could also be causing her to mind to play tricks. Bogie says she's already cited a couple of instances reminiscent of a "Spy Girl" episode. She could be confusing fiction and fact."

Rudy shifted in his seat. "But then, that means I can't tell Jean-Pierre about Sofia's suspicion that Luc may have been murdered."

"Why plant that seed if it's bogus?" Jake asked. "Why make it any rougher on JP?"

Rudy shook his head. "I can't believe I'm getting suckered into another lie."

Murphy raised a brow. "Don't be a schmuck, Gallow. It's called protecting loved ones from unnecessary hurt."

Just then headlights splashed through the office window. Rudy pushed out of his leather high-back and moved toward the door. His pulse quickened. "Depending on how Jean-Pierre takes the news, it could be a rough night, regardless."

Jean-Pierre cut the ignition of his rental car. He eyed the four-door parked next to Rudy's used Subaru and clenched his jaw against a tidal wave of anger. He glanced at the rambling inn silhouetted against a moonlight sky and tamped down a flutter of anxiety. He'd spent the entire day rehearsing for what promised to be a dramatic scene. Dozens of thoughts and feelings expressed in varying degrees of honesty and hostility. Two resolutions.

He was mentally and physically fatigued, and he had yet to confront Rudy.

Part of him wanted to get this over with. Part of him wanted to pretend like nothing was wrong. On the long, dark drive from Burlington to Rainbow Ridge, he'd almost convinced himself that Hollyberry Inn was indeed cursed with wiring problems. That Rudy hadn't been lying. That he wasn't playing around. But if the inn was not ready for guests, then why was there a strange car parked in the drive at one o'clock in the morning?

The tips of his ears burned as he exited the car and stalked toward the front door *sans* luggage. His heart thudded against his chest as months of pent-up hurt and frustration churned in his empty stomach. He curled his fingers into his sweaty palms, mounted the steps, and raised his fist to announce his arrival.

The door swung open before his knuckles connected. Rudy stood on the threshold in his velvet lounge pants and matching robe. He smoothed his hand over his dark goatee, and sighed.

"You do not look happy to see me, Bunny." Exhausted and emotionally fragile, Jean-Pierre's patience snapped. At the sound of creaking wood, he glanced around Rudy's bulked-up body and saw a silhouetted form moving up the hall, nude to the waist. He glared at the love of his life through tears of pain and exploded. "*Bâtard*!"

He struck out, landing a hard punch to Rudy's cheekbone. They both yelped in shock.

Rudy staggered back.

Ignoring his smarting knuckles, Jean-Pierre sprang forward and tackled the taller man to the hardwood floor, landing blow after blow. "I loved you, trusted you, and you betrayed me!"

Rudy didn't fight back, just tried to block the hits.

Jean-Pierre's rage gave him the upper hand.

"Whoa. Whoa," he heard a man say. Someone grabbed him by the shoulders and hauled him backwards.

Jean-Pierre swung blindly and clipped the "other man" in the balls.

"Motherfu . . ." He grabbed his crotch and stumbled back in pain.

"That hurt," noted a third male voice.

Confused, Jean-Pierre whirled around and came face to face with Lulu's husband. "Murphy?"

The bodyguard held up a hand in warning. "Take a swing, and I'll have to hurt you, Legrand."

He heard footsteps on the stairway, squinted as an overhead lamp flicked on flooding the foyer with light. He turned around for a clear look at the man he'd punched in the groin. *Jake.* "*Merde.*"

"What's going on down there?"

Winded from his tirade, Jean-Pierre fell back against the door jamb and watched as Lulu, and then Afia, came to a dead halt on the stair's landing. Sleepy-eyed, they stared at the carnage.

He glanced over at Rudy who'd pushed himself into a sitting position. Robe askew, he swiped at the blood trickling from the corner of his swollen lip. The sensitive skin beneath his right eye puffed. Overall, the man looked stunned. Jean-Pierre jammed both hands through his thick, shaggy hair. "What have I done?"

"Looks like you wigged out," Lulu said.

Now he knew what one of her red-hazed furies felt like. She blew her top and then, after cooling, regretted her rash, often hurtful actions. Ah, *oui*, regret sang through his veins.

"Put some ice on that eye, Gallow," Murphy said as he breezed by. "It's going to swell."

Afia stepped off the landing and moved toward Jake. "Are you all right, honey? You look like you're going to be sick."

"He'll live," Murphy said. He grasped Lulu's hand. "Come on, princess. Let's go back to bed."

"But, I didn't even get to say hello to Jean-Pierre."

"He'll be here in the morning." The bodyguard peered over his shoulder. "Won't you, Legrand?"

Funny. It sounded more like an order than a question. "*Oui.*"

Murphy whispered something in Lulu's ear, and whisked her up the stairs.

Afia put her arm around her husband who was still trying to catch his breath. She shot Jean-Pierre a disapproving look. "Why in the world did you hit Jake and Rudy?"

"Because he thought we were lovers," Rudy answered for him.

"That's absurd," she said.

"I know," Jean-Pierre said, feeling quite the fool.

Afia shook her head. "Honestly."

He angled his head toward Jake. "I am sorry, *mon ami.*"

"Forget it," he wheezed, while steering Afia toward the stairs. "Come on, baby."

"I'm adding this to the list of things to talk about tomorrow," she said as they scaled the landing.

"Yippee," Rudy mumbled.

"Don't forget to ice your eye, Rudy," Afia called over her shoulder. "Goodnight, Jean-Pierre. Welcome home."

Home. The word, the concept, filled Jean-Pierre with simultaneous joy and remorse. *Home* was the man he'd just wrongly pummeled. "Why did you not fight back, Bunny?"

The dark-haired man dabbed the back of his hand to his bloodied lip. "I had it coming."

"But, you did nothing wrong."

"Not tonight, no." Rudy pushed himself to his feet. "But I don't think your fury was rooted in tonight."

Jean-Pierre sighed. "Not entirely, no."

Rudy rolled back his shoulders, tightened the sash around his waist. "Are we going to be okay?"

"I do not know."

The muscled-marvel inched closer. "We need to talk about this, Jean-Pierre. I need to know what you're feeling. And I want you to know where I'm coming from."

"Ah, *oui*. Talking is what I had in mind before I . . . wigged out." He'd rehearsed this confrontation all day. Not once had he envisioned actually pummeling Rudy in a fit of rage. His violent outburst was most unexpected and made him strangely aware of the distasteful power of jealously. He tenderly brushed his thumb over Rudy's cheekbone. "I am not sure the ice will help. You are going to have, what do you call it? A shiner."

Rudy quirked a sad smile. "There are worse things, believe me." He caught Jean-Pierre's hand in his own, kissed his palm. "Come in and sit down. Before we talk, I have some news about a friend, and it isn't good."

"Are you going to tell me what's going on between Rudy and Jean-Pierre?" Lulu asked as she slipped under the cool sheets.

Murphy shucked his T-shirt and shorts and climbed into bed. "Tomorrow." He snuggled up against her, hard muscle and hot flesh.

She closed her eyes, tried to ignore the delightful tingling between her legs when he kissed the sensitive part of her wrist. "Are you going to let me talk to Sofie?"

"Eventually." He licked a sizzling path to the bend of her elbow.

"Are you trying to distract me?"

"I'm trying to make love to my wife." He captured her mouth with his own and seduced her with one of his blue ribbon kisses.

Her limbs melted and her heart bloomed. She gasped when he moved on, tonguing her neck and the soft hollow of her throat. Sex with Colin was always exciting. Before him, she'd never known kinky. Kinky for her meaning anything other than missionary sex. Seven months into their marriage and they'd already explored several of the positions in the Kama Sutra. He'd presented her with the book for their one-month anniversary, and she'd surprised him by being a quick and enthusiastic study. "Um, Colin," she whispered, while he unbuttoned her Sponge Bob pajama top. "Afia and Jake are in the next room. They'll hear us." She tended to get a little loud and aggressive in the midst of play. Something her warrior husband loved.

He grinned down at her as he palmed one of her breasts. "Maybe it will inspire them."

She squirmed in delight when he traced tickling circles around her puckered buds. "But, she's eight months pregnant."

"Trust me, that's not stopping Jake." He laughed low. "Although he's probably down for the count tonight."

She traced her fingertips along his hard jaw, over his soft lips. A man of sharp contrasts, in more ways than one. "What made Jean-Pierre wig out?"

"Tomorrow." He nipped her finger, then whispered a naughty suggestion in her ear.

Desire, fierce and hot, flowed through her pliant body, her thoughts drifting from real life to the illustrated pages of the Kama Sutra as he lavished attention on her breasts. She sucked in a sharp breath. "Be careful. They're tender."

"They are rather full." He smiled against her skin. "Not that I'm complaining."

"Yes, well, don't get too attached. It's just a pre-menstrual thing."

"Like your cravings for salty food."

"Exactly."

"I've got cravings too," he drawled, while ridding her of her pajama bottoms.

"Colin?"

"Hmm?"

"I'm sorry about tricking you into coming up here early."

"No, you're not."

She sighed. "You're right, I'm not. Rudy and Jean-Pierre need our support just now."

He smoothed her messy curls from her face. "They've got it, hon. We won't leave until they're on track."

Admiration and bone-deep love flowed through her being as she gazed up at her moonlit Prince Charming. A strong-willed champion with a heart of gold. She quirked a devilish grin, pushed him back and shifted so that she straddled his hunky body. "I've been reading about this technique called *The Black Bee*."

He smiled. "Let's rock and roll, tiger."

Rudy wasn't sure what kind of reaction he expected after relaying the details of Luc's death. But it certainly wasn't stony-faced silence. "It's all right to cry, Jean-Pierre. I know you cared about Luc." He cleared his throat. "That is, I know you were friends. I was an idiot last fall, thinking that you still had feelings for him. That he might try to steal you away from me. My reaction was childish and weak."

Jean-Pierre clasped his hands in his lap. "Let us not

talk about the indiscretion. Not now. Let me . . . let me absorb this first."

"Sure. Okay. Just . . . let me know when you're ready." Nervous, he scraped his teeth over his lower lip, and winced. Man, JP had socked him good. Who knew the gentle soul had it in him?

"I'm sorry I hit you, *mon amour*."

"I'm sorry I hurt you."

Jean-Pierre slid him a sideways glance.

"Right. Not now." Damn, this was tough. "I'm feeling a little awkward here, honey. You *are* upset about Luc, aren't you?"

Jean-Pierre twisted his thumb ring round and round . . . and round. "I am sorry that he died so horribly, of course. Passing out and hitting his head on the coffee table? How tragic."

"He might have tripped and hit his head," Rudy said, striving to make the alcohol-related death less tawdry. "They couldn't be sure." He specifically left out Sofia's scenario. Jake was right. Why imply murder? This was bad enough.

"Regardless, this was a senseless mishap. I mourn the loss of the man who used to be my friend."

"Used to be?"

The wiry Frenchman dropped his head back against the sofa, released a long sigh. "Luc changed. Hollywood changed him. He was aggressive and competitive. Shallow.

Although, I suppose if I looked back honestly on our relationship, he was always vain and selfish. Anyway, things were not going so well for Luc. Professionally. Personally." He lolled his head left, caught Rudy's gaze. "He came on to me."

Rudy swallowed hard. "Yeah?"

"More than once."

"Okay."

"I blew him away."

"Off," Rudy corrected with a slight smile.

"What?"

"You blew him off. Not away."

Jean-Pierre's lips curved into the semblance of a grin. "Ah, *oui*. Off. He was drunk at the time. He drank a lot. Too much. I tried to be patient. Tried to be his friend. I know it was difficult for him. The rejection. There is a lot of rejection in Hollywood."

"I'll bet."

"I do not like it there so much."

Rudy frowned. "Then why did you stay so long?"

Jean-Pierre looked at him as though he was dense. "I was waiting for you to make up your mind about us."

Okay. Maybe he was dense. He'd allowed his insecurities to muck up this relationship good and plenty. He shifted on the couch so that he was facing the younger man. "Look, I know you don't want to talk about this right now, but let me say this much. I never doubted *us*. I doubted me."

"Semantics."

Man, he wasn't going to make this easy. Rudy fingered his goatee and studied his partner at length. His shirt was mis-buttoned and wrinkled. His socks were mismatched and he had a fierce five-o'clock shadow. Very un-Jean-Pierre like. Dark circles marred his normally luminous brown eyes, and his skin lacked its normal peachy glow. "You look beat."

"I have not been sleeping well."

"Want to talk about it?" What the hell? He'd keep trying until he broke through.

Jean-Pierre licked his lips, surprising Rudy with a curt nod. "There is a part of me that wishes to ignore what I have been feeling. What I have been going through. It is embarrassing to admit that one is not as strong as he'd always believed. My analyst . . ."

"You've been seeing an analyst?" Rudy fisted his hands in his lap to keep from reaching out in sympathy. "Why am I just now hearing about this?"

"I did not want you to know I was having . . . trouble."

His temper flared. "Why the hell not?"

"Because you had troubles of your own, no?"

The lame helping the lame. He sighed. "No. I mean, yes. I'm sorry. Go on."

Jean-Pierre raked his fingers through his hair and cleared his throat. "I have some things to say."

Rudy braced himself.

The Frenchman squared his shoulders. "I resent that you pushed me into moving to Los Angeles to accept a job I could have lived without. Ah, *oui*, it was a chance of a lifetime, but so was my relationship with you."

Rudy swallowed a lump. "I . . ."

JP cut him off with a raised hand. "I resent that you did not trust my judgment. Nor did you trust that I would not stray and rekindle my affair with Luc. I resent that, instead of talking to me about your insecurities, you wigged out and took solace in another man's arms."

"Okay. Can I . . ."

"I resent that you did not respect me enough to call to let me know that you were alive after going AOL for hours."

"AWOL." Rudy shifted. "About that . . ."

"I resent that you did not ask me to stay after I threatened to leave you. That you did not drag me off of the airplane. That you only visited me in LA four times in six months and that you did not stay, or at some point drag me home. I resent that you tried to cancel my coming to Hollyberry Inn."

"Not cancel. Postpone. Yeah, I know," he said when Jean-Pierre smirked. "Semantics. But . . ."

"I do not like living in Los Angeles. I do not want to be a famous costume designer to the stars. I would be just as happy, *happier*, designing costumes for amateurs in regional theater. I am tired of being the strong one. The

patient one. I am at my wit's end, Rudy. I do not wish to
be jerked around any longer."

"I don't blame you."

"I want to be in a committed relationship."

Rudy smiled. "So do I."

"With you."

He laughed, his anxiety evaporating with the knowledge that Jean-Pierre still wanted to pursue their relationship. "God, I hope so. Honey, I bought this place for us.
I want us to be together. I'm sorry it took me so freaking long to come around, but I know what I want." He
grasped the other man's hand and squeezed. "You."

Jean-Pierre blinked. He shook his head and swallowed
hard. "You are making it most difficult for me to be angry,
mon amour."

"Good." Rudy sobered. "Wait. I have to . . . we need
to talk about the indiscretion. I need to wipe the slate
clean. I know you said details weren't important, but in
this case, I disagree."

Jean-Pierre glanced away. "I am most weary. Perhaps
tomorrow."

"No, now. Tomorrow is a new day. I hope." He massaged a dull throbbing in his temple, cursed the lingering
guilt. "The fact that I was even tempted to stray, that I
came so close . . . well, that in itself is unforgivable."

"No, not unforgivable. I understand more than ever
that jealousy can drive a person to most uncharacteristic

behavior." Jean-Pierre paused, crinkle his brow. "What do you mean, *came so close*?"

Rudy confessed his sins on a rush of breath. "There was some inappropriate touching, but I stopped him before things progressed. I couldn't do it. I didn't want it."

"All this time I thought . . . and you were *faithful*?"

"Did you not hear the inappropriate touching part?"

"Ah, *oui*, but . . ." Jean-Pierre fell back against the couch. "I should be angry with you, or at the very least annoyed, but I am too numb."

"It might creep up on you tomorrow. The anger."

Jean-Pierre sighed heavily. "I doubt it."

Rudy's shoulders caved with relief.

Out of the blue, his partner's eyes filled with tears. He thumbed them back, dropped his chin to his chest, and spoke to his suede clogs. "Do you think Luc suffered?"

Rudy blinked at the change of subject. "No," he lied. "His blood alcohol was through the roof. I seriously doubt he felt much of anything."

"I was supposed to meet with him today. He wanted to bounce a new story idea off of me. I forgot. He must have let himself in. Must have thought I'd stepped out. He was waiting for me." A tear coursed down his cheek. "And now he is dead."

Rudy pulled his partner into his arms and rocked him as he silently wept. His heart ached for a dozen different reasons, none of them involving jealously, all centering around love. Like Afia and Jake, and Lulu and Murphy, he and Jean-Pierre were meant to be. *I am open and ready for a long-term relationship.*

With a weary groan, Jean-Pierre pushed out of the embrace and swiped away tears. "I am sorry, Bunny. I am exhausted. I will be better . . ."

"Tomorrow?" Rudy finished with a crooked grin.

Jean-Pierre took a steadying breath and glanced around the great room. "Nice furniture."

"I'll give you the grand tour . . ."

"Tomorrow?" Jean-Pierre finished with a watery smile.

Rudy basked in that smile, tentative though it was. Holy Streisand, he'd missed this man.

"Let us go to bed."

He raised an eyebrow. "Together?"

Jean-Pierre nodded.

Rudy's heart pounded. "As lovers?"

"As friends. Just now, I am in need of a friend."

Rudy stood and offered his hand. "I can do that."

CHAPTER SEVENTEEN

Los Angeles, California

Joe spent the short walk to the mini-mart and back trying to get a handle on this insane day. Talk about action-packed. Good news: Jean-Pierre was safe. Bad news: Dupris was dead. Good news: Sofia's publicist miraculously cooled the media's attention on the *accidental* death in her home by . . . Bad news: Turning up the heat on her so-called secret affair with a former FBI agent.

At least the press thought she was still somewhere in Arizona. Unfortunately, that made his home a hot zone. The thought of reporters staking out his house and digging into his past set his teeth on edge.

He scanned the perimeter, soaked in the sights and smells of Los Angeles. The City of Angels. Home to more than 3.5 million residents. Top attractions: Hollywood, Disneyland, Beverly Hills, Venice Beach, and Malibu.

Fantasyland. The superficial haven of eager starlets, hungry actors, and greedy producers. Media-spinning publicists and fast-talking agents.

He'd never had much tolerance for the entertainment industry. Hollywood types raked in millions while police officers and teachers scraped by. Where was the justice in that? Maybe he'd spent too many years dwelling in the underworld. Unlike Sofia and her sister Lulu, he'd lost his sense of the fantastic. There was a time, long ago, when he'd been able to lose himself in the hard-hitting, fast-shooting, animated world of Dick Tracy. As a boy he'd devoured comic strips and books relaying the antics of the super intelligent police detective who butted heads with various colorful villains. Gangsters, arsonists, kidnappers. Tracy tackled them all. Later on, Tracy's creator incorporated personal wrist communicators and other futuristic gadgets.

Oh, yeah, he'd dug that techno-fantasy era bigtime.

Joe smiled. Suddenly the fact that he tuned into "Spy Girl" and occasionally *enjoyed* it, didn't seem so suspect. Although, Sofia fascinated him more than the show. He could look at her for hours on end and never tire of the vision. The sight of her kicking evil-doer ass, albeit fictional, was a bonus turn-on.

He unlocked the door of their hotel room and quietly slipped in. She'd said she was hungry, surprise confession of the year, but she'd looked dead tired when he'd left her. Understandable. It had been one hell of a day. A day that had left her exhausted, and him with a lot of questions.

He set the sack of groceries on the desk, glanced at the two double beds. She wasn't sprawled on either one. Her Gothic costume was heaped on the hunter green arm chair, the babydoll platform shoes kicked to the corner.

The bathroom door was closed. Maybe she was in the shower. He had a surreal vision of her standing naked in the stall, hot water slucing over those voluptuous curves as she shampooed that vibrant dyed hair. In his mind's eye, the water ran purple, then red. Stained water swirling into the drain.

Just like in Hitchcock's *Psycho*.

He shook off the disturbing vision of Sofia getting knifed by a crazed cowboy. Jesus, he was beat. His mind kept straying off on tangents spurred by Sofia's musings. He shrugged out of his suit jacket, slipped off his tie, and tossed it on the desk alongside the bulging plastic bag. Plastic bag. Plastic shower curtian. "Sofia? You okay in there?"

No answer.

He nabbed a beer from the six-pack he'd purchased, unscrewed the top, and took a deep swig. He glanced at the door. "Sof?"

Silence.

He rolled his head to ease a kink, moved over and knocked.

Still, no answer.

He turned the knob and peeked in. His pulse raced at the sight of her submerged in a bubble bath, head lolled to the side, eyes closed. "Sofia." She didn't stir and, Christ, his heart nearly blasted through his ribs with dread. He moved in and touched her bare shoulder. "Sof."

Her eyes flew open with a gasp. She lurched forward, one hand clasped to her throat. "Jesus, Joe. Don't scare me like that."

His heart skipped a beat, or twelve. "Ditto." He set his beer bottle on the vanity, breathed. "Christ, Marino."

"What?"

"I thought you were . . ."

"What?"

Dead. "Nothing." Christ. He took another calming breath, the heady scent of vanilla and musk filling his nostrils. Sofia's scent.

"I can't believe I fell asleep. Although . . ." She relaxed against the fluted rim of the massive tub, thick clouds of bubbles caressing the swells of her breasts. "Well, yeah, okay. I guess I get it. Between the relief of knowing JP is safe, the hot water and the pills . . ." She whistled, smiled. "Woo, yeah, I'm toast."

Joe stared at her. At her head and shoulders anyway. The rest of her was hidden beneath those frothy soap bubbles. His throat constricted. "What pills?"

"The ones I took to relax."

Fuckin' A. "Where are they?"

"The pills?"

"Yes. The goddamned pills."

"Geesh, Bogart. Chill." She pointed to her burgeoning travel case. "In there. Somewhere."

"How many did you take?"

"Five."

"Five?"

"Well, three at first, but they didn't seem to be working, so I doubled up. I'm a big girl. Figured I needed a bigger dose."

"You're not a big girl, Sofia. You're five-foot-six with a medium frame. What do you weigh? One-twenty-five? One-thirty? Give me a frickin' break." He rooted through scads of beauty products. "Dammit, where are they?"

"But earlier today you said I was fat."

"No, I didn't."

"You said, better to hide that figure than flaunt it."

Face cleanser, crème, body oil, Vitamin C, E, B . . . "Meaning you have a body people notice and envy, or notice and covet. I don't know why in the hell you starve yourself. Even if you were several pounds heavier, on a scale of ten you're a fifteen."

"You think I'm a fifteen?"

"Sof. For chrissake!"

"The other pocket," she said. "Yeah, that one."

He palmed the plastic bottle, speed-read the ingredients.

"It's a natural supplement."

"I see that."

"An over-the-counter stress reliever. I was wired tight and I didn't want to have another one of those damned attacks so, I figured what the hell? I mean it's not like they're addictive. What's wrong with you, Joe?"

"Nothing." His wobbly legs gave way. He settled on the john and stared down at the bottle in his hand. A natural supplement. He'd feared Valium or Percocet. Julietta had favored both.

"Maybe you should pop a couple of those yourself."

He set the bottle on the counter. "Pass."

She regarded him with a thoughtful frown. "All right then. Join me in here. I'll kick up the jet sprays. A hydromassage will do you good."

He blinked at his fantasy woman and the two-person Jacuzzi. "You're kidding, right?"

"No, I'm serious." She smoothed her wet hair off of her freshly-scrubbed face, exposing those killer cheekbones. Makeup free and gorgeous. She rested her bruised forearms on the rim of the tub, propped her chin on her hands, and smiled—a flash of white teeth against mocha brown skin. "It's not like I haven't seen you naked before," she purred.

His cock twitched. "Forget it."

She glanced at his crotch, wiggled her finely arched brows. "Nice package, by the way."

He grabbed his beer bottle. Took a long swallow. "You're looped."

"Funny thing, that." She angled her head. "Typically, I have a high tolerance for drugs and alcohol. Not that I've done a lot of drugs, but I have experimented, here and there, when I was younger." She frowned. "Don't tell Lulu."

"God forbid." Her older sister, a veritable teetotaler, championed the slogan, *Say No to Drugs!* Joe, especially after Julietta's overdose, supported the same view. Sofia's liberal attitude was disconcerting, although, given her progressive, needy personality, not surprising.

"I don't suppose you've ever experimented."

"Nope."

"Not even with weed?"

"Not even." Aside from the fact that it would have squelched his career as a federal agent, he'd never had the inclination. He picked at the label on his beer bottle and blatantly stared at the most beautiful woman in the world.

"Betcha don't miss the head-banger spikes and radical makeup."

"It was a clever disguise." *She* was a clever woman. He'd been duly impressed by her composure in the field. Almost as impressed as he was right now. She didn't seem to give a rat's ass that she was naked. Although, hell, it's not like he could see anything, given her position and all those bubbles. Her mouthwatering breasts were flattened against the inside of the tub. What he wouldn't give to be the inside of that tub.

She scraped her teeth across her lower lip. "I shampooed and scrubbed, but my hair's still pretty purple."

He caught a flash of insecurity in those dark brown eyes. "Hard to tell with it wet and slicked back."

"Trust me. When it dries it will still be purple." She lowered her lashes. "Less vibrant, but purple."

"Sofia?"

"What?"

"You could have an orange Mohawk, and you'd still be beautiful."

She cringed. "Am I that transparent?"

"I'm just good at reading people."

She peered up at him, forehead wrinkled in confusion. "If you feel like that, then why were you mad when I cut and dyed my hair?"

He scraped his hand along his jaw, uneasy about revealing his thoughts. "I wasn't mad. I was . . . surprised. I didn't realize you'd go to such lengths to help a friend."

She frowned. "You think I'm shallow."

"I think you're complex."

She sighed. "That's about the nicest thing anyone has ever said to me."

"I find that hard to believe."

"It's true."

He chewed on that statement for a moment. The more she gave up, the more he wanted to ask about her past, specifically her multiple rocky affairs. He'd never known her to be so relaxed and forthcoming. No doubt a result of the stress-relieving tablets. Compounded by the fact that she was operating on a post-hangover, little sleep, and no food, no wonder she was crocked. Although he wasn't thrilled that she'd relied on pills to take off the edge, he appreciated a peek at the candid, warmer side of this cynical siren.

"I like looking at you too," she said, addressing his silent appraisal. Her lush lips curled into a lazy smile. "Although, I kind of miss your goatee."

He smiled at that. "What is it with women and goatees?"

She shrugged. "I can't speak for anyone else, but it makes me think of medieval times. Knights. Protectors of the realm. Powerful and dangerous. Sexy."

"Uh-huh." That's twice in two days that she'd called him sexy. Although both times, she'd been under the influence.

"Lisa was right."

"Lisa who?"

"The cocktail waitress at the Camelback. She said you look like Johnny Depp."

"I'm surprised you remember that." He saluted her

with his beer, took another sip.

"I remember," she said with a smirk. "I remember because I thought the same thing when I first met you."

He grunted.

"That's a compliment, Bogart. Depp's frickin' hot."

Okay, so yeah, that was a boost to the ego. He suppressed a cocky smile, watched as she squeezed more scented gel into the water, and kicked up the jet-sprays with her sudsy toes. "Just an observation, but I don't think you're supposed use bubble bath in a Jacuzzi, babe."

"Yeah, well, I'm a rule-breaker from way back."

"Unlike your sister."

"Lulu's a throwback to the Victorian age. I used to call her Mary Poppins." Sofia laughed. "She hated that. Thought I was making fun of her. I was, sort of. But secretly, I admired her. All that optimism. Priceless."

Her laughter, rich and genuine, caught him off guard. He swigged the last of his beer, hoping to cool the heat of desire rushing to his loins. It was as if they were caught in a time warp. As if she'd never tangled with those cowboys. As if Dupris wasn't dead.

Denial.

Not entirely healthy, then again the kid deserved a break. Tomorrow would come soon enough and with it reality, although he wasn't entirely sure what that entailed. Tomorrow they'd have to crack that memory block.

"She takes after her mother, a comedic actress," Sofia

continued with a smile. "We never knew Camille. She died when Lulu was two, before I was born. But Viv said she was a hoot."

"You had different mothers, but the same father, I know that. I also know that your mother—a dancer from Spain, right?—and Dante Marino died in a car accident when you girls were very young. Your grandmother . . ."

"Viv," Sofia interrupted. "She likes to be called Viv. Grandma or *Nona* makes her feel old."

Joe raised a brow. "Isn't she seventy-something?"

"Age is a state of mind." She added with a wistful sigh, "According to Viv."

Age, he surmised, like weight, was probably a sensitive spot with Sofia given Hollywood's love affair with youth. It pissed him off, but if he stated his views, like earlier today on Fremont Saddle, she'd get defensive—she came from generations of entertainers, after all—and climb up on her soapbox. He wasn't ready for the return of defensive, cynical Sofia.

He braced his forearms on his knees and leaned forward, determined to know this woman. "*Viv* raised you and your sister together. Same maternal influence. How is it you turned out such opposites?"

"Wanna know my life story? Climb in. Get comfortable."

He'd rather climb in and get busy. "No."

"How old are you?"

He stood. Time to end this cozy chat. She was, after all, *looped*. "Old enough to know better."

She rolled her eyes. "Give it up, Bogart."

"Almost forty."

"That explains a lot."

He frowned. "Like what?"

"Like why you're such an old-fashioned fuddy-duddy."

"I'm not a fuddy-duddy." Christ almighty. He was a former undercover agent with the Federal Bureau of Investigation.

"Prove it." She smiled, beckoned him forward with a crooked finger.

"*You* are dangerous." Contemplating his sanity, he summoned the control of a monk and exited the sexually-charged room. Maybe he wasn't such a bastard after all.

He'll be back, Sofia smugly thought. As she'd once told Lulu, no man could say no to a naked and willing woman. And boy, was she willing. Eager and willing. She'd been dreaming about him when he'd woken her. About that kiss earlier today. A kiss as wild and haunting as the Superstition Mountains and as wondrous as that desert sunset. She wanted more. When Joe kissed her he transported her conscious being to an alternate plane.

Time ceased to exist. Troubles disappeared.

Just now she needed very badly to escape. To obliterate lingering thoughts of Luc and two homicidal cowboys. Just now she needed Joe.

She glanced at the open doorway. What the hell was he doing out there? Being a gentleman? Resisting a woman in a vulnerable state? *Being respectful*. Well, damn.

Just then he strode back into the room.

She tried to suppress a cheeky smile and failed.

He blew out a frustrated breath. "What am I going to do with you?"

Jesus, he was handsome. "I can give you a couple of ideas if you're really stuck." Desire pulsed hot and rapid through her veins. Racy scenarios burned away her no-sex resolution like wildfire.

"I'm not stripping down and getting in that tub," he said, refusing to take the bait. "On the other hand, I'm not leaving you in here alone. What if you fall asleep again? Slide under the water? What if you slip getting out of the tub and whack your head like Dupris?"

"What if." Sofia blocked out thoughts of Luc and focused on her agenda. "You sound like Lulu. A fuddy-duddy *and* a worrywart." Maybe if she needled him enough he'd kiss her just to shut her up. It would be a start.

He snatched up a folded bath towel and snapped it open. "Come on, kid. Out of the tub."

She turned off the jet sprays and frowned up at him.

"Kid? Is that what's troubling you? Our age difference? Ten years." She snorted. "Big deal, Bogart."

"More like eleven, but who's counting?"

"You." Jeez, he was conservative. She eyed the bottle of stress-reliever pills he'd set on the counter. Understanding clicked. Conservative and haunted. "Ah."

"What, ah?"

"You don't want to get naked with me because you think I'm, what did you call it? Looped." Admittedly, the pills had made her a little slow on the uptake. She should've sensed the connection long before this.

"I don't think it, I know it. Get out of the tub."

Water sloshed as she pushed herself up, less than gracefully, to her feet. "I'm not chemically dependent, Joe."

"Nice to know."

She read the male approval, the lustful desire flickering in his eyes before he averted his gaze. Apparently her bruised arms and dinged-up legs, compliments of the mysterious scuffle, didn't diminish her appeal in his eyes. Knowing that he liked her body even though she wasn't a size three was a supreme high. Knowing that he'd find her just as attractive even if she were several pounds heavier blew her mind. And was almost beyond her comprehension.

Even though men had been sniffing after her since she was fifteen, she'd always been self-conscious about her hour-glass figure. Between fashion magazines, film and television, and the brutal assessments of several casting directors, she had a firm vision of the ideal body. She'd been striving for perfection for years. Since moving to LA, she'd been insanely obsessed with staying fifteen pounds under her healthy weight.

God, she was hungry. And for more than just food.

She stepped out of the tub, and when Joe wrapped the towel around her, she wrapped her arms around his neck. She waited until he made eye contact to make her point. "I'm not Julietta."

"No," he said after a long, tense moment. "But you are needy."

"I can't argue that. It's something I've been working on and I thought I had a pretty good handle on it." *Until we hooked up again.* "Until recently." She pressed her body flush against him, acknowledged his blatant desire with a satisfied grin.

He closed his eyes briefly. Valiantly fighting the inevitable, she thought as she rose on the balls of her bare feet and angled her mouth close to his.

He met her gaze then and his body tensed. "We're not going to do this, Sofia."

"Yes, we are. I'm not the only needy one in this room." She pressed her lips to his and poured her heart and soul into a kiss meant to soothe. A kiss meant to ignite. She wanted this, *him,* so badly her entire body trembled.

She vibrated with frustration when he eased back.

"You're cold," he said, tightening the towel and reaching for her silk robe hooked over the back of the door.

Her temper flared. "For someone who reads people well, you're not getting me at all, Joe."

"Wrong." He maneuvered her into the robe with all the intimacy of an overworked medical intern. "I know exactly what you want."

"Are you saying you don't want the same thing?" Exasperated, she boldly cupped his bulge. "Because that would be a lie."

He grasped her hand and anchored her palm against his chest while he visibly fought for calm. "I'm saying I don't want to take advantage."

She marveled at his control, her pulse quickening at the feel of his heart thumping beneath her hand. "I know exactly what I'm doing."

"The pills . . ."

"Relaxed me but didn't rob me of my senses. In fact, I'm quite certain the euphoric effect is wearing off. I'm feeling more stressed by the minute."

She waited for him to cave, to make a wisecrack about sex as a stress reliever, but the infuriating man just stood there looking guilty and anxious as hell. It was petty of her, but she couldn't help feeling jealous of Julietta. He must've really cared about her to be this twisted over her death. And to think she'd once blasted him for being a heartless manipulator.

"Oh, forget it." Feeling foolish and sorry for herself, she tightened the sash around her waist and stalked into the bedroom. "All I wanted was an orgasmic night in your bed instead of a troubled night in my own. I was stupid enough to think that we would both benefit. Christ," she snapped, choking back tears, "it's not like it had to mean anything."

It was the wrong thing to say.

Or maybe the right thing. Joe moved in behind her and spun her around so fast she saw stars. He framed her face in his hands, and branded her heart with an intense, sizzling expression.

"I wanted you the moment I saw you. A day hasn't gone by that I haven't fantasized about you. At night, you monopolize my dreams. Goddammit, Sofia, you're in my blood. If you think our making love wouldn't mean anything, you're dead wrong."

Never had a man rocked her so utterly with a confessed infatuation. "I don't know what to say."

He brushed his thumbs over her cheekbones, tempered his tone. "Say stop. No. Say, I've changed my mind, Bogart. I don't want to have sex. I don't want to have anything to do with you."

She blinked back tears and willed her knees not to buckle. If this were a scene in a movie, the women in the audience would hopelessly fall for this man.

His heated gaze slid to her mouth. "Last chance."

She untied her sash and allowed her robe to slide off

her shoulders and pool at her ankles. Something told her that she was going to regret this, but she was too carried away, too seduced by Joe's honesty and desire to listen to the distant nagging voice of reason that sounded an awful lot like Jean-Pierre.

She expected him to sweep her off her feet, to toss her on the bed. She expected swift, hot, and heavy.

She got molten lava slow.

Gazing deeply into her eyes, he cradled the back of her head with one hand, while the other smoothed over her shoulders and down her back, stopping at the swell of her hip. He pressed his lips to her forehead, lingering a moment before brushing whisper soft kisses across her eyelids, her cheeks. *Sweet ecstasy.* Her breath stalled in her lungs when he nipped her lower lip, then gently suckled. The anticipation of a mind-warping kiss rendered her boneless.

Attuned to her body, he held her close, preventing a total, knee-buckling meltdown. His hand, splayed at the small of her back, felt warm, solid, *possessive*. In their past encounters, his hands had always immediately slid to her ass, but not now. This unexpected restraint was far more seductive.

She felt savored and cherished when he claimed her mouth in a slow, seeking kiss. He tasted of tell-tale spearmint and heady beer, his tongue skillful, and as soft as cashmere. The earth fell away, and she floated. He'd yet to touch her intimately and still she floated on an orgasmic cloud.

She wanted more. She wanted him naked. She wanted to slide her hands over hot flesh and corded muscles. So rugged. So manly. She too wanted to savor and cherish. She maneuvered one hand between them, tried to work the buttons of his white Oxford shirt. She'd always been able to rid a man of his shirt, one-handed. A sexy little trick that she'd practiced to perfection. Tonight, her fingers trembled so badly she was forced to rely on both hands, and even that didn't work.

Joe eased back and smiled down at her, eyes twinkling with tender amusement.

"I don't know what's wrong with me." Her cheeks heated and her voice cracked. "I've never been nervous about lovemaking. I'm actually quite skilled. I . . ."

He silenced her with another open-mouthed kiss, freed his own damn buttons. She at least had the dexterity to push the material off his strong shoulders and down his arms. The shirt fell to the floor and she concentrated on his belt buckle while his lips and teeth worked some sort of spellbinding magic on her earlobe, neck, and shoulder. "Dammit," she muttered. Was there some sort of trick to unfastening this particular buckle? She dropped her forehead to his bare chest and sighed. "This is so embarrassing."

"Actually," Joe countered, tangling his fingers in her wet hair, "it's a helluva turn-on."

She didn't see how. What kind of man fancied an inept lover? Her heart pounded against her ribs when he lifted her into his arms and carried her to the bed. She swallowed an anxious giggle. She couldn't even remember the last time she'd *giggled*. "You'd think I'd never done this before."

He gently laid her on the mattress. "Exactly." He pressed his lips to hers before she could comment, scattered her thoughts before she could fret herself into a panic.

Somewhere in the midst of what seemed an eternal kiss, he freed himself of his trousers and shorts. He was not inept. He was focused and confident and supremely skilled in the art of seduction. He worshiped her body with his hands and mouth, spending an inordinate amount of time on her breasts and cootch. His long fingers danced over her damp skin, caressed and teased. His tongue tasted and probed. Time blurred into a euphoric mix of decadent sensations and sexy endearments. When he massaged her feet and sucked her big toe, she squirmed with shock and erotic delight. By the time he eased away to tear open a foiled packet, she'd already come twice.

Skin tingling, breath labored, she watched as he rolled on a Trojan. "I'd offer to do that for you but I'd probably snap your dick in two. You look that hard, and tonight I'm that clumsy."

He laughed softly. "Your candor never ceases to amaze."

"Call 'em as I see 'em."

"I like that." He shifted so that he was lying on top of her, nudged her legs wide. "And not clumsy, Sofia. Perfect."

Heart beating with the ferocity of tribal drums, she caressed the chiseled planes of his face. "I've never known a man like you."

"Good." With that, he sank deep inside.

She gasped at the feel of him, thick, long, and hard, filling her, stretching her and propelling her to new and exquisite heights. He didn't just take her to an alternate plane. He showed her the Milky Way and asked for nothing in return. She trembled with awe and mindless pleasure as Joe made love to her with fierce tenderness and affection.

She came . . . and came. Wave after wave of delicious ecstasy. So this is what an out-of-body-experience felt like.

He climaxed with a raw, masculine groan that stoked a fire in her belly. Home fire, she thought hazily, as he rolled onto his back, bringing her with him, and pulling her flush against his warm, muscled body.

She tingled from head to toe. One, maybe two brain cells sparked, the rest had shut down. He'd pleasured her into a state of exhaustion. In her dreams it had been the other way around. "I've fantasized about this moment," she confessed in a sleepy whisper. "It never went quite like this."

"Same here."

"Are you disappointed?'

"Far from it, Sofia." He smoothed his palm over her cheek, kissed her forehead. "It exceeded my dreams, and then some."

CHAPTER EIGHTEEN

Pittsburg, Pennsylvania

This blows."

Frank claimed the keys from the car rental agent and turned to face his red-eyed, slack-jawed brother. "I'm not getting back on that plane, Jess." His gut clenched when he heard the female agent whispering behind his back to another female agent. Something about his battered face. He heard pity in that whisper. Made him feel like a goddamned freak. "I need a drink."

Jesse fell in beside him while he sought out the nearest airport lounge. "Don't you think you've had enough?"

"No."

"It's one in the morning. You've been bending your elbow since noon. If you think I'm letting you get behind the wheel, you're nuts. You're plastered, Frank."

"I ain't seein' double, so I guess that makes me fit enough to drive. Besides, it's a stick and you've only got one good hand."

"Thanks for the reminder." Jesse shrugged his tote carryall higher on his shoulder as they ascended an escalator. He started to grasp the banister then jerked back, no doubt obsessing on the countless other hands that had gripped that rubber—germ count in the zillions. "Do you know how long it's going to take us to drive from Pennsylvania to Vermont?"

"We'll drive straight through."

"It'll still take something like fifteen hours," Jesse said, as they hit the main floor and started down the semi-deserted hall of shops. "If we fly, we can be there in less than two."

Frank tightened his grip on his duffle bag and made a bee-line toward the Wings and Things Bar. "Bitch all you want, I am not getting back on a plane. First we're delayed, twice, in Los Angeles. Then, after barely making our connecting flight here in Pittsburg, we sit on the runway forty minutes due to structural problems."

"The door on the luggage bay, or whatever they called it, was stuck open." Jesse snorted. "Big deal. It's not like the landing gear broke or an engine blew."

The muscles in Frank's shoulders knotted. "What if they get the door shut and then it springs open mid-flight?"

"They were switching us to another plane."

"Forget it. It's a sign."

"Since when did you get superstitious?"

"Since you botched the Cavendish job."

Jesse stopped in his tracks. "That's right. Blame me."

Frank spun around, putting himself toe to toe with his pain-in-the-ass brother. He tipped up his Stetson and glared down at the man. "You're the one who freaked."

"He was marked to die anyway."

"But not in his house, and not in front of a witness."

"Speaking of . . . ain't that her?"

Frank whipped his head left, then right. "Where?"

Jesse pointed over Frank's shoulder. "There, on the television."

He whirled, stalked into Wings and Things, and pointed to the plasma screen anchored above the bar. "Turn that thing up, will ya, Mac," he said to the bartender, "and give me a shot of whiskey."

"Nothing for me." Jesse set his bag on the floor alongside Frank's, and settled on a bar stool.

They both stared at the screen.

Frank couldn't believe his ears. The celebrity slut was still in Arizona. What's worse, she'd shacked up with a fed, their exact whereabouts unknown. The news piece focused on their so-called steamy affair. Nothing about

Cavendish. Only a minor blurb about gay-boy.

Jesse shook his head. "It's like it never happened."

Frank elbowed him to shut up, paid the bartender, and sipped his whiskey. He listened to the rest of the report, then nudged his brother, and angled his head toward an isolated table.

"Maybe it's a sign," Jesse said as they settled in the corner.

"You making fun of me?"

"Seeing I suffer from a phobia myself," Jesse said, wiping down the table with a sanitized towelette, "I'd be a fool to do so."

"Damn straight."

"I'm just saying that if she's not talking, maybe it's a sign that we should call it quits and head to Mexico. I've got a bad feeling."

Frank leaned forward, voice low. "She's not just gonna forget what she saw and let lying dogs lie. She's up to something. I say she's plotting with that fed."

"Former fed," Jesse pointed out.

"Bet he's still got connections and I've got a record. Won't take much for him to track me down."

"And why would he want to do that?"

"Blackmail."

Jesse scratched the dark whiskers shadowing his dimpled chin. "Come again?"

"She's an eyewitness to a murder. Any law abiding citizen would've hightailed it to the cops and spewed their story. She's soaking up the desert sun and screwing some shifty prick. It doesn't track."

Jesse yawned, stretched. "The guy looked like a hippy, what with that long hair and beard, but that doesn't make him shifty."

"Former fed," Frank reminded his brother. "You ever known someone to retire from the Bureau at thirty-something? They must have forced him out."

"So, you think he's crooked?"

Frank flashed back on the photo of the stormy-eyed man and the dark-skinned beauty. Dread shot from his balding head to the toes of his snakeskin boots. "I think he's trouble. The longer she's with him, the bigger the risk to us."

Jesse nodded, as if he'd recognized the same dangerous vibe in the man the newscaster had announced as former Special Agent Joseph Bogart. "So, you think Bogart and Marino are plotting to blackmail us. Meaning, you think she knows about the quarter-mill Mrs. Cavendish shelled out?"

Frank shrugged. "I don't know about that. Maybe they're looking to enlist us on trade. Marino's silence for services rendered."

"You think they got someone they want us to cap?" Jesse angled his head. "I don't know, Frank. Seems pretty farfetched."

"Got any other ideas on why the bitch hasn't spilled

her guts to the law?"

"Maybe she's scared. Maybe she asked this Bogart dude to protect her, just in case we came looking. Which we did. You know, like a bodyguard. She is a star, after all. Those Hollywood-types probably have flings with their bodyguards all the time."

"You could be right. I hope you are." Frank threw back the remainder of his whiskey. "Still, I don't plan to spend the rest of my life wondering and looking over my shoulder. Not to mention that bitch should pay for what she did to my face. I ain't gonna rest until she does."

"So, we're going to Arizona then." He whistled low. "That's gonna be one hell of a long drive, Frank."

"If the press can't sniff out her exact location, who says we can? No. We're sticking to our plan." He patted the journal in his inner jacket pocket. "We'll make her come to us."

"And then?"

Frank fingered his marred face, fury swirling in his liquored-up gut. "Payback time."

CHAPTER NINETEEN

<u>Los Angeles, California</u>

*Y*ou're even more beautiful in person."

She didn't mind the compliment. She minded the way he looked at her. Like a wolf salivating over a lamb. She should be flattered . . . that's what he was thinking. She could tell by the arrogant tilt of his silvery head. He was handsome, wealthy, and powerful. He was in the position to make her a star. A respected cinematic star.

He was also married.

He topped off her wine. "Did you enjoy dinner?"

"Very much." She reached for the wine glass, needing, hoping to soften her brittle nerves. Keep it casual, Sofia.

Keep it business. "So, when are the others arriving?"

"Soon." He stood and lowered the lights. "In the meantime, let's relax and watch a movie."

"One of yours?" *Maybe he wanted to familiarize her with his work. Would she sound like a kiss-up if she said she'd seen every one? She didn't want to fall back on compliments, no matter how sincere, coy smiles or fluttering eyelashes. She wanted to do this right.*

"A classic, actually." He settled beside her on the screening room couch. "I understand you're a fan of Hitchcock."

Music swelled. Her muscles tensed. Don't touch me, she thought as he casually draped his arm across the back of the couch. She closed her eyes, breathed deep, and listened to the haunting score, the cryptic dialogue. She knew every scene, every line.

She knew that slightly accented voice.

Sofia bolted upright, eyes wide. Ingrid Bergman spoke to her from a nineteen-inch television. No, wait. Ms. Bergman posing as Dr. Constance Peterson talking to her mentor about the man she loves, her patient, John Ballantine, AKA Dr. Anthony Edwardes, AKA John Brown. A man with assumed personalities.

A man with amnesia.

Her muscles bunched at the brush of a hand. "Don't touch me!"

"Easy, baby."

Her heart raged in her ears as Joe smoothed a reassuring

palm down her rigid spine. Ingrid Bergman's voice faded to a drone as the man in her bed took center stage.

"You had a bad dream."

She pulled the sheet to her chin, remnants of the nightmare causing her to feel exposed, chilled. "Trapped."

Joe pulled her into his arms and leaned back against the headboard. He eased her head to his chest. "Relax, Sofia. You're safe."

Her racing heart said differently. She clung to the man who'd made reverent love to her. The man who'd admitted a soul-stirring attraction. She soaked in his body heat, his strength. She listened to the steady beat of his heart and willed hers to beat in tandem. *Center yourself,* she heard Master Chai whisper. "What time is it?"

"Close to four in the morning." He held her close, stroked her hair.

The room was dark save for the light from the television. She wondered how long Joe had been awake. Wondered if he regretted their lovemaking. Or maybe he'd been pondering her lost hours. Trying to analyze her sketchy memories. After all, he had been schooled in psychology.

Bergman and Gregory Peck conversed in the background. Psychologist and amnesiac. The parallel was ironic. Uncomfortable with the notion, she focused on the nightstand. Her stomach fluttered at the sight of a portable book light and a stack of printed pages. "You read my script."

"I did." He rested his chin on her head, continued to soothe her trembling body with sure, tender strokes. "When I have trouble falling asleep, I like to read. *From Venice With Love* was sticking out of the pocket of your backpack. Looked more interesting than the phone book. Hope you don't mind."

She wasn't sure. She tipped her head back and squinted up at him. "What did you think?"

"Chick flick."

"And?"

He shrugged. "Not bad, if you like chick flicks." He quirked a faint smile and her pulse slowed to a bearable rate. "Are you going to do it?"

"I'd have to audition."

"You'll smoke the audition. You'll smoke this part."

She balked at the total confidence in his voice. "How do you know? You've never seen me act. Maybe I suck."

He broke eye contact, glanced toward the screen. "You don't suck."

"How do you . . ."

"Tell me about the dream."

"What?"

"What were you dreaming about?"

She realized then that he'd been talking her down from an anxiety high, putting her at ease before questioning her on whatever had disturbed her sleep. "Planning on psychoanalyzing me?"

He gazed down at her, serious as sin. "I can help you through this, Sofia. But you need to work with me. I have to know what happened back in Phoenix."

It seemed like a lifetime ago. It had been less than two days. A forty-eight hour nightmare from which she was no longer certain she wanted to awake. She snuggled closer to Joe, holding tight to the better part of something awful. "I can't remember." She worried her bottom lip. "Not everything, anyway."

"That's okay. We'll fit the puzzle together piece by piece. Tell me about the dream."

She wished she could say she couldn't remember, that the details of the dream had faded. Sadly, the conversation and actions, the realization of where she'd been and what could have happened, were painfully clear. Not wanting to look Joe in the eyes, she settled her cheek against his chest and absentmindedly stroked the dark, soft matting of hair on his defined pecs. Fuzzy-headed, she stared at the night owl movie. "We were watching *Spellbound*," she said in a soft voice. Another irony.

Joe laid his hand over hers, stilled her nervous fingers. "No, hon. You'd already fallen asleep by the time I turned on the TV. I kept the volume low, but not low enough. It must have seeped into your subconscious."

How easy it would be to change the subject. Naked as they were, how easy it would be to distract him. But the need to know how those cowboys figured in, what threat, if any, they posed to her friends and family overrode her embarrassment. "No, you don't understand. In my dream, we were in a screening room. We were watching *Spellbound*. He knew about my fascination with Hitchcock."

Joe rubbed a hand over her goosepimply arm. "He, who?"

"The man with no face." Her temples throbbed mercilessly. "Why can't I remember what he looked like, Joe? Who he was specifically? It's as if I don't *want* to see his face."

"You don't. We'll figure out why. Back up. Take it slow. You said you were in a screening room. A movie theater?"

"No. A private screening room." She swallowed hard. "In his house. The house where the limo driver dropped me. He's a director, or maybe a producer. He makes films. Award-winning films. That much I know. He's wealthy, powerful."

"Powerful enough to make you a star."

His tone revealed nothing, but she felt the subtle tension in his body. Her stomach turned. "I know what you're thinking. Casting couch. Sleeping my way to the top. But, it wasn't like that." Her face flushed with an ugly realization. She pushed out of Joe's arms, leaned forward, and clutched her knees to her chest. "Who am I kidding? It *was* like that." She dropped her forehead to her knees and rocked. "How could I be so stupid? So trusting? He lied to me. Just like Chaz. Just like . . . " *All of them*.

Joe gently rubbed the base of her neck.

She released a shaky breath. This wasn't about the men in her past. This was about the man with no face.

"I can hear his voice in my head," she said, her thoughts loosening as Joe kneaded her tight muscles. "A phone call. I remember being shocked and flattered. He told me that he'd seen me in "Spy Girl". Said he thought I'd be perfect for a role in his next movie. He invited me to his home in Paradise Valley. "*Come for the weekend*," he said. "*I invited a half-a-dozen other actors*." He said that the film called for an ensemble cast and he wanted to see how we interacted."

"But, the other actors didn't show," Joe surmised. "It was just you and this movie mogul."

She rested her chin on her knees and stared into space. "He said they'd be arriving later. We had dinner, wine. I remember he was very talkative. Very charming. I tried to relax. It was, after all, an audition of sorts. But, I was so damned nervous. Something felt wrong." She curled her fingernails into her palms, mentally slugging herself for being so dense. Of course, something was wrong. Her gut had known what her brain refused to acknowledge. He'd invited her there for sex.

Joe's hands stilled. "Keep going, Sofia. This is important."

She looked over her shoulder, shivered at the grim set

of his jaw. "You won't like it. I don't like it."

"All the more reason for me to hear it."

She didn't know what to make of that. All she knew was that she didn't want him to think the worst. "Nothing happened . . . sexually," she said with absolute certainty. "I wouldn't have agreed. He's married. I don't do married men." She winced at her word choice.

Joe dragged a hand down his face, waited a beat, then said, "What if he didn't take no for an answer? *That's* my concern, Sofia."

Her heart warmed at the genuine affection in his eyes. At least, she thought it was genuine. She'd been fooled before. So many men. So many lies.

He gently skimmed a hand down her forearm. "How did you get these bruises?"

Her stomach clenched. "Fighting the cowboys."

"Not the producer?"

"No. It never came to that." She massaged a dull throbbing in her temples. "We were watching the movie. He was sitting next to me. Close. Too close. Don't touch me, I thought. And then . . . "

"What?"

"Someone's here."

She smiled. "It must be them."

"We were interrupted." The pain in Sofia's head intensified. Her skin prickled with sweat as she fought a bout of dizziness.

"Interrupted by who?" Joe asked. "The cowboys?"

He rose from the couch. "I wasn't expecting, that is . . ."
He touched her shoulder, a brief intimate squeeze. "Wait here,
Sofia. Enjoy the movie. I'll be right back."

"I waited, but . . . he didn't come back, so I went looking and . . ." Her memories spun out, a wild cyclone of
jumbled images. Red seeping into orange and white. Blue
splattered with red. Colors collided into a wall of black.

"What is it, Sofia? What do see?"

"Dark. Overwhelmed. I'm sinking. Suffocating."
She shook her head. "Can't breathe. Need to come up.
Need air." Tears pricked her eyes as she clutched at her
aching chest.

Suddenly Joe was sitting in front of her, his hands
framing her face. "Look at me, Sofia. Listen to what I'm
saying. You're having a panic attack. It can't stop your
heart or your breathing. Focus on something good."

"You," she whispered, concentrating on his gentle
touch, his earnest gaze. Visions of their lovemaking slowly
overrode the ugliness, the horror. She thought about the
way, he'd touched her, cherished her. She thought about
his whispered endearments, and her raging pulse tempered. Her breathing eased. Exhausted, embarrassed, she
slumped against him. "I'm so sorry," she said in a thick,
raspy voice. "I know it's important for me to remember.
I tried. I . . . Shit." She knocked a limp fist against his
shoulder. "What's wrong with me?"

"Nothing." He held her close, rocked her gently. "You did good."

"But, I didn't tell you anything of consequence."

"More than you know. Don't worry, the rest will come." He eased her back on the bed. "Just not tonight. You need to sleep. You're exhausted mentally and physically."

He was right. Her body ached and she lacked focus and energy. "But . . . if I sleep, I'll dream."

"I'll be right here."

She hated herself for asking. Hated that she cared. "For how long?"

"For as long as you need me."

"I'm going to kick your fucking ass when I see you." Joe glanced at Sofia to make sure she was still asleep, before taking the conversation outside.

"You can try," Murphy said, amusement lacing his tone. "Should be fun. So, what's got your shorts in a bunch this morning? Wait. Let me guess." He paused, his breath audibly labored. "What did Sofia do now?"

She burrowed her way into my heart. "She fell for another asshole's bullshit." Cell phone pressed to his ear, Joe relaxed against the brick façade of the motel and used his free hand to massage his chest. There wasn't enough antacid in the world to cure this ache. No suppressing, no denying.

He was in love.

In all brutal honesty, he'd fallen months ago when he'd first seen her on her casino gig, dressed in a glitzy bustier, fishnets, and heels, relaying sarcastic directions to the nickel slots and the all-you-can-eat buffet to an impatient patron. Frickin' love at first sight.

Knowing and dealing were two different animals. What the hell was he supposed to do with all these *feelings*? A minor in psychology had not prepared him for this mind-bending dilemma. Wasn't he supposed to be walking on air, quoting Shakespearean sonnets or some romantic shit? Where was the goddamned euphoria? Murphy would know. *"Love warps a man,"* he'd said. That's why, after an hour of solitary hell, Joe had decided to sneak outside and ring him up. He'd meant to ask his big brother's advice. Instead, he'd threatened him with an ass-whooping. Hell. "Sounds like I caught you in the middle of something. Dare I ask?"

"Morning run," Murphy said. "Thought I'd take advantage while everyone's still asleep."

"Legrand made it to the inn all right?"

"He showed. There was a scuffle between him and Gallow. Things are tense. I'm not sure what's going on, but I promised Lulu we'd stay until the waters stilled."

"Not exactly the relaxing getaway you were anticipating," Joe said.

"No, but it's not boring either. So," he said after a significant pause. "What's going on? It's barely five a.m. on the west coast. What are you doing up at this hour?"

"Researching an asshole." He'd waited until Sofia had fallen asleep and then he'd fired up his laptop and utilized the motel's wireless Internet. "A movie producer," he ground out. He needed to talk about this, to work the anger out of his system before Sofia woke up. Murphy could handle whatever he spewed. Better him than a woman who was holding onto her composure by a thread. "She's blocked out his face and name, but she gave me enough information to narrow the field."

"You better bring me up to date."

"You better sit down."

"Done," Murphy said. "Let's have it."

"There's still a chunk missing due to Sofia's amnesia, but here's the general scenario." Joe took a deep breath and began to pace. "An influential movie mogul invited her to his home under the pretense of an informal audition for his next movie. Claimed other actors under consideration would be joining them for the weekend."

"Un-huh."

"Exactly," Joe said, acknowledging Murphy's sarcasm. "After dinner and wine, he invited her into his private screening room to watch a movie."

"Smooth."

"Yeah." Joe ignored a jealous pang, pushed on. "But,

they were interrupted before he could make his move."

"The cowboys?"

"This is where it gets sketchy. She couldn't say for certain. I'm guessing, yes. Where else would they figure in? So, the producer guy left to greet the guests, intruders, whatever. When he didn't return, Sofia went to find him." He massaged the back of his neck, his muscles knotting at the memory of her gasping for air and losing control. "I don't know what she saw, bro, but it's bad. Bad enough to incite amnesia and subsequent panic attacks."

"Hard to imagine a woman who once threatened my balls with a pair of scissors having a panic attack."

"Yeah, well, she's not as tough as she pretends. Although if you ever hurt her sister, I'm sure she'll make good on the threat. She's got a fierce streak when it comes to friends and family."

"Admirable trait," Murphy noted.

Joe agreed, but didn't comment.

"Sounds like we're talking about an act of violence. I assume you checked news reports, touched base with your local connections?

"And came up with zilch."

"Huh."

Joe could envision his brother, sitting under a tree, slick with sweat from his run, brain buzzing. He'd always enjoyed a good mystery. Probably why he got along with Jake Leeds, another puzzle-solver. "She remembers tussling with the cowboys," he continued. "She's got the scrapes and bruises to support an actual struggle. She woke up in a tool shed with a Beretta. The magazine was down three rounds. No prints other than hers. She said she remembers aiming and shooting."

"At the cowboys?"

"I'm guessing. Although if that's the case, she missed her mark. If there's really a connection, then Luc Dupris's last words suggest they're alive and hunting Sofia."

"The Beretta's not hers, so it has to belong to the producer or one of the cowboys. Since there were no prints, the owner must've worn gloves," Murphy said. "My money's on one of the cowboys."

"My thoughts exactly. That would also explain why their prints weren't found in Sofia's apartment. That's if they *were* in her apartment."

"I assume this movie mogul's rich."

Joe grunted. "Paradise Valley. We're talking million dollar homes."

"Did Sofia say if she heard knocking? A doorbell?"

"No. Just that her host announced that they had company."

"A silent alarm, maybe."

Joe shrugged. "Possibly. Maybe they were there to rob the house. Or to shake the guy down. Maybe he owed them money. Drugs. Loan sharking. Who knows?" He'd seen it all.

"And Sofia walked in on whatever went down."

The probability made him sick. "Here's another thing. The film they were watching was *Spellbound*. Sofia's a fan of Hitchcock. She's probably seen that movie a few times."

"Refresh my memory."

"Gregory Peck played a guy who witnessed something traumatic, then blocked it out."

"Right. I remember," Murphy said, voice grim. "Sounds like reality imitating fiction."

"A weird-ass parallel," Joe confirmed.

"Huh." His brother blew out a breath. "So, are you thinking what I'm thinking?"

Joe jammed his hand in his pants pocket, stared at a crack in the asphalt, experienced a crack in his composure. "Yeah. Although I don't have proof that any of this happened, my gut says it did. I'm thinking the movie bastard's dead. Can't say I'm sorry. I wonder how many other women that smooth-talking fuck lured into his bed with promises of fame?"

Silence greeted his snarled outburst.

Joe worked his jaw. "What?"

"You tell me."

He shook his head, paced two steps, and stopped. "Goddammit."

"That bad, huh?"

Well, hey, okay, what the hell? Isn't this why he'd called his brother in the first place. "I love her, Murph."

"I know. I saw it in your eyes months ago."

"Thanks for cluing me in."

"Where love is concerned, a man's gotta come around on his own."

Joe sighed. "It's kicking my ass."

Murphy laughed softly. "It'll do that. So, where is she now?"

"Sleeping. She's wiped out. I'll be surprised if she wakes before noon."

"I guess you're going to Paradise Valley."

Joe frowned. "I have to help her face whatever happened. I don't want to involve the authorities until I know exactly what we're dealing with. Right now, I don't know what's real or imagined."

"Understood. That's why I'm not sharing any of this with Lulu. As far as she knows, you and Sofia are having a torrid affair, period. Speaking of, according to the morning talk shows you two are shacked up somewhere in Arizona. If those cowboys really are on the hunt, then the media pointed them straight in your direction."

A muscle jumped under Joe's left eye. "Let them come."

"Right." Murphy whistled low. "You're in the mood to kick some ass."

CHAPTER TWENTY

Rainbow Ridge, Vermont

Let me get this straight," Jean-Pierre said. "You are telling me Hollyberry Inn is haunted?"

Rudy propped himself up on one elbow and stared down at his bedmate. Even though they hadn't made love last night, he felt incredibly close to his partner this sunny morning. Continued honesty, he'd thought upon wakening next to the man, was a good way to start the day. Instead of jumping in headfirst and declaring his love and intentions, he decided to ease his way in via Casper the-not-so-friendly ghost. "I know it sounds crazy. That's why I didn't tell you over the phone."

"Ah, *oui*. It sounds magnificent, this story of Casper Montegue. But, I prefer dealing with a ghost rather than a . . . a . . ."

Rudy stared down at Jean-Pierre, hoping the Frenchman recognized the affection burning in his heart and eyes. "You're the only man in my life, Jean-Pierre." Normally, he would have followed up that statement with a caress, a kiss—but he didn't want to risk rejection. He needed a sign or, even better, a verbal go ahead.

Jean-Pierre scratched his whiskered jaw, poked his tongue in his cheek. "What of Jake?"

Rudy smirked. "You know what I mean."

The corners of the younger man's lips twitched upward.

The smile was weak, but there, and instilled Rudy with hope. Hope that they were on the road to complete recovery and a blissful future.

"Do you think Jake is angry with me?"

"For punching him in the nuts?" Rudy grinned. With the heat of the moment behind them, he was able to find humor in last night's brawl. He didn't even mind that he had a shiner, a badge of black and blue fury that showed JP cared. Jake on the other hand . . . "I don't know about angry, but you might not want to ask him any favors for awhile."

"Perhaps a gift would help to make amends?"

Rudy shrugged. "He's not like that, but there is a fabulous antique barn not too far from here. You know how he feels about antiques."

"Perhaps a sugar and creamer to augment his demi-tasse cup and saucer collection."

"Maybe. Or else . . ."

A scream rent the air, propelling both men into a sitting position.

"*Merde*," Jean-Pierre exclaimed, a hand pressed to his chest.

Another shrill shriek had Rudy throwing aside the patchwork comforter and scrambling out of the crocheted-canopy bed. Foregoing his robe, he raced out of the door in his striped boxers, sailed down the hall, and nearly collided with Jake—also in his shorts. The P.I. shoved through the door of Murphy's assigned suite and then into private bathroom, Rudy on his heels, Jean-Pierre close behind.

The scene that greeted them was straight out of a Farrelly brothers' movie. The men froze in shock.

A buck-naked Lulu danced around in the bathtub, squealing while struggling to reaffix the showerhead. In the chaos, she'd knocked aside the shower curtain. Water sprayed everywhere soaking the walls, the bath mat, the guest towels . . .

Rudy palmed his forehead. "What the . . ."

Lulu jerked around, screamed at the sight of the three men, and quickly gave them her back. "Get out! Get out!" Realizing she was showing them her bare butt, she squealed louder, dropped the shower head, and slapped her palms to her cheeks. Yeah. Like that was going to help.

Jake recovered first. He snatched an oversized bath towel and slung it around her body, heaved her out of the tub, and into Rudy's arms. "Dammit," he said, struggling with the chrome lever. "The faucet's broken."

"I know," Lulu yelled. "Why do you think I was fussing with the showerhead?"

"Beats the hell out of me!" Jake shouted. "Christ, this water's freezing." Soaked to the bone, he continued to wrestle with the out-dated plumbing.

Rudy passed Lulu off to Jean-Pierre, barely containing a bout of laughter. "Let me try." He shouldered his way in, twisted, pushed, pulled, and somehow managed to cut off the water. Then again, he'd been wrestling with faulty plumbing and wiring for weeks. Thanks to the century-old property and a meddlesome ghost.

"You are shivering, *Chaton*." Jean-Pierre briskly rubbed his hands over Lulu's bare arms.

"The hot water cut out," she said through chattering teeth. "I thought someone flushed a toilet in another bathroom, so I tried to adjust the showerhead away from me, you know, just until the hot water returned, but it broke. The showerhead," she clarified, staring at her toes, the sink, anything, Rudy thought, other than the three half-naked men surrounding her.

Jake snagged a towel from the rack and mopped his face and hair. "Why the hell didn't you just get out of the tub?"

"I did, but then the water was . . . I thought I should . . . " Her lower lip trembled.

Uh-oh, Rudy thought. "Um, honey. Where's Murphy?"

Lulu wiggled out of Jean-Pierre's arms, shoved her wet ringlets off of her stricken face. "Jogging."

Just then Afia stepped over the threshold wearing zebra pajama bottoms and a matching Tee. Hands folded protectively over her rounded stomach, she looked harried and out-of-breath. "What's going . . . " her blood-shot gaze slid from a soaked, towel-clad Lulu to her wet, half-naked husband, ". . . on?"

Lulu's cheeks burned red.

"Oh, no," Rudy mumbled, just as the straight-laced storyteller burst into tears.

"Aw, hell," Jake complained, tossing aside the towel.

Jean-Pierre scrambled for tissues. "Do not cry, *Chaton*."

Afia moved toward the weepy storyteller and slipped on the wet tile.

Rudy caught her, no harm done, but Jake blew his cork.

"Dammit, Afia, I told you to stay in bed! As in *don't move*. But no, you just had to investigate!" Panicked, he grasped her shoulders, inspected her head to toe. "Are you all right? Did you pull a muscle or anything?"

She batted away his hands. "No, I didn't pull a muscle or anything. Stop treating me like an invalid. And stop being such a worrywart!"

"I'm not a worrywart!"

Rudy snorted. "And I'm not gay."

Lulu blew her nose in a wad of tissues and glared at Jake. "Stop yelling at Afia!"

"I yell because I care. I'm irritated because I'm tired." Jake nailed the dripping-wet sprite with an exasperated look. "If you and Murphy hadn't been going at it like bunnies last night . . . "

Lulu gasped as if slapped. Mortified, she clutched the bath towel tighter and fled the bathroom in a teary huff.

Afia frowned at her husband. "Nice going, Mr. Sensitive." She strode after Lulu.

Jake took off after his wife. "Ah, baby. Don't get agitated. It's not good for you and the . . ."

"Stuff a sock in it!" she cried before her voice faded down the hall.

One door slammed and then another. Lulu must've taken refuge in an empty suite.

Eyes wide, lips pressed together, Rudy glanced at Jean-Pierre. "It's not funny."

The Frenchman's shoulders shook with restrained mirth. His eyes twinkled. "No. It is most serious. This unfortunate," he fluttered a hand toward the shower, "incident."

They held out another two seconds before covering their mouths and doubling over with muffled laughter.

Barely able to catch his breath, Jean-Pierre pointed to the broken plumbing. "Casper's handiwork?"

"Possibly." Rudy thumbed away amused tears.

"We must take action," the Frenchman said on a giggling snort. "We cannot allow an embittered spirit to distress our guests." He whistled low. "I cannot believe I saw *Chaton* naked. But of course, I have seen her *nearly* naked, what with her costume fittings, but, *merde*, Jake! How are we going to break it to Murphy?"

We. Our. In that moment, Rudy's heart took flight. He shook a mental fist at Casper. *Take that, Montegue.* Instead of driving a bigger wedge between him and his lover, the ghost had just pushed them closer together.

Afia handed Lulu another Kleenex. At this rate, they'd tear through the box of tissues in the next five minutes. "Jake can be pretty blunt when he's sleep deprived. Not that he didn't sleep because of you and Murphy," she hastily added. Obviously, the woman was embarrassed that her nocturnal activities had been overheard. Although, gosh, they had been pretty loud. She'd ended up putting a pillow over her face to muffle her own laughter as much as the noise.

"Honestly, Lulu. If anyone's to blame for Jake's lack of sleep, it's me." She smoothed her hand over her rounded belly. "I'm not the best bedmate these days. I get up to go to the bathroom three times a night, sometimes more.

And then, because I can only sleep on my left side, I get restless and uncomfortable, so I fidget. Oh! And then there are the muscle spasms in my calves. Not pleasant." She stopped because she was rambling. And instead of making Lulu feel better, she only seemed to be making things worse. "Anyway, please don't worry about Jake's insensitive crack."

"It's not that," Lulu said, sobbing into crumpled tissues. "Well, it is partially, and I do apologize because, jeez, crap, how embarrassing is *that*?"

"Don't be embarrassed." Afia sank down on the bed next to the towel clad woman. "It's sweet. I thought it was sweet, anyway. Jake, I think he was a little turned on. He wanted to fool around and I . . . well, I didn't. Which is unusual for me, because I really love fooling around with Jake. But lately . . . " She paused. She'd never confided in a girlfriend before. She didn't really have any girlfriends, except for Rudy. And since he had a penis she supposed he didn't officially count.

Lulu looked at her expectantly through teary eyes. "What?"

Afia shrugged. "Well . . . look at me."

She looked, blinked. "You're beautiful."

"I'm a cow."

"A beautiful cow. I mean, you're big, but it's all in your belly, and that's your baby, so who cares? Surely, not your husband. I've seen the way he looks at you. The way he hovers. It might get annoying at times, but it's because he loves you so much." She grasped Afia's hands and squeezed. "A baby? Do you know how lucky you are?"

In that instant, Afia felt incredibly contrite. She'd been lamenting the negative aspects of pregnancy, her unattractive figure—her big, really huge belly—and this woman couldn't even *have* a baby. According to Jake who'd heard it from Rudy who knew it straight from the source, Lulu was infertile. Or, at least she thought she was. Tests had been inconclusive, but her ex-husband and his girlfriend just had a baby, so the fault, Lulu concluded was with her.

Afia sighed. "That was petty of me. You're right. I am very fortunate. And so are you. You have Murphy. You have hordes of children who adore you. Unlike you, I am *not* naturally gifted with kids, although I seem to be getting better." Her work at the daycare center proved an excellent way of gaining experience with wee ones. Hoping to direct the topic in a more cheerful direction, she said, "Hey, aren't you and Murphy planning to adopt?"

Lulu sniffed back tears and quirked a bright smile. "We want a whole brood."

Afia smiled too. "I think that's wonderful. There are so many children desperate for a loving home. You and Murphy will make wonderful parents."

"So will you and Jake. I look forward to creating stories for your kids. We'll create one together, you and I. It'll be fun."

✦

"Yes, it will." Afia's spirits lifted along with her new friend's. "Feeling better?"

"Yeah." She blew out a breath, rolled her eyes. "Sorry about that. I guess, well, I guess a few things set me off. For one, as of last night, only two men had ever seen me entirely nude, not counting my dad who saw me as a baby, or any doctors. This morning the count is up to five."

Afia laughed. "No offense, but I doubt you made much of an impression on Rudy and Jean-Pierre, and as for Jake, I'm sure he's just as embarrassed as you are."

Lulu blinked. "You're not mad?"

"That Jake saw you naked?" She snorted. "He's seen lots of naked women. Before me the man was a hound. Anyway, this was in the line of duty, so to speak. I'm not mad at all."

"I hope Colin's as open-minded as you."

"Why does he even have to know? Use that imagination of yours, for goodness sake. I'm thinking you already had a towel around you when the men busted in. Just put that incident out of your mind. I'm certain the guys are doing the same." Afia pushed her long, fine hair over her shoulders, blew her bangs out of her eyes. "You said a few things were bothering you."

"Well, for one, I'm worried about my sister."

"She'll be fine. She's with Joe Bogart. Jake describes him as a real tough guy. I wouldn't worry overly much. What else?"

Lulu shrugged. "It's stupid. I can't even explain it. It's just, lately, I've been feeling off."

"Off?"

"Stressed and overemotional. Achy. Kind of like PMS, but different. The past week I've woken up feeling queasy. I thought I was coming down with something, but it always passes. I certainly haven't lost my appetite." She sighed. "I've been eating like a horse."

Afia pressed her hand over her mouth to hide a smile. Could it be? And was it possible this woman could be that naïve? "Um, forgive me for being personal, but when was your last, that is, is your cycle normal?"

"It's never been normal, and it was . . ." She scrunched her brow. "Hmm. Well, it's definitely on its way. Why? Wait." She bolted to her feet, eyes wide. "You can't be thinking . . . It's not possible."

"You don't have medical proof of that."

"But, I tried for ten years, and zip!"

Afia grinned. "But you didn't try with Murphy. Have you been practicing any kind of birth control?"

Lulu blushed. "No. I . . . I didn't think we needed to." She chewed her fingernail, stalked to the bureau, and pulled out a pair of cargo pants and a cartoon T-shirt. "I can't even go there, Afia. I don't want to get my hopes up and then . . ." She shook her head. "I don't want to talk about this anymore."

Fine, Afia thought. But later, they'd go shopping and

pick up one of those home pregnancy tests. She'd beg Lulu to humor her, and she wouldn't feel one bit guilty. She had a feeling. A very good feeling. On top of that, Jean-Pierre and Rudy weren't snarling at each other, so perhaps they were on the mend. Perhaps she'd done a very good thing by showing up early at Hollyberry Inn. For once in her jinxed life, maybe she'd actually instigated a string of *good* luck. Afia Leeds: Miracle Worker. She liked the sound of that.

Suddenly, she wasn't so tired and cranky. Nope, she was revved and ready for a big plate of waffles. *This* was going to be a spectacular day. "I'm going to get dressed too," she said casually. "Meet you downstairs. Oh, and about that naked thing. Don't worry. I'm sure the guys aren't stupid enough to breathe a word to Murphy."

"Heads or tails?"

Jake leaned back in his chair and drummed his fingers on the kitchen table. "Forget it, Gallow. I'm not flipping for the chance to get my ass kicked."

Rudy balanced the quarter on the back of his thumb. "Don't be such a pansy. It won't come to that. It's not like we stood there ogling."

"Although there was a time lapse," Jean-Pierre pointed out from his lookout station. Rudy had told him to watch out the back window and to warn them when he saw Murphy jogging up the trail. "Those few moments when we stood motionless. That could be construed by some such as a possessive husband, as ogling, *mon ami*."

The smirking P.I. looked over his shoulder at Jean Pierre. "The woman was prancing around like an idiot shrieking at the top of her lungs."

"You forgot about the naked part," Rudy said, still balancing that quarter.

Jake shot him an exasperated glare. "Not yet, but I'm trying."

"He is coming!" Jean-Pierre let the curtain fall back into place, hurried over to the coffee grinder and started pulverizing scoops of fresh beans.

Rudy stared down at his friend. "Heads or tails?"

"I'm not . . ."

"Yes, you are." He tossed the coin high.

"Didn't I suffer enough last night when JP . . ."

"Heads or tails?" Rudy asked as he caught the quarter and smacked it to the back of his hand.

The back door knob jiggled.

"Tails," Jake muttered.

Smiling, Rudy flashed him the flipside of cherry-tree chopping GW.

"Hell."

"*Bon jour*, Murphy," Jean-Pierre called a little too brightly.

Visibly exerted from a hard run, the bodyguard moved into the kitchen and eyed the three men. "Morning."

Rudy was glad they'd all dressed and weren't sitting round in their boxers. That wouldn't have helped, no sir.

Murphy leaned back against the counter and dabbed his forearm to his sweaty brow. "Smells good, Legrand. Cinnamon?"

"Ah, *oui*," JP answered without making eye contact. "Cinnamon Viennese. *Café* will be ready *momentanément*."

"Great. I could use a cup."

Rudy dropped into the chair across from Jake, and nodded at Murphy in greeting. "You were up and out early."

"Slept like a baby last night. I was pretty wiped."

Jake snorted. "Wonder why?"

Rudy kicked him under the table.

Jean-Pierre stopped grinding. "Where do you keep the filters, Bunny?"

"The walk-in pantry." He started to push out of his chair.

"Do not trouble yourself," his partner said. "Which way? Which door?"

Rudy pointed. "Second door to the left. Third shelf. Beside the paper napkins and towels."

Murphy reached beneath his army-green T-shirt, unclipped his cell phone from the waistband of his sweatpants. When Jean-Pierre was out of earshot, he said, "Bogie called."

Jake sobered, and swiveled in his chair. "Any more specifics?"

"Sofia's memories are trickling back, but they're still sketchy." He set the phone on the counter, moved to the sink, and washed his hands. "We're pretty certain she witnessed a crime and that she scuffled with those cowboys. It's possible that they're tracking her."

Jake frowned. "Damn."

Rudy's pulse raced. "If anything happens to her . . ."

"Bogie will protect her," Jake said.

"If he needs help, he'll reach out to me or to his southwestern contacts." Murphy dried his hands with a dish towel and turned, brow raised. "No way in hell is he going to risk her safety."

Jean-Pierre came back in waving a coffee filter. "Found it."

"Where's Lulu?" Murphy asked, pointedly changing the subject. "She was up when I left. I'm surprised she's not down here raiding your fridge. She's had quite the appetite lately."

Jean-Pierre busied himself with the coffeemaker.

"The women are upstairs," Rudy said. "Dressing and . . . talking. You see . . . there was . . . that is, we were . . ." He tapped the quarter on the table, silently beckoning Jake to jump in at anytime.

"There was an unfortunate incident," Jean-Pierre said as he turned on the kitchen faucet.

Murphy frowned, and Rudy knew he was thinking back on the time Lulu had thrown up on his shoes after she'd been drugged by a mobster. At the time, Jean-Pierre had labeled the occurrence an *unfortunate incident*. "She's fine," Rudy insisted while glaring at Jake. "Just embarrassed."

Murphy crossed his arms over his chest, angled his head. "Why?"

Silence.

Murphy moistened his lips, studied each man at length. "Why is my wife embarrassed? So much so that she's hiding upstairs while you three lounge down here. Someone spit it out."

Rudy kicked Jake under the table. Hard.

"Ow. All right. All right." He cursed. "We saw Lulu naked."

Rudy groaned.

Jean-Pierre turned, eyes-wide.

"What? Why sugarcoat it?" Jake shifted, draped one arm over the back of his chair, and laid it out for Murphy. "We heard screaming. Christ, it was shrill, so naturally we rushed toward the source. Fortunately, nothing was wrong except that the hot water heater went on the blink and the showerhead and faucet malfunctioned. Unfortunately," he spread his hands in a what-are-ya-gonna-do fashion, "Lulu was in her birthday suit."

Murphy scraped his teeth over his bottom lip, his voice low and thoughtful. "You saw my wife in the buff."

"Not just me. *We.* All three of us," Jake emphasized, looking annoyed.

"*They're* gay."

Jake poked his thumb in his chest. "*I'm* married."

Murphy braced his hands on his hips. "Did you look?"

"A wee time lapse," Jean-Pierre answered. "You see . . ."

Murphy cut him off. "I'm not talking to you." He looked pointedly at Jake.

"What kind of asinine question is that? Of course, I looked. You see a freak accident, you look!"

Rudy slapped a palm to his forehead. Why did he flip that coin? He should've sucked it up and broken the news himself.

Then, Jake made it worse. "For chrissake, Murphy. I'm a happily married man. I saw your wife naked. So what? You saw my sister naked. Let's just call it even."

Rudy glanced from man to man. "You saw Joni naked?"

Murphy rolled his eyes. "We had a thing."

"You slept with Jake's sister?" came a female voice. *Lulu's* voice.

All eyes shifted to the threshold. She and Afia stood side by side. Complete opposites.

Waif-like Afia had pulled her long, dark hair into a classic ponytail. She looked like a petite model for designer maternity clothes in her black flared capris and a black halter top splashed with Victorian roses.

Cupie-doll Lulu had donned funky cargo pants and

a tight-fitting cartoon T-shirt. Her golden curls were still wet, but at least her eyes were dry. Red, but dry. She glanced at Afia. "Did you know?"

The dark-haired woman smirked. "No one tells me anything."

Rudy inwardly cringed.

"I try not to think about it." Jake stood and pulled out a chair for his wife. "Sit down, baby. I'll get you a glass of . . ." He noted her frown. "Right. You'll sit when you're good and ready."

Smiling now, she moved in, kissed her husband on the mouth, and sat down. "A glass of milk would be great. Thanks."

"Sure." Brow scrunched, the poor man moved toward the fridge.

"You had an affair with Jake's *sister*?" Lulu repeated, still hovering on the threshold.

"A long time ago, princess," Murphy said. "Ancient history."

"Speaking of ancient history," Rudy said, jumping on a chance to change the subject. "Remember last night when I said Hollyberry Inn was haunted?"

Afia shoved her bangs out of her doe-like eyes. "Not that again. Can we eat first? I'm starving."

"I need to shower," Murphy said.

Cheeks burning red, Lulu twirled a damp curl around her finger. "Don't use our bathroom. There was, um, an incident."

He moved to her now, pulled her into his arms, and kissed the top of her head. "I heard."

Afia gawked at the other men. "You told him?"

"About that," Rudy tried again. "More specifically, the hot water heater and the showerhead." He really wanted to come clean on this Casper thing. The ghost's antics were escalating, and he wanted everyone to be aware. God forbid anyone got hurt.

"JP, is that coffee ready yet?" Jake asked after presenting Afia with a glass of milk.

"Ah, *oui*. I will pour you a cup. Murphy?"

"Please."

"Me too," Lulu said, snuggling deeper into her husband's arms.

"No!" Afia narrowed her eyes, frowned. "You don't want coffee, Lulu. Caffeine is bad for . . . it's bad. Jake, get her a glass of juice."

The P.I. shook his head. "Fine. Sure."

Rudy sighed. "About the water heater . . ."

"Oh!" Afia gasped once, twice.

Jake nearly dropped the pitcher of freshly squeezed orange. "What?"

She gasped again and placed her hands over her stomach.

Rudy stood so fast his chair tipped over. "Should I call a doctor?"

"Are you okay?" Lulu asked, pushing out of Murphy's arms.

"I'm fine. Fine. He just kicked. Hard. And then . . . Ooh! There's another." She giggled.

"Jesus," Jake said, plopping into the chair next to her. "Don't scare me like that."

"*Le bébé* is a boy?"

"We don't know, Jean-Pierre. We want it to be a surprise. But, I keep thinking boy. Ooh! Gosh, he's active today."

Jake grinned, leaned down, and kissed her belly.

"Does it hurt when he kicks?" Rudy asked.

"No. Come here." She rolled her eyes. "Don't look so nervous. Come here. You too Jean-Pierre."

Rudy couldn't believe it. She lifted her shirt, right there in the kitchen in front of everyone and exposed her lily white, massively pregnant stomach. His awe skyrocketed when she took both his and JP's hands and placed them on her belly. It felt so warm and . . . hard. Then he felt the kick. "Oh, man."

Jean-Pierre's wonder was evident in his smile and twinkling eyes.

Rudy's heart bloomed as their fingertips connected. The baby kicked again, and they bonded not only with each other, but with Afia and Jake's unborn child. "Wow."

Afia smiled. "Come here, Lulu."

All eyes turned to the petite storyteller, the woman who loved children and whom children adored. A woman unable to have her own baby. Rudy swallowed an emotional lump when she actually moved forward. He and JP linked hands and stepped aside.

"You too, Murphy."

Rudy watched the man exchange a look with Jake.

The P.I. sighed. "Go ahead. But, now we're definitely even."

Afia placed the couple's palms on her tummy and held them secure. "Just wait. Wait. There!"

Tears swam in Lulu's big eyes, but a grin split her face ear to ear. "Gee."

Murphy traced his free hand along her cheek, then smiled down at Afia. "Thanks, hon. It's not every day that you get to experience a miracle first hand."

Afia beamed at the couple, her husband, then JP and Rudy. "Today is going to be a spectacular day."

CHAPTER TWENTY-ONE

Los Angeles, California

Today was going to suck. Every day after today, for the rest of her freaking life was going to suck sand. Sleeping with Joe had been a mistake. They had no future as a couple, yet she would spend eternity, here and beyond, craving the man. *This* is what she got for breaking her no-sex-for-a-year resolution. Although, if she were entirely honest, it wasn't the physical act, but the intimacy, the intensity, that had been her doom. She wasn't emotionally equipped to handle Joseph Bogart. He wasn't like any man, any *person*, she'd ever known.

She heard him thanking someone. His voice alone

triggered a sensual heat that slithered through her entire prone body. The door clicked shut, and though she couldn't hear his footsteps in the plush carpet, she envisioned him carrying a tray of food to the table near the window. She smelled fresh coffee, eggs, and buttered toast. A heavenly smell that transported her back to childhood. Viv wouldn't think of sending her granddaughters off to school without a fortifying breakfast. Sofia's stomach rumbled. She couldn't remember the last time she'd eaten buttered toast. But, even the promise of a bracing cup of java and a hearty meal couldn't lure her to open her eyes.

She lay on the bed, stiff as a board, fists clenched at her sides, feigning sleep. Call her a coward. Call her immature. She didn't want to face Joe. What would she say? *"Thanks for the great lay?"* She sensed he wouldn't appreciate the flip compliment. So, what was left? Sincerity? *"You captured my heart with the most magical experience of my life. I am now and forever a slave to the memory."* A tad over-dramatic. Then again, drama was in her blood.

She could go with a simple, heartfelt, *"I'll never be the same."* But, that would give him too much power. Like, he didn't already have the capability to crush her heart with *goodbye*, but he didn't have to know that.

Denial. Yeah, that was the way to go. Pretending like last night never happened wouldn't fly, so she'd pretend like it didn't matter. She could do that. She was, after all, a trained actress.

Her mind stumbled and skipped back to Joe admitting he'd read *From_Venice with Love*, of his supreme confidence that she'd land the part and, what's more, *nail* the part. Again, how could he be so sure? He'd never seen her perform. He'd never tuned into "Spy Girl", even though it had run every week for several months. The more she thought about it, the greater her annoyance. He was family, for chrissake. Family, at least her family, supported one another. Lulu and Viv never missed an episode of "Spy Girl", and what's more, they'd attended every play she'd ever been in, no matter how minor the part, no matter the quality of the production. Joe could have tuned into her television show at least *once*.

She clenched her fists tighter, fought an audible growl. She did not however, fight the anger. Better anger than depression. Better anger than wistful dreaming. She could not, *would not* love Joe Bogart.

"Do you want to talk about it?"

Startled, her eyes flew open. Dressed in jeans and a white oxford with the tails hanging out, the former fed stood next to the bed, hands on hips, staring down at her with concern and something she couldn't decipher. Her voice stuck in her throat. Her insides twisted when she looked into those soulful eyes and reflected on the way he'd made love to her, as if she were fragile and pure. Amazingly, she'd felt as though she'd been making love for the first time. The morning after and she still felt like an insecure virgin. The bad dreams and the panic attack were a cakewalk compared to this frazzling dilemma. She summoned sarcasm to veil her nervousness. "Watching me sleep, Bogart? That's a little creepy, don't you think?"

"You weren't sleeping. You were thinking. And whatever you were thinking about was upsetting."

"I'm not upset."

"Okay then, agitated." He studied her long and hard. She blushed under his blatant scrutiny.

"Have something you want to get off your chest?"

She realized then that she was massaging her breastbone, trying to soothe a bothersome ache. "Heartburn," she muttered, sidestepping his question. "What time is it?"

"Ten-thirty."

She glanced at the windows. The curtains were drawn, but sunshine streaked through a fractional parting. "Why did you let me sleep so late?" she complained, pushing herself up to her elbows.

"You'd been going strong for almost forty-eight hours, Sofia. You needed the rest. You also need to eat." He gestured toward the table. "I ordered omelets. Coffee. Throw something on. We'll eat and talk about what's bothering you."

"*You're* what's bothering me," she snapped. She didn't want him to be thoughtful and caring. It would only make things harder when he dumped her. He'd been up front. He only aimed on sticking around for as long as she needed him. Once the mystery was solved, once she was out of danger, he'd be on his way. Back to his jeep tour gig, back to his isolated desert home. Well, at least he'd been honest. More than she could say for past lovers. "Stop hovering, Bogart. Just because we slept together doesn't mean that you have to be nice."

He rubbed the back of his neck, narrowed his eyes. "You're starting to piss me off."

"Good. No reason why I should be the only miserable one in this room." Desperate for breathing space, she shooed him aside and slid out of bed in one graceful move. Grace proved a true feat this morning. Ignoring stiff muscles, various aches, and the fact that she was naked, she brushed past Joe and into the bathroom.

She sensed his gaze sliding over her body, felt a delicious tug in her stomach, and a shameless tingling between her legs. She wondered if he suffered similar symptoms. Of course, instead of thinking about sex he could be exercising his psychology chops. *Textbook exhibitionist. Someone desperate for attention.*

She belatedly considered her robe. Although her robe was in the other room . . . with Dr. Bogart. Screw it. She'd never been overly modest. Viv said she took after her mother, a native born Brazilian. Gabriela had always been comfortable with her body, and sexuality in general. Sofia had inherited her liberal views, whereas Lulu wouldn't even wear a bikini. The difference in the two girls had always been a mixed source of amusement and frustration to Viv.

Sofia imagined her grandmother's twinkling eyes and Lulu's infectious smile and experienced a pang of loneliness. Damn. Now, on top of everything else, she was homesick! She blew out a disgusted breath while snagging her toothpaste and brush. "This day sucks."

"It's only going to get worse," Joe said as she started scrubbing her teeth. "As of today, I'm taking off the gloves."

She didn't know what that meant. Just now she didn't care. She was two seconds from crying and she didn't want him witnessing the breakdown. She rinsed and spit. "Will you please go away?"

"You're scared."

"Of course, I'm scared!" She clanged her toothbrush into an empty glass and splashed water on her face. "I was involved in some sort of heinous crime and now I'm being hunted by a couple of lunatics! Any sane person would be rattled."

"I'm not talking about that. I'm talking about you and me. What's happening between us."

She angled her head and found him leaning against the door jamb with his arms folded over his chest. Handsome, confident, and caring. She'd give anything to wake up with this man every morning until she was six feet under. Talk about a pipe dream. *Fight the tears. Fight the heartache.* "Nothing's happening." She swiped the bottle of antacid off the counter and poured four tablets into her hand.

"Those won't help," Joe said with a sympathetic nod. "Trust me."

Those two words snapped what was left of her control. She looked away and tossed the pills in the waste can. "We had sex. Great sex, but that's all it was. It didn't mean anything." She opened the glass door of the shower stall, stepped in. Heart pounding, she shut the door and shut out the world—specifically, Joe Bogart. *This isn't real. This isn't happening.* She turned on the faucet. The spray of water hit her face just as the first tear fell.

The door wrenched open. "Bullshit." The look on his face had her backing flush against the wall. "I warned you last night, Sofia. It's too late to back out now."

As much as she tried to feign conviction, her voice trembled. "Last night was a mistake."

"No, it was inevitable."

She shook her head, choked out another lie. "I don't want this. I don't want you."

"Wrong again." He stepped into the shower fully clothed. The moment he laid hands on her she was lost. He pulled her into his arms and ravaged her mouth with a punishing kiss. Brutally possessive. Terrifying in its intensity. Hot water pummeled their bodies, yet it was Joe's stormy kiss that washed away one failed affair after another, leaving her as untainted and vulnerable as a newborn.

His strong hands framed her face as he eased back and issued a throaty challenge. "Look me in the eyes, Sofia, and tell me you don't want me."

She gripped his shoulders to keep from sliding down the wall. Her bones had dissolved with most of her brain cells. They were crammed into an acrylic shower module, water blasting from the super pressure showerhead. He was soaked, his shirt and jeans plastered to his skin, his testosterone level fierce enough to warp the frosted pane of the door. Hands down, this was the sexiest moment of her life. The need to join with this man, here, now, was excruciating. "What I want," she managed past the lump in her throat, "is a normal relationship."

His gaze slipped to her tingling mouth. "Describe normal."

"A relationship based on mutual respect and adoration. A relationship based on love. Not lust," she clarified as every nerve ending pulsed with maddening desire, "*love*. But what I want, and what I seem destined to have are two different things."

Joe stared down at her with a mixture of anger and pity. "Who the hell brainwashed you into thinking you don't deserve to be loved?"

Her body trembled with the God-awful truth. "Every man I ever cared about, and who claimed to care about me."

He dropped his forehead to hers, cursed under his breath. She felt the tension in his shoulders, in the air.

"I've got news for you, babe. Sometimes lust and love come in one package."

Apprehension stiffened her spine even as hope blossomed in her chest. "I'm not ready to risk it."

"I am."

No mercy. The man showed no mercy whatsoever, blindsiding her with another torrid kiss. She tried to fight the sensations, the primal calling. Damn him, she thought hazily as he plundered her mouth, his lips and tongue pirating the last of her clear thoughts.

One hand molded to the back of her neck, while the other roamed her wet, naked curves. His fingers trailed up her thighs, caressed her slick heat. She clung while he stroked her to climax, groaned when he kissed a hot trail to her breast and suckled.

Breathless and desperate with raw need, she shoved him back and ripped open his shirt. Buttons flew. She nipped and kissed his shoulders, his chest, while deftly working his fly. In a heated blur, she shoved the sodden jeans down his lean hips to his ankles, wrapped her hand around his delicious cock and sighed with the anticipation of making this man plead for mercy. She wanted to pleasure him, to torture him as he'd tortured her, and her mouth was the ultimate weapon.

Her mind glitched when he grasped her forearms and pulled her to her feet. "Not now," he rasped, while spinning her around to face the wall. He grasped both of her wrists with one hand, anchored them high above her head. Her body quaked with anticipation as he smoothed his free palm down her back and paid lingering homage to her ass, before nudging her legs wide.

Sweat beaded on her forehead as the hot water pulsed and steam swirled. Her stomach knotted and her thighs quivered as his skilled fingers worked erotic magic. "Joe, please . . . I . . ." She gasped when the tip of his shaft grazed her pulsing folds, cried out when he slid home. Her heart raced as he drove into her hard and fast, again and again. He pressed his upper body flush against her back, and she trembled beneath his solid strength. Her breath stalled when he kissed the back of her neck, bit her shoulder, and whispered graphic instructions close to her ear.

This was nothing like last night. *This* was hot and dirty. He pounded her mercilessly until she screamed his name and her body quaked with an earth-rocking orgasm.

Sweet Jesus. She couldn't think. She couldn't move. Her eyes glazed over when Joe turned off the faucet and swept her up in his arms. Her pulse thrummed when he carried her into the bedroom and laid her gently on the bed.

"That was lust," he said, reclaiming her body in a position as old as time. "This is love." He smoothed her wet hair from her cheeks and gazed deeply into her eyes as he entered her once more. Only this time he made love— slow, deep, and with a tenderness that brought tears to her eyes.

She'd never felt anything like it. This crazy mix of sensual and sweet. Maybe he's right, she thought as she pulled his head down for a soulful kiss. Maybe this was love.

He knew the moment she gave in, the moment she relinquished her heart. He saw it in her eyes, felt it in her touch. She wrapped her long legs around him, matched his languid rhythm. Her hands floated up and over his shoulders to cup the back of his head, and then she kissed him, a leisurely, impassioned kiss that pushed him over the edge. He'd never felt anything like it. This yearning, this bone-deep affection. She peaked and he followed. One last thrust and he was spent. Sweet Christ. Euphoria followed by contentment. So, this was what had his cynical brother spouting sappy drivel.

His joy was short lived.

A tear slipped through Sofia's lowered lashes and his heart slowed to a grinding halt. Had he been too rough in the shower? The way she'd responded, he'd assumed she was turned on. But, Christ, what if he'd been wrong? What if he'd let passion cloud his judgment.

"Oh, God, Joe. What have we done?"

In an instant, he realized he had indeed allowed his heart to rule his head. He'd forgotten a condom. Well, damn. He thumbed away her tears. "Sofia, I . . ."

"I know. I didn't think about it either. It happened so fast. I should get up and . . . " She bit her lower lip, glanced away. "I should clean up."

He stroked a thumb over her cheek, strived for calm in the face of a potential crisis. "Does this mean you're not on the pill?"

She shook her head. "After Chaz, I vowed off sex for a year. I wanted to prove to myself that I wasn't addicted to sex. I wanted to prove that I didn't need to be in a relationship to be happy."

Stunned, he absorbed and examined the news. How had he ever thought this complicated woman shallow? He couldn't help asking, "How long has it been?"

"Eight months."

"Were you happy?"

At last she met his gaze. "Most of the time."

Knowing that she hadn't been with anyone in months selfishly rocked his world. "I'm trying to feel guilty about making you break your vow, but it's not working."

Her full lips curled into a sad smile. "I really need to get up."

Cursing himself as an insensitive jerk, he rolled off of her and watched as she snatched up her robe and escaped into the bathroom. She closed the door and he swung up into a sitting position. What the hell was wrong with him? He'd screwed up royally, yet he was having a hard time feeling bad. It had been a very long time since he'd felt this *good*. It wasn't just the sex, although, damn, it had been nothing short of amazing. It was the emotional aspect, the connection he felt with Sofia that pegged this as a life-altering moment.

It wasn't the first time he'd told a woman he loved her. He, like Sofia, had been in more than a few relationships, one of them serious. But, he'd never been so obsessed. So consumed. He'd never lost himself so completely in the moment as to forget protection. What if he'd gotten her pregnant? Again, he was having a hard time feeling bad.

Well, hell.

The door opened. Sofia stepped out looking particularly young and vulnerable. The pale blue robe complimented her dark skin. Her purple hair, though not as vivid as yesterday, proved an interesting contrast. Still damp, she'd combed the thick, shoulder-length mass back and behind her ears, exposing that gorgeous face. The face that would haunt his dreams for eternity. His heart slammed against his ribs when she regarded him with a shy smile. "Bathroom's all yours. Can I pour you a cup of coffee?"

He blinked at her calm demeanor. So different from the angry, fiery woman he'd mauled in the shower. He dragged his hand over his wet hair, collected his thoughts, and stood. "We need to talk, hon."

"I know . . . I just . . . could we talk over breakfast? I'm starving."

Hallelujah. Getting food into this perpetually dieting

woman took priority. Their discussion could wait. "Dig in." He squeezed her hand as he walked past. "I'll be right out." He paused before shutting the bathroom door. "And coffee would be great. Thanks. I take it . . ."

"Black. I noticed yesterday."

He was still smiling when he moved to the sink to wash up. The fact that she wasn't cursing him or sobbing uncontrollably was a promising sign. He turned on the faucet and grabbed a washcloth and soap.

So, where did they go from here? He wasn't about to ask her to give up her career, even though he wished she would. He couldn't help feeling the entertainment industry was a destructive environment for someone as sensitive as Sofia. She cared and felt deeply. In turn, her outbursts were melodramatic by most people's standards.

Joe found those flashes of sarcasm and temper challenging. He realized now that simple and peaceful had never been his ideal. Murphy was right. He'd spent the last several months avoiding rather than handling life. He'd been wallowing in self-pity while Sofia had made a self-improving vow and attacked a dream with conviction. It was a sobering realization.

Contemplating the future, he returned to the bedroom and tugged on shorts and dry trousers.

"It's good," Sofia said, around a mouthful of food. "Cold, but good."

"Hard to go wrong with an omelet." He tugged a

T-shirt over his head and moved to sit across from her. "Sorry about the toast. I ordered it dry, but . . ."

"That's okay," she bit into a butter-slathered slice, and smiled. "Fattening, but good."

He sipped his coffee and watched as the woman ate with gusto. Not wanting to spoil her appetite, he picked at his own omelet and enjoyed the view. Having breakfast with Sofia Marino. He could get used to this. "Sofia, about what I did in the shower . . ."

"It was very sexy."

"Yeah?"

Her lips twitched. "I take back the fuddy-duddy crack."

A trace of a grin touched his lips before he sobered. He swiped both hands over his face, steeled himself for part two. "About . . ."

"I don't think I'm . . . I think we're okay." She laid aside her fork, hooked the coffee mug with slender fingers. "My cycle, the timing, I don't think I'm ovulating."

Leave it to Sofia to be blunt.

"I just panicked for a minute. I thought about it when I was in the bathroom, and I think we're okay. Besides, one time." She shrugged. "What are the chances?"

"I know you're not that naïve." He watched as she lifted the mug to her lips, noticed the slight trembling of her hand. Okay, so maybe she wasn't so calm.

She sipped, regarded him over the rim. "I'm not pregnant."

"What if you are?"

"I'm not."

He studied her at length, keyed in on a pattern. "This isn't real. This isn't happening."

Her cheeks flushed. "What?"

"You've said that a couple of times over the past two days. Like a mantra." He leaned forward and laid his right hand over her left. "You can't wish something away, Sofia."

She slowly set down her coffee, her gaze riveted on the hunter green mug. "According to Rudy, affirmations are powerful. See it, be it. I guess, subconsciously, I hoped it would work in reverse. I wanted to spin reality into a bad dream."

"Better to face your demons and conquer them, hon. Otherwise, they'll linger or sneak back when you're least expecting and bite you in the ass. It's something I'm just realizing myself." He smoothed his thumb over her knuckles. "We're heading back to Phoenix today. We're going to face what you've blocked out, together. Later, if it turns out you're pregnant, we'll face that together too."

"Later?" She met his gaze, crinkled her forehead. "You mean you want to continue this," she fluttered a hand, "whatever it is, after we solve the mystery?"

She blinked back tears, and his heart cracked. "I didn't make that clear?"

"Last night when I asked how long you'd be around? You said, *'as long as you need me'*. I just thought . . . " She refocused on the mug, traced a finger around the rim. "It's pretty standard in my world. Actors work together on a project. Weeks go by, sometimes months. It's like living in this bubble. Friendships form, affairs flare. They seem genuine, but then the production ends and, well, people drift."

"You think what's happening between us is a result of being thrown together in a highly stressful situation? Once the adventure's over the thrill is gone? Something like that?"

"I just know that things aren't always what they seem."

Then it clicked. Her reluctance to accept his amorous feelings as gospel, unfortunately, made perfect sense. She knew that he'd weaseled his way into the Falcone family by conning Julietta into believing he loved her. She'd been disgusted by his behavior. The lie. He'd been disgusted too. But, he'd been focused on the greater good. Christ, no wonder she didn't trust him. "As long as we're talking about worlds, maybe this would be a good time to clear the air about Julietta."

Her gaze flew to his. Sympathy swirled in those big brown eyes. Sympathy and kindness. "You aren't responsible for that woman's death, Joe."

"A wise person once said to me, and I quote: *'Logically, I know that. But surely you of all people understand why I feel somewhat responsible'.*"

She flipped her hand over so that their palms connected,

curled her fingers around his hand in silent unity.

Touched, he forced a smile and continued. "That same wise person pointed out, just yesterday as a matter of fact, that I've spent the last few months dodging life."

She blushed. "So, on top of all your other talents, you have total memory recall?"

"Let's just say important things stick." He rolled his head to ease a kink. "Christ, I really don't want to talk about this, but I need you to understand, Sofia. What I did, conning Julietta, I did in the line of duty. I didn't feel good about it, but then again, over the years I've pulled some damned unethical stunts in order to eliminate some sick, dangerous scum. I had every intention . . ." he paused, closed his eyes, and summoned composure. Battling guilt and self-disgust, he refocused on Sofia. "I had every intention of letting her down easy. Once the sting was over, I planned to get her into counseling. She had an insecurity issue that exacerbated her drug and alcohol problem. I wanted to help, but . . ."

"She wouldn't let you."

"When she learned of my betrayal, she took refuge in her great-uncle's home. The Falcone ranks closed in. I couldn't get to her. I told myself maybe it was for the better. A clean break. I figured she'd be pissed at me for awhile and then move on to a new boyfriend. She'd moved on plenty of times before. Meanwhile, I hoped one of her uncles would bully her into laying off the booze and drugs." He frowned. "A few weeks later, she overdosed."

"You've been punishing yourself ever since." Sofia shook her head. "I feel so heartless for chastising you like I did last fall. I didn't know all the facts. Frankly, I didn't care. I was having a hard time . . . Chaz had just . . . well, he lied to me. I still can't believe I fell for his bullshit. What's worse, it wasn't the first time I'd been duped by a man." She rolled her eyes. "I can't believe I'm telling you this. I never confided in anyone, not even Lulu. But since we're clearing the air, I want you to know why I was so hostile."

"You don't owe me . . ."

"Please. Let me get it out. Chaz told me he loved me, promised me the moon personally and professional-ly. Meanwhile, he promised several other actresses on his roster the same thing." She groaned. "I was a blind fool."

"No. You were trusting. You believed the best in someone who claimed to care about you. In that regard, you're very much like your sister. All that optimism," he said, quoting her from last night. "Priceless."

And Chaz Bradley had taken advantage. Joe fisted his free hand in his lap. He'd clocked the bastard once. He should've done worse. "I knew Bradley was a prick the moment I laid eyes on him." He frowned. "Okay. So I can see where you'd compare me to the guy."

"Yes, well there's a big difference between the two of you. I know that now. You actually feel bad about what you did. But quitting your job, Joe, a vital job. Was that really necessary?"

"I quit the Bureau because I didn't like who I'd become, the depths I'd sink to to make a bust. I needed time away, time to reevaluate my life."

"And I interrupted the process."

"No, you kicked the process into high gear." He wasn't one for talking out his problems, wasn't one for laying his emotional cards on the table, but he'd come this far. This woman, who'd been jerked around by a string of men, deserved complete honesty. "Sofia, I understand your reservations, but I assure you my feelings are genuine. Deep down, I was, I _am_ hoping you'll need me for a very long time." He interlaced his fingers with hers, crawled out on a limb. "Like . . . forever."

She tried to pull away, but he held her firm. "Please, don't joke about that," she said in a soft voice. "Out of the several months we've known each other we've spent, what, maybe sixty hours together? Once you get to know me better, you may end up hating me. Maybe you'll grow bored. Crave variety."

Inwardly, he cursed Chaz Bradley and every other bastard who'd treated her poorly. "Not gonna happen."

"How can you be so sure?"

"I just am."

She glanced at the ceiling, shook her head. "How's this going to work? We live in separate states."

At least she was considering the possibility. "Come here." He tugged on her hand, and when she rose, he pulled her down onto his lap. He wrapped his arms around her and pressed her head to his shoulder, soaked in her warmth, her scent. "I don't have all the answers, Sofia. All I can say is, one step at a time."

She traced her fingers over his lips. "I'm sorry I over-reacted before. You're right. I'm scared. About a lot of things."

"I know."

"We need to solve the mystery."

He grasped her hand, kissed her palm. "Yes, we do."

"I can't remember his name, Joe. I can't remember his face."

"I think I can help you with that. Based on what you told me last night, I did some research, and narrowed the field to two strong possibilities." He felt her shiver and strengthened his embrace. "Don't worry, babe. We'll face this together."

"Together," she whispered.

"Having a hard time with that, aren't you?"

"I'm sorry. You don't know how much I want to believe . . . I'm just, I'm not ready."

"It's okay." He kissed her forehead, his body vibrating with optimism. "I'll wait."

CHAPTER TWENTY-TWO

Rainbow Ridge, Vermont

Patience rated low on Rudy's list of admirable qualities. Not always. Just today. When chaos reined supreme at Hollyberry Inn. And though it was pleasant chaos, it ill afforded him even five secluded minutes with Jean-Pierre.

It started with breakfast—a crowded, noisy affair, Rudy's idea of heaven. At first. Even though everyone had offered to pitch in, he and Jean-Pierre had taken charge. They'd worked seamlessly together, creating a smorgasbord of breakfast entrees. Rudy had concentrated on vegetable omelets, using fresh eggs from a nearby farm and Vermont's award-winning cheddar, while Jean-Pierre whipped up a family favorite: *Crêpe Millefeuille* with Apple Compote and Apricot Jam. Since Afia had mentioned waffles, they'd served up a batch of those too, along with pure maple syrup and seasonal fruit.

Twice in the kitchen, he'd come close to saying, *I love you*. The three words he'd never spoken to any man. The three words he longed to say to Jean-Pierre, a no-turning-back declaration. But both times, they'd been interrupted. Even at the dining room table, it had been hard to get a word in edgewise, not that he wanted to declare his love publicly, but he had hoped to address the ghost issue.

No dice.

Talk had revolved around children. Afia and Jake's up-coming birth. Lulu and Murphy's plans to adopt. Afia's work with HIV babies and Lulu's specialized Loonytale, an anti-drug interactive story geared toward grammar students. In between, Jake and Murphy had swapped stories regarding recent cases, lapsing once into sports, which spurred Jean-Pierre to pipe in with his take on the highly publicized Super Bowl "wardrobe malfunction".

Before Rudy knew it, breakfast was over. When the gang had offered to clear the table and clean the dishes, he'd accepted. Yes! Time alone with Jean-Pierre. The sooner he proposed, the sooner they could start making plans. He had his heart set on a small, intimate civil ceremony, but if Jean-Pierre wanted lavish, he'd have it. After all he'd put this man through, he'd deny him nothing.

Wanting to give him the grand tour of their new home as a prelude to his proposal, Rudy had escorted Jean-Pierre room to room explaining that he'd only purchased essential furniture and had left the decorating up to the creative genius. Jean-Pierre, thank goodness, had been duly impressed and touched.

He'd quickly ushered the man to the outer deck overlooking the Worchester Mountains. The sun shone, birds sang, and the pristine, green view was nothing short of magnificent. The perfect moment. But just as Rudy had prepared to drop to one knee, Afia and Lulu had winged open the sliding glass doors to announce they wanted to go into town. Unfortunately, Jean-Pierre expressed interest as well and before he knew it, Rudy had been sweet-talked into driving them into the quaint town of Rainbow Ridge while Murphy and Jake stayed behind to look further into the prowler issue and the faulty water heater. He started to tell them Casper was to blame, but why bother? Either they wouldn't believe him or they'd interrupt him mid sentence. *That's* the kind of day he was having.

"I'm still disappointed that Jake and I never made it out to LA, Jean-Pierre," Afia said from the back seat of Rudy's Subaru. "Not that I'd want to live there myself, but I can imagine it must be very exciting. All those celebrities."

"Sofie told me she was ordering a decaf espresso at Starbucks one day," Lulu said, "and when she looked over her shoulder, who was waiting in line behind her? Me ibson! Can you imagine?"

"I would have gawked," Afia said.

Jean-Pierre fidgeted in the front passenger seat, read-
sted his seatbelt. "Sofia gawked. I was standing beside
er, waiting for my Pumpkin Spice Crème. I think she
en sighed."

Rudy navigated a curve in the road, glanced sideways
his mate. "Did you gawk?"

"Wouldn't you?"

He smiled. "Yeah. I guess I would."

"So, what other celebrities did you run into out there?"
fia asked.

Lulu reached forward and squeezed JP's shoulder.
Tell us some of your favorite stories. You must have some
eat dish. I know Sofie always does."

Knowing JP despised the City of Angels, Rudy tried to
mmandeer the conversation. "Actually, I was hoping to
ll you more about Casper."

"The cat?" Afia asked.

"No, the ghost."

"Casper the Ghost," Lulu said. "I used to watch that
rtoon. He's not exactly what I'd call a celebrity."

Rudy frowned at her via the rearview mirror. "I'm
lking about Casper Montegue, the artist. A local celeb-
y. Dead."

"Don't know him," she said, swiping her wild curls out
her eyes.

"Did you ever shop in Beverly Hills?" Afia asked Jean-Pierre.

"You would be in heaven, *Chou à la crème*." JP reached over and squeezed Rudy's thigh, letting him know he was up to the discussion. In fact, he spent the next fifteen minutes enthusiastically conveying the wonders of Disneyland and Rodeo Drive, appealing to Lulu and Afia's personal interests.

When Lulu asked about Jean-Pierre's screenwriter friend, Rudy cringed. But Jean-Pierre simply answered, "Sadly, he recently passed on," and moved the conversation forward.

Rudy reached over and squeezed his hand, then announced to all that they'd be in town shortly.

After an awkward silence, Afia asked, "Did Sofia ever take you on the set of 'Spy Girl'?"

"Ah, *oui*. Most interesting. I particularly enjoyed the filming of action sequences. Sofia is most skilled in martial arts. Sometimes I think she gleans more satisfaction from the stunts than the acting."

"That's because the scripts aren't so great," Lulu said. "But that's okay. They're bringing on a new head writer. The second season should prove more challenging."

"That's if she decides to do the second season."

Lulu leaned forward, frowned. "What do you mean?"

Jean-Pierre craned his head around. "She did not tell you? She has not yet signed her contract. They want her to sign for three years. I think she is hoping to move on to film much sooner. She is . . . " he shrugged. "Restless."

Lulu snorted. "Maybe that's why she's messing around with Colin's brother. For the thrill. Jeez, they don't even *like* each other."

Jean-Pierre crinkled his brow. "Sofia is seeing Agent Bogart?"

Afia leaned forward too. "You didn't know?"

"She said nothing of this to me."

Lulu patted his shoulder. "Don't feel bad. No one tells us anything either."

Guilt tickled Rudy's conscience, causing him to blurt like an overenthusiastic tour guide. "Here we are, gang! Rainbow Ridge!"

"Swap your Stetson for one of those ball caps we bought back in New York." Frank parallel parked the rental car in front of a two-story brick building with a porch boasting colorful flags and pots of flowers—General Pat's General Store. He rolled down his window and breathed in the smells of brewed coffee and baked goods.

His stomach rumbled.

He was hungry and bone tired, but he'd pushed hard and they'd made it from Pittsburg to Rainbow Ridge in well under Jesse's projected fifteen hours. Thing was, between

the booze, pills, and lack of sleep, he was in no shape to proceed until he got some shut eye. They'd taken a wrong turn
a few miles back and had stumbled upon an abandoned
cabin. The perfect hideaway. But before they settled in,
they needed supplies and directions to Hollyberry Inn.

He tossed his Stetson in the back seat, smoothed his
hand over his thinning hair. His head and nose hurt like
a mother. He glanced over to ask his brother if he had any
aspirin and noticed he'd yet to switch hats. "Listen, Jess. I
know how you feel about your Stet, but we're in the north-
east now and we need to blend." He motioned to the men
and women crowding the cobblestone sidewalks. "You see
anyone wearing a cowboy hat?"

"What I see are a bunch of liberal pansies."

They were all kind of prissy looking. And their politics, he knew from watching the news, differed greatly
from his. "I won't argue with you there, but I will ask you
to mind my direction. If we do this right, we can be on
our way to Mexico in two days, tops."

"Ah, hell." The younger man swiped off his Stetson,
and Frank felt a pang of envy. Unlike him, his brother had
a full head of thick wavy hair. "But goddammit, Frank,
we're flying."

Stiff from the long ride, he wasn't about to argue. Besides, once they exacted revenge on Sofia Marino, a good
portion of his anxiety would be alleviated. With no witness, no evidence, and a cool quarter mil in their pockets

in addition to their nest-egg, he and Jesse would be on Easy Street.

They tugged on their Yankee ball caps at the same time, and grimaced. Frank felt like a traitor, being a Texas Ranger fan and all, but a man's gotta do what a man's gotta do.

Jesse leaned forward and squinted through the front window at a couple walking toward them. Two men dressed in black jeans and bright colored shirts. Trendy haircuts and those rectangular, European-type sunglasses you see in glossy menswear magazines. "Holy shit, are they holding hands?"

"Heard there were a lot of queers in Vermont." Frank glanced back at the general store. "We need to go in there, buy some food, while discreetly inquiring about that Hollyberry Inn."

"The address is in the journal."

"I know. But that doesn't help me much when I don't know the area." He pocketed the car keys and reached for the door. "Don't touch anything around here without your gloves, not that you would."

"Nice that you care, Frank, but AIDS is transmitted through sexual contact with an infected person, transfusions of blood, or by sharing syringes, not by everyday contact."

He rolled his eyes. "Figures you'd know particulars, seeing that disease attacks the immune system, making a body open-season for *germs*, but I was talking about fingerprints. I don't want to leave behind any evidence that we were ever here. No loose threads."

Jesse worked a glove onto his left hand and then wiggled the fingers of his right. "Can't wear a glove on this hand because of the cast. I'll be mindful, don't worry."

Frank frowned at his brother's smart-ass expression. "What the hell are you grinning at?"

"The fact that you knew AIDS attacks the immune system," he said, using a bandanna to open the car door. "I'm impressed."

Frank shoved open his own door. "How could I not know? I'm related to a walking, talking encyclopedia on germs."

Leaving the car, they paused on the sidewalk and took in the sights of Rainbow Ridge.

"Looks like that town on the Andy Griffith Show," Jesse said.

Frank nodded. "Mayberry." Old-fashioned and sugary sweet. "Gives me the creeps." He slid on a pair of oversized aviator sunglasses. Couldn't do much about his swollen, discolored nose, but he could hide his blackened eyes. "Anyone asks," he said to his brother as they scaled the steps of General Pat's General Store, "we were in a car accident."

"Check."

They were in and out in less than ten minutes with a bag of groceries, a box of supplies, and directions to Hollyberry Inn which, according to the short-haired, soft-voiced, unisex-dressed proprietor of the store, wasn't yet open for business.

Jesse elbowed him as they descended the porch steps. "So, was Pat a man or a woman?

Frank grunted. "Damned if I know." He tossed their booty in the back seat, then opened the driver's door.

"Hold up, Frank. Isn't that . . . shit, yeah. Over there, the open air café, sitting at the table far left. It's the fruitcake we saw on that photo strip with Sofia. What's his name?"

"Jean-Pierre." Frank peered over the rim of his sunglasses. "You're right. Damn. That other guy, the one that looks like a young Sylvester Stallone, that's Rudy. The pretty dark-haired lady with the black sunglasses, that's Afia."

"How do you know?"

"Sofia described her friends in the journal. The descriptions are pretty detailed. The peppy woman, the animated one with the blond curls, that's Lulu."

Jesse nodded. "Sofia's sister."

Frank's lips curved into a wicked grin. "Looks like our luck's on the upswing."

Paradise Valley, Arizona

Bernard Cavendish.

The moment Joe had said the name, Sofia flashed on the movie producer's face, his voice. She remembered the house, the address. She recalled in vivid detail every moment right up until the womanizing bastard left her sitting in the screening room, and then she drew a blank. She'd spent the short flight from LA to Phoenix repeating her recollection to Joe over and over, hoping to break through. But every time she tried to think beyond that screening room, her mind shut down.

By the time they'd landed at Sky Harbor International and located Joe's jeep in the long-term parking garage, Sofia had fallen into thoughtful silence. She didn't want to go back to the house, but she knew it was the only way to jar her memory. She needed to confront and deal with whatever had happened in order to move on.

And she very much wanted to move on.

This thing with Joe . . . what the hell *was* this thing with Joe? He hadn't verbally declared love by way of those three specials words, but he had shown her love, and lust, in a manner that had rooted in her soul and twined throughout her body like a glorious vine. Something new and beyond description. It occurred that if he had tossed those words out, maybe she wouldn't be taking him so seriously. She'd heard a hundred lines, including "I love you," from various men at various stages of a relationship. More than once she'd been fooled into believing there was potential for a lifetime union. For all her liberal attitudes, she was old-fashioned when it came to wanting to settle down with one man.

Hence, her avid search for the *right* man.

Unfortunately, her determination to succeed in the entertainment world always steered her toward men in the business. Powerful men who stroked her ego and spoke her language, but who never tapped in beyond the superficial. She'd never truly connected with any of her exes.

She connected with Joe.

He challenged and intrigued her and, amazingly, he took her temperamental personality in stride.

He'd mentioned forever and she'd vibrated with warring emotions. Her cynical self jumped on the notion that he'd only said that because there was a slim chance he'd gotten her pregnant. She didn't know Joe well, but she knew he was a gentleman. His antiquated sensibilities would dictate that he marry the mother of his child. Then again, though conservative, a rebel dwelled within. Maybe marriage wasn't his agenda, but simply living together. The latter, whether she was pregnant or not, wasn't good enough. She wanted more.

She realized suddenly that she'd spent her entire life wanting more. Even her success on "Spy Girl" hadn't sated a hunger that gnawed at her night and day. She felt like she was destined for something bigger. Something more important. That's why she'd jumped at Cavendish's weekend invitation. "*I can give you the recognition you deserve.*" He'd tempted her with legitimacy.

But, as they neared the mansion that represented prestige and wealth, the vacation home of a man who'd dazzled audiences and critics worldwide with several blockbuster films, she faced the frightening possibility that, no matter her level of artistic success, it might never bring her complete joy and contentment. If this were true, then what the hell was she supposed to be doing with her life?

Her cell phone chimed . . . and chimed.

Joe shifted gears as he drove the jeep up the steep private driveway. "Babe. Your cell's ringing."

"I hear it." She reached into the handbag she'd snagged from her apartment last night and thumbed off the phone's power. Recharging her cell had been a mixed blessing. It had allowed her the freedom to leave Lulu a short message on her cell phone, assuring her that she was fine, not to worry. And to retrieve several messages, most of which she chose not to return. Unfortunately, her publicist and agent refused to be ignored.

"Might be important."

She fixated on the decorative wrought iron gates up ahead. "Discovering the truth about that night is important. Friends and family are important. Aside from Viv, the people I care about most are with your brother. If they truly need me, he'll call you."

He peered at her over the rim of his Ray Bans.

Her heart stuttered at the concern in his eyes. "It's

like I'm preparing to go on," she said, trying to make him understand. "I need to focus. No distractions."

"Just remember this isn't a one-woman show. I'll be with you all the way." He reached over and brushed the back of his fingers over her cheek, then shifted the jeep into park. "Security fencing. Wait here."

She readjusted the dark glasses she'd donned as part of her disguise and watched as Joe, who'd changed into an ebony suit and fresh white oxford, walked toward a field-stone post. Today, instead of polar opposites, they looked like a team. Dipping into the suitcase she'd packed from home, she'd dressed in a tailored black suit and a white Dolce and Gabanna cotton crew-neck T-shirt. Her hair was now jet black, compliments of a semi-permanent dye, and slicked back into sleek, low ponytail.

Sharp and sophisticated, they looked like a pair of high-end real estate agents . . . or trendy feds.

A minute later, the electronic gates swung open and Joe hopped back into the jeep.

"How did you do that?"

"Specialized training."

"Like picking locks." She cocked a brow. "They teach that kind of stuff at Quantico?"

He shifted gears and accelerated through the gates, up the paved drive that led to a large parking courtyard. "Let's just say I'm a student of the world I chose."

"More like a master, I'd say. Your hand-to-hand

combat skills are top-notch and I'd venture you were holding back the couple of times we tussled."

He shot her a sidelong glance, his lips curved in a soft smile. "You held your own."

He probably thought she was rambling. But talking about anything other than what they might find in that house, was the only thing keeping her from hurling. The closer they got to the southwestern structure, the tighter her stomach knotted. "You know what I like best about 'Spy Girl'?"

He parked the jeep alongside the garage and chuckled. "The scenes where you get to kick ass?"

Her lips twitched. "How'd you know?"

"There's an energy to your moves, a fierce expression on your face. An intensity that explodes through the television screen and grabs the viewer by the throat. Great execution, by the way."

"Thanks. Although it's not the fighting *per se* that gets me jazzed. It's *what* I'm fighting. Evil. And *who* I'm fighting for. The innocent. I know it's pretend, but it makes me feel like I'm doing something important. Something worthwhile."

"I know the feeling."

Then it hit her. "Wait a minute." She blinked after him as he exited, rounded the jeep, and opened her door. "You've watched 'Spy Girl'?"

He handed her out. "Once or twice."

Her pulse quickened.

"Okay. That's a lie. Every episode."

"But . . ."

"I told you, Sofia. You're in my blood. I also visit your fan sites regularly. I would have told you before, but we weren't on the best of terms and I didn't want you thinking I was some kind of perv."

She stared up at him, heart in throat. "You continually surprise me."

"You fascinate me." He skimmed his lips over hers, then angled his head toward the rambling mansion. "Ready?"

She interlaced her fingers with his. "Let's get this over with."

He escorted her toward the front door, knocked. When no one answered, he whipped out his slim black case of tools. "I'll have to deal with a security system once I get in. Just hang tight until I call you."

She shook off a chill. Crazy. It had to be eighty degrees. "You're sure no one's home?"

"I called his main residence in Carmel. Mrs. Cavendish is on holiday in Paris. Mr. Cavendish, according to his assistant, is spending the weekend here. A quiet getaway. He gave the housekeeping staff a few days off."

Sofia's cheeks heated. "I'm such an idiot."

"Stop saying that." He worked the lock. "When I called here, I got an answering machine. No car in the drive. No answer when I knocked."

The knob turned and he quickly disappeared inside.

Sofia concentrated on detaching emotionally. She turned inward and away from Sofia Chiquita Marino. Affected the mindset of a clear thinking, federal agent. She was certainly dressed for the part.

A few seconds later, Joe returned and ushered her inside. "The security system was already deactivated." He paused in the foyer, scanned the high ceilings and spacious open air rooms. "Nice."

"That's putting it mildly." She swiped a trembling hand over her clammy brow. "Five bedrooms, four bathrooms, jetted tubs, and a private tanning solarium. A billiard room, library, office, and, of course, the screening room."

Joe took off his sunglasses and slid them in his jacket pocket. "Sounds like he gave you the grand tour."

"There's a guest house out back, beyond the pool. I ran past it when . . ." Her voice drifted off as she gravitated toward a painting on the wall. Arms and legs. A nose. An eye. Disjointed images. "Picasso," she said softly. "This painting is by Picasso. I passed it when I came down to find Cavendish. I remember thinking it was an odd work. Then I heard voices. Coming from there." She pointed toward the kitchen. "I thought the other guests, other actors had arrived. Maybe someone I knew. I was curious. I thought I would surprise them and . . ." Her fingertips tingled as she moved toward the Country French kitchen. Her heart raced. "In there."

Joe pulled her back. "Let me look first." He stepped in ahead of her, then called over his shoulder, "All clear."

She entered, only to be slammed by an oppressive wave of chaotic visions. "I stepped around the corner and aimed just as the gun fired and . . ." she glanced down at the orange ceramic tile. The white grouting. "Red seeping into orange and white." She glanced down at her pants and envisioned the skirt she was wearing that night. "Blue splattered with red. Blood. Oh, God, Joe. There was so much blood."

He moved in and touched her arm. "Sofia. Who was in this kitchen?"

"Cavendish and the two cowboys."

"And you shot one of them?"

She shook her head. "No, no. The man wearing the brown cowboy hat, the shorter of the two, he shot Cavendish." She gasped. "In the face. Oh, Jesus. The man with no face was Cavendish!" She lurched for the kitchen sink and vomited.

Joe turned on the cold water, splashed it on her face, and smoothed a damp towel over the back of her neck. "Easy, baby."

She sucked in a deep breath, nudged him aside. "I'm okay. I'm sorry. I . . ." Head throbbing, she pushed off of the counter and whirled. "Where's the blood? Where's the body?"

Joe rammed both of his hands through his hair. "The

cowboys must've cleaned the scene, disposed of the body, unless . . ."

"Unless what?" She caught a glimpse of skepticism in his eyes. "Unless it didn't happen? Why would I make up something like that?"

"I don't know. I'm not saying you did. I just think you're still confused. First you said you aimed and shot, but then you said the cowboy fired at Cavendish."

"He *did*." She massaged her throbbing temples, strove for calm. Why was the evening still such a jumble? "I gasped, or screamed, or something. That's when they saw me. I ran." She pointed toward the den, started walking. "This way. Through here." She wrenched open a sliding glass door and stepped outside, desperate for fresh air. Joe was right behind her.

"I ran across the lawn, toward the back wall."

"Slow down. Take a breath." He grasped her shoulders and pulled her back against his solid body.

She closed her eyes and leaned into him, absorbed his calm as she tried to relive the sequence of events. "Two men. Two guns. They caught up to me just past the pool. I reacted. I just *reacted*. A flurry of kicks and thrusts. I disarmed both of them." *Heel to bone.* "Broke the tall one's nose. Knocked him out. The short one, the killer, he dove for his gun, and I stomped on his hand." *Spike through flesh.* She cringed and turned in Joe's arms. "I drove the heel of my shoe into his hand. I can still hear him screaming."

"Then what?"

"I was afraid he'd crawl to the gun and shoot me in the back, so I grabbed the weapon, and scaled the back wall." *Run, run, run!* "Then I ran."

Joe led her across the lawn. He looked over the wall. "Pretty steep slope."

"I remember falling, sliding. It was dark. When I reached the road below, I crossed over and headed toward that housing development."

"And ended up taking refuge in that shed, where you blacked out."

For the first time since they'd entered the house, tears stung her eyes. "You believe me?"

"Hold on." He scaled the fence, worked his way down the slope toward a patch of prickly pear cactus.

She leaned over the chest-high wall. "What do see? What is it?"

He squatted down, then stood and held up a blue three-inch, spike-heeled pump. He smiled. "Evidence."

CHAPTER TWENTY-THREE

Rainbow Ridge, Vermont

"What do you think, *Chou à la crème?*" Jean-Pierre held up a vintage set of salt and pepper shakers for Afia's inspection. "The vendor says they are handmade. Early 1900s. No chips or scratches."

"Jake would love them." Exhausted, Afia reached back and tightened her drooping ponytail. "He'd love any one of the several items you've already shown me. Honestly, Jean-Pierre. A gift isn't necessary. You were upset last night. Jake understands."

"I tried to tell him," Rudy said, bristling as a crush of shoppers closed in on them. It occurred to Afia that his patience was as tapped as her energy.

"Jean-Pierre! Over here!" They all turned to see Lulu waving at them from four rows over. She held up a ceramic knick-knack. "It's perfect!"

The Frenchman set down the salt and pepper shakers, and Afia and Rudy groaned. After lunch and a bit of shopping, they'd piled back into the car and headed home, only to be waylaid by a flea market. Hordes of tourists and residents packed the outdoor fair on this sunny Sunday afternoon in search of bargain antiques. Normally, Afia would have been in heaven. She loved to shop, whether it be for designer clothes or vintage collectibles, it really didn't matter. She'd even gotten a charge out of purchasing a home pregnancy test for Lulu when everyone else was perusing postcards on the other side of the drugstore. Shopping was shopping. But this afternoon her abdomen sporadically tightened like a fist and she had a low, dull backache. She must be overdoing it. She tugged on Rudy's sleeve. "I really need to sit down."

He looked down at her with concern. "Are you okay?"

She nodded. "Just tired."

He tapped Jean-Pierre on the shoulder. "Afia needs to get off of her feet. Meet us back at the car."

Jean-Pierre studied her, brow crinkled with worry.

She conjured a smile. "I'm fine."

"I will examine whatever Lulu found and make up my mind post haste. We'll join you in ten minutes, no more."

He kissed Afia, and then Rudy, and zipped off through the crowd.

"Seems like you two have worked things out," Afia noted as Rudy ushered her through the masses.

"We're on the mend." He interlaced his fingers with hers, sighed. "I've been trying to get him alone all day. I want to make it legal, Afia. I want to propose, have a civil ceremony, a reception. Cake and champagne, the whole enchilada." He paused. "You're frowning. You don't approve?"

She squeezed his big hand, relishing the contact. It soothed her soul to know that they were as close as ever. "Of course, I approve. I'm just not convinced the timing is right. He just lost a friend. He made light of it, but I could tell he's upset. Plus, he just got here. Let him settle in, get his bearings. Don't force the moment. When the time is right, you'll feel it."

He opened the front passenger door and helped her in. "You're right. I know you're right. I just feel like I've wasted so much time."

"As a very enlightened man once said to me, everything happens for a reason."

He leaned down and brushed a kiss across her forehead. "I love you, Afia."

Her heart raced with joy. "I love you too, Rudy. And so does Jean-Pierre. You're meant to be together. Remember that. And don't worry about rushing things. You have all the time in the world."

Phoenix, Arizona

Joe glanced at his watch as he stepped out of the Phoenix Field Office. He'd spent more time with Creed than he'd planned, but the SAC had been ripe with questions about Cavendish. Joe didn't blame him. The only evidence to support Sofia's story was the dried blood on the heel of her shoe. Hopefully, forensics would be able to match DNA and identify at least one of the movie producer's alleged murderers. Creed had been hot to interview Sofia in person, but Joe had begged off until morning. There were still gaps in her memory. Given a little more time, he was certain he could help her remember what he suspected was a key element. Knowing Joe excelled in the interviewing process, Creed had reluctantly agreed.

Meanwhile, he'd touch base with the LAPD to request a detailed report on Dupris' death, and instigate a proper investigation into a possible Interstate double homicide.

Joe gunned the Jeep down East Indianola, anxious to get back to Sofia. He hadn't been crazy about leaving her alone at the motel, but she'd been shaken and exhausted. He reminded himself that she wasn't defenseless. When threatened, she retaliated. He could almost envision her disarming those cowboys, and couldn't help but smile. "That's my girl."

His cell phone rang. He noted the incoming number. Murphy. He slowed for a stop light and slipped on a headset. "I left a message for you over an hour ago, bro."

"I just got it. Sorry. The reception in this area's iffy. What's up?"

Joe rattled off a succinct version of Sofia's revelation as he navigated a patch of heavy traffic.

"No wonder she blocked it out," Murphy said. "Seeing a man shot in the face? That's rough."

"Yeah." He hated that she'd witnessed an atrocity that would probably haunt her for life. But even as he ached for her, his heart swelled with admiration. A weaker person might have lacked the courage and wherewithal to get out of that situation alive. Sofia didn't just flee, she fought. She had the instincts of a warrior.

"Any further signs that those cowboys are tracking her?"

"No." Joe rolled back tense shoulders. "If it weren't for that bloody shoe and Sofia's conviction, I'd have to wonder if they weren't a figment of her imagination. I know Creed's wondering. We've got an honest to God mystery on our hands, Murph."

"Got one of those here ourselves."

Steering one handed, Joe shifted and accelerated onto the highway while Murphy explained how he and Jake had spent the afternoon inspecting the bed and breakfast property.

"Someone tampered with this place. The wiring. The plumbing. There's a storm door on the back side of the house, a passageway leading down to the basement. No lock. They might be getting in that way. Last night they mangled a gutter while vandalizing the satellite dish."

"They who?"

"I have no idea. But someone's messing with Gallow's head. He thinks Hollyberry Inn's haunted."

Joe grunted. "It has to be someone with a personal grudge. Maybe the neighbors aren't thrilled about having a gay B&B owner in their backyard."

Murphy chuckled. "Most of his neighbors *are* gay."

"Hmm. Okay. Business grudge, maybe? Someone trying to run off the competition?"

"Maybe. The thought did cross my mind. Jake and I are heading over to a tavern down the road to pick up some wine for dinner. We'll ask around. See what we can find out."

"What's Gallow got to say about the rigged wiring?"

"He doesn't know yet. He took Legrand and the women into town to do some shopping. They should be back shortly."

"Does Lulu know anything about the mess her sister's in?"

Murphy cleared his throat. "No. I was holding out until we knew more."

"Creed issued an APB on Cavendish. It's only a matter of time before this case busts wide open and leaks to the press."

"I'll have a talk with Lulu tonight. Bernard Cavendish. Christ. I hope Sofia's prepared."

"A scandal. I know." Exactly what she didn't want. She was in for a rough few weeks. Maybe months. Depending on how this all affected her work. "Listen, Murph, that job you mentioned, is it still open?"

"Absolutely. You want it?"

"Thinking about it. Just so you know, I might be relocating to LA."

"Huh."

Joe raised a brow. "You're smiling, aren't you?"

"Hell, yeah. Welcome back to the living, bro."

"This is crazy." Rudy checked his watch. "It's been twenty minutes. JP said ten minutes, no more."

Afia shifted in her seat, wiped beads of sweat from her pert, little nose. "Maybe the checkout line is long."

"There is no checkout line. You pay the individual vendor."

She shifted again, rubbed her stomach.

Rudy angled his head. "Are you sure you feel okay?"

"I'm fine. Just uncomfortable. You'd be uncomfortable, too, if you had someone inside of you squirming and kicking."

Images from the movie *Alien* flashed through his mind. He shuddered. "I can't imagine."

She rolled her eyes. "Men."

"Speaking of, if I don't get you home soon, Jake's going to call, again. He's already checked in twice." He opened his car door. "I'm going to go find JP and Lulu."

"I'll come with you. Maybe if I stretch . . ." She shoved open her door, winced.

Rudy blanched. "What's wrong?"

"Nothing. Just a cramp. Will you stop? You're as bad as Jake."

"No one's as bad as Jake," he mumbled as he circled the car and helped Afia to her feet. He took it slow and they moved back into to the main hub of activity.

"I don't see them," she said, sounding worried.

Neither did Rudy. Concern twisted his gut when he noticed an excited cluster of people hovering near the table where he'd last seen Jean-Pierre. Someone shouted for a doctor. He put his arm around Afia and practically carried her toward the ruckus. He elbowed his way in, swearing when he saw Jean-Pierre sitting on the ground, pale as a sheet, face covered with sweat. "What happened?"

"Someone broke his arm," the lady behind him said. "I think someone already called for help."

"I did," another man said. "Paramedics are on their way."

Rudy shifted so that he was sitting behind Jean-Pierre and holding him steady, while trying to keep an eye on Afia who also looked as though she were in pain. Although, maybe, hopefully, she was just upset. "Someone broke your arm on purpose?" he asked Jean-Pierre.

The man weakly nodded. "It happened so fast. I decided I wanted the salt and pepper set, so I came back here while Lulu made her purchases. It was so crowded. I did not think anything of it when someone pressed up against me from behind. But then he whispered in my ear, '*This is for my brother.*' He grabbed my arm, twisted. Snap. Crunch. The pain was excruciating. I think I blacked out."

Rudy scanned the surrounding people. "Did anyone see this happen?"

Everyone shook their heads no.

"I'm calling Jake." Afia pulled her cell phone out of her purse. "Where's Lulu?"

Jean-Pierre cradled his arm, licked dry lips. "Four rows over."

Afia whirled. "I don't see her. I don't see her anywhere!"

Rudy was torn between comforting his partner and best friend. "Afia, honey, don't get upset."

"I can't get a signal." Her eyes filled with tears. "I can't . . ." She dropped the phone and wrapped her arms around her stomach. "Oh, God."

She doubled over just as the paramedics pushed

hough. Their gazes bounced from Afia to Jean-Pierre.
Who are we here for?"

"Both of them," Rudy said as he scrambled for his own
ell phone.

Sofia folded her arms across her chest and tucked her
ands beneath her pits so as not to gnaw her fingernails.
Nervous energy had her pacing back and forth across the
mall motel room. At this rate, she'd soon wear a visi-
le path in the dingy brown Berber carpet. She glanced
oward the pressed-wood desk and eyed her phone. She'd
lugged it in to recharge, but she hadn't turned it on. She
idn't have the energy to endure her publicist's media up-
ates or her agent's insistence that she make a decision on
he "Spy Girl" contract.

She was in the middle of a real life crisis.

Bone chilling apprehension had kept her from falling
sleep, even though the visit to Cavendish's house had been
motionally exhausting. After checking them into an in-
onspicuous motel near the airport, Joe had left to handle
usiness. He'd instructed her to lock the door behind him
nd not to leave, or to let anyone in the room under any
ircumstances.

She'd witnessed a crime. She could send those cow-
oys to prison for life. No wonder they'd tracked her to

LA. They wanted to silence her. Permanently. Instead they'd found Luc.

She shook off the guilt. His death was tragic, but it wasn't her fault. Put the blame where it belongs, she told herself. On the cowboys. Focus on the cowboys.

Funny, how she still thought of them in that stereotypical category, but a more vivid description eluded her. Everything had happened so fast, and the tussle in the backyard had taken place in complete darkness except for a smattering of moonlight. She'd never gotten a good hard look at either of the men's faces. Truth told, she wasn't one-hundred percent sure she could identify them in a line-up. What stuck out in her mind was their attire. Blue jeans. Denim jackets. Cowboy hats.

Still, obviously they thought she could ID them or they wouldn't be going to so much trouble to track her down. They had to be wondering why she hadn't gone to the cops with her story. If she had, the Hollywood icon's death would have been all over the news. Again, she wondered about Cavendish's body. She wondered about a lot of things. Like, why no one had reported the man missing. And why those cowboys had been in the house to begin with. It could have been an attempted burglary. The house was loaded with artwork, and probably a safe or strongbox containing jewelry and cash. Cavendish had seemed surprised that someone was on property. Maybe he'd interrupted the pair. But then, why wouldn't they have just tied him up, or otherwise incapacitated him? That way, they could have still burgled the house and gotten away. Why complicate things with murder?

Sofia paused at the window and peeked through the curtain. What was taking Joe so long? What if she'd somehow unwittingly gotten him in trouble with Special Agent Creed? Not that Joe couldn't handle himself, but she hated to think that she'd complicated his life by making him an accessory to a crime. He'd provided Creed with a gun, a bloodied shoe. Was he breaking the law by not turning an eyewitness over to the authorities?

She worried her bottom lip and searched the moderate traffic for his Jeep. An uglier thought occurred. For the past two days his picture had been splashed all over television, compliments of that damned front desk clerk and her own publicist. She and Joe were a hot item. The fantasy cable spy and a real life government agent. What if the cowboys had been following the gossip shows? What if they'd staked out the Phoenix Field Office? What if they'd followed Joe?

She strode to the desk and powered on her cell. She needed to hear his voice. If anything happened to him she'd never forgive herself. But, her phone chimed before she could punch in his number. She checked the incoming number. Lulu. She was tempted to ignore it, but the need to connect to something good just now was overwhelming. "Hi, squirt. How's things in boonie-ville?"

"Looking up," came an unfamiliar male voice. "I've been trying to connect with you for a good hour, Sofia."

"Who is this?"

"You broke my nose."

"I . . ."

"And my brother's hand. We've got some unfinished business."

She detected an accent. Southwestern. Texas. *Cowboy.* Disgust and anger overrode all fear. "You shot Bernard Cavendish in the face and then you tried to shoot me. You broke into my apartment and killed another defenseless man, and you're whining because of a few busted bones?"

"I left you three messages," he said, ignoring her question. "Why didn't you call me back?"

"I haven't listened to my messages." Holy hell, what did he want? She balled her free hand into a fist, tamped down the panic. "How did you get my sister's phone?"

"She threw it at me." He snorted his amusement. "Luckily for us, she's not a trained fighter like you. Although if looks could kill, me and Jesse would be pushing up daisies."

Her blood ran cold. "What are you talking about?" Lulu was in Vermont. He had to be bluffing. How could he possibly know about Rainbow Ridge?

She flashed on the note she'd taped to the fridge for Jean-Pierre. *See you in Vermont.* Her skin prickled with dread.

"That journal of yours, the one you keep hidden in our nightstand? That was some real interesting reading. By the way, we didn't kill gay-boy. The pansy fainted and hit his head. At first, I thought he was your friend, Jean-Pierre. Course, I noticed the difference right off when we finally met up."

"If you hurt Jean-Pierre . . ."

"Oops. Too late." He laughed. "Squealed like a sissy when I snapped his arm."

She pressed fingertips to her throbbing temples. *This is real. This is happening. I will annihilate your ass.*

"I don't know why you haven't gone to the cops, but I appreciate it, sugar. So much so, that I haven't hurt your little sister. Yet."

The obvious threat had an adverse effect. Instead of falling apart, Sofia rallied. This was no longer about her. This was about family. "What do you want?"

"For starters, I want you to hop the next plane to Burlington, Vermont. Bring your phone and call me on your sister's cell when you arrive. Reception sucks up here. If you don't get me, leave a message. I'll call you with further instructions. Oh, and Sofia, come alone. I see hide or hair of your fed boyfriend or any other tagalongs, I'm going to go to work on your sister."

"I want to talk to her, you son of a bitch, or I'm not going anywhere." But she was already checking her purse for the emergency cash and credit card she'd swiped from her apartment.

"Figured."

She heard jostling, then a groggy mumble. "Sofie?"

Her heart pounded. "Lulu? Are you all right? You sound funny."

"Just tired. Can't focus. Bad men. Don't come. Don't . . ."

"Bad advice," said the cowboy, after commandeering the phone.

"What the hell did you give her?"

"Just something to keep her quiet. Time's ticking, Spy Girl." He signed off.

Sofia snatched up her purse and slid her phone inside. Her phone. The link to her sister's kidnappers, Cavendish's murderers. The link, the link.

She had an epiphany just as the door opened and Joe stepped inside. She dropped her purse on the bed behind her, heart and mind racing as they locked gazes.

"What's wrong?"

She dug deep and affected calm. "Nothing."

He angled his head, closed the space between them. "Nice try." He smoothed his hands over her shoulders, down her arms. "You're flushed. You're upset. Talk to me, babe."

Sweet Jesus, how she wanted to confide in him, but if she did, no way would he let her face the cowboys alone. She could hear him now. *Trust me.* In a blinding rush, she

alized she did. She trusted Joe Bogart with her heart.
he trusted him with her sister's life.

But, she didn't trust the cowboys.

"I was just . . . I was worried about you." That, at least,
as true.

He smiled and brushed his lips across her forehead.
Good to know you care."

She more than cared. She eased back and framed his
ce in her hands, her course clear. He was going to be mad
; hell, but she refused to risk his life anymore than Lulu's.
he pressed her lips to his and poured her heart and soul
to a kiss that said *I love you*. A kiss that had him moan-
g and melting against her. A kiss that said *I'm sorry* as she
ilized a pressure point and knocked him unconscious.

CHAPTER TWENTY-FOUR

Rainbow Ridge, Vermont

By the time Jake got to the hospital, Afia was in a operating room.

"What took you so long?" she asked in a soft, rasp voice.

"I'm sorry, honey. Murphy and I were at a neighbo ing bed and breakfast putting the fear of God into Rudy *ghost*. My cell wasn't receiving signal and . . ." He shoo his head, laid a comforting hand to her furrowed brow. " doesn't matter. I'm here now."

Exhausted from labor and groggy from pain med cation, she looked up at him with teary eyes. "Is Jea

Pierre okay?"

"He's fine. He and Rudy are pacing in the waiting room. They'd rather be in here. They send their love."

She quirked a lopsided smile, then frowned. "What about Lulu?"

He didn't flinch. "I'm sure she's fine. Murphy's on it."

She didn't know what to make of that. "They're having a baby."

"No honey, we're having a baby."

She lolled her head to the right. The anaesthetist winked. She looked back at Jake, acknowledged the flash of worry in his beautiful green eyes. "Don't be scared. You can't be scared, because I'm scared. One of us has to be brave. I pick you."

He chuckled at that, a hoarse, nervous sound that warmed her heart.

"I went into pre-term labor. The baby kept pushing to get out, but my cervix wouldn't dilate enough." A tear slid down her temple. "He's turned around and his heart rate dropped."

"Shh. I know. The nurse explained. It's all right, Afia. The baby's breech. The doctor's performing a caesarean section."

She couldn't see anything. Thanks to an epidural, she couldn't feel anything aside from a strange pressure. "Does he look like he knows what he doing?" She heard amused chuckles from south of her waist. "No offense, doctor."

"None taken," she heard him say. "You're doing fine, Mrs. Leeds. Almost there."

Not that she didn't believe him, but . . . "Can you see, Jake?"

He looked over the cloth barrier. "Yes, honey. I can see."

His voice sounded gruff. She imagined what it must look like. The incision, the blood. A baby being pulled from her stomach. "You're not going to faint, are you?"

"No, sweetheart. I'm watching a miracle. I'm good. Everything's good. Right, Doc?"

"Everything's great," he said.

She felt more pressure, tugging, heard commotion, conversation. She closed her eyes and prayed, but something disturbed her mantra.

A baby's cry. A croaky wail that shouted, *hello world!*

The doctor and staff were offering congratulations when Jake turned back to her, tears shimmering in his eyes.

She swallowed hard. "Are those tears of joy?"

"Absolutely."

"Does he have ten toes and ten fingers? Does he look healthy?"

"Looks like a fighter." Jake leaned down and rested his forehead against hers. "And sweetheart, he's a she. We just had a daughter."

She smiled, sighed. "Rainbow. We have to call her Rainbow."

"Uh." He looked shell-shocked. "I thought we decided

on Samantha."

"*Please.*"

"Just because she was born in Rainbow Ridge?"

"No, because Rainbow represents hope. Oh! Maybe we should go with Hope."

He caressed her cheek, his eyes twinkling with relief and affection. "Hope it is."

Her heart soared when the nurse cleared her throat, and Afia caught the first glimpse of her little girl. "I knew this was going to be a spectacular day."

"If anything happens to Afia or the baby, I'll never forgive myself."

Jean-Pierre watched as the man he loved wore a path in the waiting room carpet. "You, of all people, should know better than to toss negative thoughts into the universe, Bunny."

"I'm having an off day. What can I say? First, some crazy person breaks your arm, then Afia goes into premature labor, and Lulu disappears. Then, I learn from Murphy that 'Casper' is really the team of Parker and Lewis, competing B&B owners hoping to 'scare' me into selling Hollyberry Inn cheap!" He snorted. "Haunted, my ass. I can't believe I fell for that ghost crap."

"First of all," Jean-Pierre said, "although it is unfortunate that the baby saw fit to come early, I am optimistic all will be well. Jake is with Afia, and any moment he will plow through those double doors, announcing we are uncles. As for Lulu, Murphy is looking for her. He is most competent and most determined when it comes to *Chaton*. He *will* find her." He glanced over at Rudy. "How am I doing so far with my pep talk?"

Thankfully, the sullen man's lips twitched. "Not bad. What else have you got?"

"That part about Parker and Lewis, that is good news, no?" Jean-Pierre adjusted his sling, and fidgeted to get comfortable on what the hospital dared to call a couch. A bench with cushions was a more apt description. "The disappearing wine bottles. The faulty wiring and plumbing. All the mishaps that were making you crazy will now cease and desist. Jake and Murphy confronted those vandalizing jerks and told them you would press trespassing charges should they ever again set foot on your property."

"Our property," Rudy corrected.

Jean-Pierre smiled. "Murphy is certain there will be no more problems. Hollyberry Inn is not haunted. *We* can finish preparing and open the inn for business within a month."

Rudy shot him a glance. "You mean you still want to live here knowing that we're stuck with a couple of jerks for neighbors?"

"I can live next to a couple of jerks. I cannot live

without you. You are here. Our new home and business is here. I am not going anywhere." To think two days ago, he'd been relying on Valium and an analyst to ease his nerves. All he'd really needed was a heart-to-heart talk with Rudy and to get the hell out of Los Angeles. Since arriving in Rainbow Ridge his nerves had calmed significantly. He realized suddenly that Rudy had stopped pacing and was now staring down at him. "What?"

"I love you, Jean-Pierre."

He blinked. Blinked again.

"Yeah, you heard me right. I should have told you months ago. But, I'm a little slow in the commitment area." Rudy closed the space between them and got down on one knee.

His heart stuttered. "What are you doing?"

"What's it look like? Although, damn, I don't have . . . shit." Rudy stroked a hand down his goatee, sighed. "Wait. Take off your thumb ring and give it to me."

Jean-Pierre glanced around the waiting room. Two other families awaited news about a loved one's birth, and yet the two gay guys were suddenly the center of attention.

"The longer I'm down here on bended knee, the more attention we're going to attract. Give me your freaking ring." He smiled. "Please."

The knuckle to shoulder cast slowed his progress, or maybe it was his shaking hands, but he managed to twist off the ring and hand it to Rudy whose blue eyes twinkled with amused affection.

"Jean-Pierre Legrand, you light up my life. Sometimes you annoy me, and I know I sure as hell annoy you, but the good times outweigh the bad, and quite frankly I'm miserable when you're not around. I love you. I want us to be together forever. I want to make it legal. Will you . . .?"

"*Oui*!"

Rudy eyebrows shot up. "I didn't even finish . . ."

"*Oui*, I will marry you, Bunny." Heart pounding, his leg started to bounce with nervous excitement. "This is the part where you put the ring on my finger."

"But, I didn't even . . ."

"Put the freaking ring on my finger." He smiled. "Please."

Rudy rolled his eyes and slid the ring back on Jean-Pierre's thumb.

The surrounding audience broke into applause just as Jake plowed through the double doors with a wide-as-a-mile smile. "Congratulation, Uncles!"

Beaming, the two men stood and approached Jake. "Boy? Girl?"

"Girl. Her name's Hope."

"That is a beautiful name, *mon ami*."

Jake jammed a hand through his spiky blond hair, chuckled. "At least it's not Rainbow. Rainbow Leeds. Can you imagine?"

"How's Afia?" Rudy asked.

"Thank God, Mamma and baby are doing well. Although, the doctor wants to keep them in the hospital for a few days. Not unusual with a preemie, so they tell me." He wiped away a renegade tear. "You should have seen it, guys. The way they pulled Hope out of Afia's belly. It was . . I was so freaking scared and then . . . there she was. This tiny little baby. My *daughter*."

"I cannot wait to see them," Jean-Pierre said.

"You can stay with us as long as you like, Jake. You know that." Rudy interlaced his fingers with Jean-Pierre's. "Our home is your home."

"Thanks, I . . ." He licked his lips, narrowed his eyes. "What the hell just happened here? Why's everybody smiling at you and why the hell were they applauding?"

Rudy blushed. "I just asked, well, I didn't really ask, he didn't let me finish, but . . ."

"We are getting, how do you say it?" Jean-Pierre smiled. "Hitched."

Jake blinked. "No shit? Well, hell. Congratulations." He processed a second, then threw his arms around both men and hugged them tight. "Wait till Afia hears. You just bumped her spectacular day up to stupendous."

CHAPTER TWENTY-FIVE

Pittsburgh, Pennsylvania

Sofia stared at the digital picture on her cell phone and relived the worst night of her life for the umpteenth time as her plane rolled up to the gate. If she thought about it enough, stared at the graphic evidence enough, she'd desensitize herself to the horror. At least, that was the theory.

To think all this time she'd had the hard evidence to convince Joe, to condemn the cowboys. Her mind had twisted everything around, making her think she'd aimed and shot a gun, when she'd really aimed and shot a picture. She'd aimed and shot at the precise moment the cowboy had shot and killed Cavendish.

She rarely used the camera function, but her cell had been in her jacket pocket when she'd ventured out of the screening room in search of her host. On a whim, she'd plucked it out to snap a picture of that Picasso painting. She had no idea if it was an original, she doubted it, but it had struck her as unusual and she wanted to document the work so that she could research it later.

Then she'd heard voices.

"Are you for real?" she heard Cavendish ask. Then he laughed. *"Forget it."*

She'd assumed he was joshing with a couple of actors. The guests he'd claimed he'd invited. She'd stepped around the corner to snap a candid shot. A memento of the weekend. Something they could all laugh about later.

Only, no one was laughing now.

The flight attendant jerked Sofia out of her thoughts as she instructed passengers not to forget whatever they'd stored in the overhead compartments. Swallowing hard, she snapped shut her phone and unfastened her safety belt. She wondered if the cowboys realized that she'd taken the grisly shot. Doubtful, as they'd noticed her *after* she'd screamed, *after* she'd taken the picture. A split second later she'd fled for her life. Would they really have made the connection in all that chaos?

Then again, the man who'd called her *had* instructed her to bring her cell along to Vermont. Maybe he wanted to make a trade. The phone for Lulu. Or, maybe it was simply because Lulu had her on speed dial and vice versa. Maybe he just wanted to be able to easily reach her with instructions on where to meet.

Regardless, she'd taken precautions. Back in Phoenix, after driving like a maniac to the airport, she'd acted on her epiphany and checked the pictures stored on her phone while waiting to purchase a ticket to Vermont. As soon as she saw what she had, she'd emailed a copy to her home computer as well as Murphy's and Joe's. She'd also left a voice mail on Joe's home phone explaining why she'd knocked him out and acted on her own. At least he'd know the entire story and would be able to pass on the evidence to Special Agent Creed. She probably shouldn't have ended the call with "I love you" but, dammit, it had just come out and she wanted him to know her heart should things go badly in Vermont.

With any luck, she'd rescue Lulu before he even heard the message. Even if he'd recovered consciousness within minutes, she'd delayed him further by securing his wrists and ankles with his tie and her pantyhose. She'd also stolen his Jeep, leaving him without transportation or an immediate clue as to where she was going.

Luckily, she'd been able to score an express flight. Four hours to Pittsburgh, change planes, and two more hours to Burlington. Factoring in time zones, she'd arrive before midnight.

Before she'd boarded she'd tried to call Murphy. He was probably sick with worry wondering where Lulu was. He had no reason to suspect a kidnapping. All the same, she had to keep him from contacting the authorities. She couldn't risk the cowboy following through on his threat to harm Lulu should he spot anyone but Sofia. Unfortunately, she'd gotten Murphy's voice mail, so she'd left a brief, succinct message.

Adrenaline surging, she shoved her tinted glasses higher up her nose as passengers stood and shuffled down the narrow aisle. As soon as she deplaned, she'd try Murphy again. Still dressed in her dark suit, sin-black hair tethered in a low ponytail, she strove to blend with other businessmen as they flowed into the terminal. Her connecting flight was two gates over. She focused on Lulu. Focused on her mission.

She was zoning, channeling Cherry Onatop's special operative persona and skills, when two men flanked her and physically veered her off course.

"Special Agent Earl Creed. FBI," the man to her left said before she could react. "Just keep walking, Ms. Marino."

Stunned, she blinked up at the dark suited man on her right. *Joe.*

He glared down at her. "Not a word. Not one fucking word."

Her heart hammered. She knew he'd be pissed, but this was more than she'd bargained for. He looked eager and ready to wring her neck. It rattled her for all of two minutes, then she remembered the cowboy's warning. "You have to let me go. I have a plane to catch."

"We have a plane waiting for you, Ms. Marino," Creed said calmly, as they escorted her down a stairwell, outside onto the tarmac, and toward a private jet.

She shook her head, dragged her feet. "I can't go back to Arizona. Not now. Not yet."

"We know where you need to go, ma'am. We're speeding things along."

"Murphy got your message," Joe snapped. "He called me. I called Creed." He squeezed her forearm and propelled her toward the jet. "It's called teamwork."

Realizing their intent, she jerked free and backed away. "You can't come with me. Absolutely not."

Creed glanced at Joe. "We're wasting time."

"You'll compromise my mission!" she railed.

Joe lunged forward and threw her over his shoulder so fast that he knocked the wind out her. She was still gasping for air when he boarded the jet and tossed her in a seat. Her heart stuttered when he grasped the armrests, leaned down, and got in her face.

"This isn't fucking "Spy Girl". This is real life, Sofia. The FBI located Cavendish's body. Those cowboys buried the body in the middle of the desert, only the idiots didn't bury him deep enough and the fucking coyotes dug him up. If you thought he looked bad the last time you saw him, you should see Cavendish now." Red-faced, Joe leaned closer, his voice growing louder with every word. "We're talking about a couple of dimwitted, cold-blooded killers, and they've got your sister. <u>My</u> sister-in-law. My *brother's* wife. Yet you saw fit to handle this on your own? Murphy and I are trained to negotiate with kidnappers. We're trained in hostage extractions. What the hell are your qualifications? You're an actress, for Christ's sake!"

Hurt and fury raged in her blood, but she swallowed every sarcastic, nasty reply that welled in her throat, because he was absolutely right. She hadn't been thinking clearly. She'd been thinking with her heart.

And now her heart was breaking. "I fucked up."

Joe continued to stare down at her. "Is that all you've got to say?"

Creed squeezed his shoulder. "Lay off and take a seat. Over there," he added, pointing to a cluster of seats further back. "I need to talk to Ms. Marino." He raised an impatient brow. "Alone."

She breathed easier when Joe backed away, taking all that hostility and judgmental bullshit with him. But then her cheeks burned brighter when she noticed five other men, all of whom had witnessed Joe's tirade. Some looked amused, others embarrassed, but they were all studying her with interest.

Creed leveled them with a frown. "What are you looking at? Sit down. Buckle up. We're taking off."

On cue, the jet roared down a runway and the nose tipped up. Once airborne, Creed regarded Sofia with a sympathetic smile. "Bogart's aggravated because he cares," he said in low voice.

Sofia bristled. "He's pissed because I knocked him out and tied him up."

"He told me about that." He grinned. "I'm impressed. And when that bonehead cools off, he'll be impressed too."

"I doubt it."

"I know Bogie pretty well."

Another chip broke off her heart. "I don't." He'd hurt her deeply by insinuating she didn't know the difference between fantasy and reality. Actress did not equal airhead. But, he'd been right about her not being trained to negotiate with kidnappers. She aimed to rectify that right now. "The men who are holding my sister hostage threatened to hurt her if I didn't show up in Burlington alone."

"I assure you, they'll be under the impression that you're alone."

She blinked at the Special Agent in Charge. "So, you're going to let me go though with this? You think I can hold my own with the cowboys?"

"With your acting skills and fighter instincts? Yes. I do." Creed angled his head. "And so does Bogie. He's just not happy about it."

She refused to look over at the man. Composure was essential just now, and he could easily blow hers away. She was too fragile. *"He's aggravated because he cares."* She understood that. She knew he'd spoken in anger and she believed he cared deeply, maybe even loved her. But it wasn't enough. She'd told him before she wanted a relationship based on mutual respect and adoration. She refused to spend the rest of her life with someone who could make her feel like a failure with one wrong word, one skeptical look. This moment, she wasn't sure if the problem was with him or her.

"Bogie said that you emailed his brother visual evidence of the shooting," Creed said.

Sofia nodded. "I emailed a copy to Joe as well. I snapped a shot with my cell phone just as . . . well, I can show you after we land."

"Let me have it now." He snapped his fingers. "Agent Benson. I need the photos off of this cam phone."

Sofie handed Benson her phone. "How . . .?"

"He's a tech genius," Creed explained as Benson took off with her phone. "He'll be the one wiring you for sound."

"I have to wear a wire?"

"We need to hear what's being said. We'll also fit you with a wireless ear bud so that we can talk you through whatever happens." Creed glanced at Joe, then back to Sofia. "We'll get your sister back alive and well. There's just one catch."

"What is it?"

"You have to listen to what we say and follow through."

He crossed his arms, gave a curt nod. "You have to take direction."

At last she risked Joe's gaze and matched his stern expression. "I can do that."

Burlington, Vermont

Allowing Sofia to deplane and proceed into the airport without him or the obvious protection of an Agent, had been excruciating for Joe. He'd kept his distance while Creed had issued her last minute instructions on procedure. Honoring her need to mentally prepare, he'd let her go without kissing her goodbye, without words of encouragement—no distractions. Meanwhile, his body hummed with dread. He'd been furious that she hadn't confided in him back in Phoenix after she'd first received the threatening call. Instead of trusting him, she'd acted rashly yet again. He'd nurtured his anger for as long as he could because beneath the anger lurked fear. Fear that something would go wrong and she'd end up hurt, or worse.

Now the wheels were in motion and he had to detach and trust in the team's competence. Pushing aside negative thoughts, he dialed his brother. "Hey, Murph."

"You in Burlington?"

"Just landed." Joe pressed the phone close to his ear as he and Creed climbed into a surveillance van provided and manned by Agents from the Albany Field Office. They were joined by Agent Benson. Two Phoenix Agents split off in unmarked cars. The remaining two stayed behind in the terminal to shadow Sofia. "She's been briefed," he told Murphy. "She knows what to do. What she's *supposed* to do."

"Sofia's a smart woman," Murphy said. "She's not going to endanger the safety of her sister. Is she wired? What about a tracking device?"

"Yes and yes."

"Okay then."

Joe marveled at his brother's calm. Then again, Murphy never panicked in a crisis situation. That's what made him so damned good at his job. Only this time it wasn't a client's life at risk, but his wife's. "How you holding up?"

"I'm guessing, about the same as you."

Which meant, on the inside, his brother was a frickin' nervous wreck.

"She's got the cowboy on the line," Benson said, adjusting his headphones and signaling for quiet.

"I heard that," Murphy said to Joe. "Call me back with the info."

"You made excellent time." Frank swiped the back of his hand over his drool covered chin and struggled to focus. Exhausted and experiencing the lingering effects of drugs and alcohol, he'd fallen asleep sitting straight up.

"I want my sister back," Sofia stated plainly. "I'm standing outside the terminal, near a taxi stand. Tell me where to go."

Straight to hell, came to mind, but instead he directed her to a diner midway between the airport and the cabin he and Jesse were holed up in. "No taxi. Rent a car. Once you get to the diner, pull into the middle of the parking lot and wait. I'll call you with further instructions."

"I look different," she said. "Just so you know. I dyed my hair black. I didn't want anyone to recognize me on the flight."

He supposed that was smart, seeing that she was a celebrity and all. "What are you wearing?"

"Black suit. White T-shirt. I'm carrying a black shoulder bag."

He gingerly touched his mangled face, glanced over at Jesse's casted hand. His blood boiled. "What kind of shoes are you wearing?"

"Boots."

"With spiky heels?"

"Um, well, yes. Sort of."

"Once you get to the diner, take them off." He rose from his chair, moved to the threadbare couch, and nudged his brother awake. "When you meet up with us you best be in your stocking feet, Sofia . . ." He paused for dramatic effect. "Or else."

"Put Lulu on. I'm not going anywhere until I know she's okay."

Frank cursed under his breath, schlepped over to the bed, and shook the drugged-up pipsqueak. "It's your sister," he told her while placing the phone near her ear. "Tell her you're okay."

Disorientated, she slurred, "I don't feel so good."

He rolled his eyes, took back the phone. "She's fine," he told Sofia. "Flying high on Percocet. It'll take us thirty minutes to get to that diner. You've got forty-five. Don't be late."

He signed off then, looked at Jesse, who looked like hell. "Once we get to Mexico you can sleep for two days," he told his brother while scooping up their groggy hostage. "Grab the hunting knife we bought at General Pat's and let's go."

Joe traded a look with Creed as the team sprang into action. His muscles loosened as he called his brother. "Lulu's fine. Said she wasn't feeling well, but that's probably due to the Percocet. They drugged her to keep her quiet. Didn't you tell me that she's hypersensitive to medication?"

"Yeah." Murphy blew out a tense breath. "She's going to be sick as a dog. The good news is, she's probably too out of it to be scared."

"I've got more good news." Joe relayed the address of the diner.

"I'm at the local police station with a couple of the boys from Albany," Murphy told him. "We've got a chopper at our disposal. I can be there in fifteen."

"Same here." Joe smiled. "We're dealing with amateurs, Murph."

"Yeah, well. One misstep and you'll be looking at a couple of dead amateurs."

He glanced over his shoulder at Creed. "Understood."

Sofia parked the rental car near the sole security light in the deserted lot of the closed diner. She cut the engine, took off her boots, and shook off a chill. Her sister was at the mercy of the same coldhearted men who'd murdered Cavendish. The same monsters who'd left Luc to bleed to death.

She'd memorized Creed's instructions. She had every intention of following the FBI's directive. But, what if something went wrong? She couldn't imagine life without Lulu. A world without all that sunshine and goodness. Why the hell hadn't she spent more time with her sister over the last few years?

Because she'd been too obsessed with her own life. With trying to land the right man and the plum role. She'd moved to the other side of the country in a last ditch effort to attain stardom before hitting thirty. She'd succeeded by snaring the part of Cherry Onatop. She'd thrown herself into her job, socialized and networked with directors, producers, agents, publicists, screenwriters—you name it. Meanwhile, aside from weekly phone calls, she'd sorely neglected Lulu and Viv. She could've snuck away for sporadic visits to New Jersey. She could've invited them to California, could have taken them to Disneyland, for a tour of Universal Studios. They would have loved that.

She'd sacrificed family for career. A rocky career that was currently on the upswing, but entertainment, no matter the venue, was a risky business. A finicky, unpredictable business. If she hadn't been so hungry to secure another connection, a higher connection within the industry, she wouldn't have accepted Cavendish's invitation in the first place. She knew he was a womanizer, yet she'd ignored her gut. Now, she was paying the price. Or rather, her sister was paying the price.

She blew out a tense breath and scanned the area. Deserted diner. Deserted parking lot. It was well past midnight and she was surrounded by dense woods. *Lone girl faces crazy killers.* She could almost hear a Hitchcockesque score swelling in the background.

Except, she wasn't alone.

Joe, Special Agent Creed, and several other officials were out there somewhere. Snipers were stationed on the roof. She wouldn't be surprised if her brother-in-law was nearby as well. Knowing she was backed by an expert team bolstered her confidence, but even so anxiety simmered just below the surface. To think she'd been ready to step into this situation solo.

She placed her phone on the dashboard table, glanced at her watch. The cowboys would be calling any minute.

Just then Creed spoke in her ear via the tiny receiver. "Relax, Ms. Marino," he said in a reassuring voice. "Remember, this isn't a one-woman show."

She blinked back tears. A message from Joe. *"I'll be with you all the way."* Was it just this morning that he'd made soul-stirring love to her? He'd mentioned forever. She could barely wrap her mind around this moment. One thing was certain. The last forty-eight hours had changed her entire lookout on life.

Her phone chimed. "I'm here," she said calmly. "Where are you?"

"Right behind you," the cowboy said.

She glanced in the rearview mirror, but saw nothing.

"Step out of the car, Sofia. Into the light. Let us see that you're alone."

She sat tight, just as Creed had instructed. "I'm not stepping into the wide open so that you can gun me down.

That's the idea, right? Dispose of the eyewitness?"

"If you want your sister to live, you'll step out and away from the car."

"If you want me to step out of the car, show me my sister."

He cursed foully.

She waited.

"Fine. But one wrong move and I'll slit her throat." He severed the phone connection.

Her stomach churned as she laid her phone on the seat. "He said he'll slit her throat if I make a wrong move," Sofia whispered into the darkness. "He must have a knife instead of a gun."

She waited for Creed to say something reassuring in her ear. Instead, she got Joe. "If he hurts Lulu, he knows he won't get you, Sofia. You're the one he wants. Remember Creed's directive. You can do this, babe." Gone was the man who'd been royally pissed at her two hours before. This was the Joe who made her feel cherished and special. The man who believed her to be capable and clever.

She held tight to that notion when headlights flashed in her rearview mirror. A car crept into the lot, parking several yards away from her own. Every muscle in her body tensed when a tall, lanky man exited the driver's side and rounded the car.

She got a glimpse of his battered face and shuddered. Had she done that? Jesus.

He held up his hands to show her he was unarmed, then redialed her cell.

She answered before it even rang. "I see you. I don't see Lulu."

"She's in the back seat. Look hard."

Joe spoke in her ear. "We see her, Sofia. But the second cowboy's sitting next to her. He's probably the one with the knife. You need to get them, all of them, out in the open. We need a clear shot."

"All I see is a limp woman with gold curls," she said to the grotesque cowboy. "She could be dead for all I know. Bring her out and send her over to this car. When she's three-quarters of the way here, I'll come to you. Her for me."

He laughed. "Do I look stupid?"

She resisted the obvious retort. "I'm no idiot, either," she said into the cell. "If I come over there, you'll kill us both."

"If you *don't* come over here," he growled, "we'll kill your sister."

Her heart pounded. Her upper lip and underarms moistened with nervous sweat.

Joe's voice rang softly, but firmly in her right ear. "Don't cave."

"If you so much as bruise her," she told the cowboy, "I'll drive off like a bat out of hell."

"You're bluffing."

She keyed the ignition.

"Crazy bitch." He opened the back door, grabbed Lulu's hand, and yanked her out of the car and into his arms.

The second cowboy swiftly followed, a vicious knife glinting in his left hand.

Sofia ignored a swift surge of anxiety and the urge to give herself up. In her heart, she knew that once she was within striking distance she could disarm that bastard and take them both down. She'd done it before.

If only her drugged-up sister wasn't in the mix.

She resigned herself to following Creed's directive. Then, the freakiest thing happened. Lulu lurched forward and threw up all over the man with the cast.

He screamed like a stuck pig and backed away in horror, the knife clattering from his limp hand to the pavement. Thwarted by projectile vomit.

"Goddammit, Jesse!" When the lanky cowboy scrambled for the weapon, the snipers took their shots.

Sofia was halfway to their car by the time the wounded men slumped to the ground. She kicked the knife out of their reach and grabbed up her sister before she fainted dead away.

The night exploded with screeching tires, blaring headlights, and dozens of feds.

Lulu wrapped her arms around Sofia and clung. "I knew you'd outsmart them," she said in a soft voice.

Sofia swallowed an emotional lump. "You're the one

who provided the distraction. I can't believe he freaked like that just because you puked on him."

"He has a thing about germs," she said, easing back and pushing her hair out of her glassy eyes. "I heard him whining earlier. What a wimp."

Sofia laughed at that. Being married to a hard-ass like Murphy had given her goody-two-shoes sister an amusing edge.

"Where's Colin," she asked as if reading Sofia's mind.

"Right here, princess." He swiftly moved in and took her into his arms. "Are you hurt?"

"Just sick."

"I saw." Murphy smoothed his hand up and down her back. "That was one weird-ass takedown, honey. Once I get over the coronary I've been suffering for the last several hours, I'm sure I'll see the humor."

Joe moved in, kissed Lulu's temple, and smiled. "Tangling with the Marino sisters. Those idiots never stood a chance."

He glanced at Sofia and her heart jumped up to her throat. She just stood there, frozen.

"Are you okay?" he asked.

She nodded.

"She's a natural," Murphy said with an appreciative wink.

"I won't argue with that," Creed said, stepping into the mix. "Well done, Ms. Marino."

"Teamwork," she said, holding Joe's gaze.

Creed turned to Murphy, gestured toward Lulu. "I have a couple of Agents waiting for you at the chopper. Take her to the hospital. Have her checked out."

"Are you the man in charge?" Lulu asked weakly.

He nodded. "Special Agent Earl Creed."

"I overheard something when they thought I was sleeping." Lulu leaned into Murphy for support, but focused on Creed. "The man they killed? His wife hired them. She caught them trying to rob her house last month and, instead of calling the cops, she hired them to kill her husband. Apparently, he cheated on her. A lot. She didn't want a divorce. She wanted revenge. Oh, and the insurance money."

"I can't believe they talked so freely in front of you," Murphy said.

Joe shook his head. "Amateurs."

Lulu shivered. "Like I said, they thought I was sleeping. They argued a lot. They were creepy." She shifted in Murphy's arms and looked at Sofia. "When we got here, Frank told Jesse he was going to mess up your face worse than you marred his. Said no man would ever want you again. I knew I had to do something. But, I was so nauseous. I'd already thrown up once back at their cabin. When they hauled me out of the car, I remember how disgusted Jesse had been, something about bacteria. So, I stopped trying to hold it in and spewed."

"This is one for the books, I'll tell you that." Creed scraped his hand along his jaw. "Is that it, Mrs. Murphy?"

"Isn't that enough?" Sofia asked.

He smiled. "More than enough. Needless to say, we'll be contacting Mrs. Cavendish." He squeezed Lulu's shoulder. "In the meantime, get some rest. We'll talk again in the morning."

Sofia smoothed the back of her hand over her sweaty brow. "What about me?"

Creed looked over his shoulder at Joe, then turned back to her. "Morning will do." He raised a hand in farewell and disappeared into the fray.

Murphy swept Lulu up into his arms, glanced at his brother. "We'll meet you at the chopper. Don't be long."

Sofia's pulse quickened as Joe tenderly grasped her hand and led her away from the structured chaos.

He paused in the shadows, turned and faced her. "I'm sorry for being so rough on you back on the plane. What can I say? I'm a bastard. I thought about you facing those assholes alone, and I freaked."

She nodded. "I understand. I do. That's what happened to me back in Phoenix after I got their call. Only, I was worried about them hurting you and Lulu."

He smiled at that. "Sweetheart, I can take care of myself."

"I know that. My reaction was . . . rash. I didn't think things through. You were right. The only crisis I'm qualified to handle is one concocted for film."

He winced. "That came out a little harsh."

She shrugged. "It's the truth. And it's okay. You actually helped me reach a decision. I know what I want to do with my life. It involves some major changes, but I think, no, I know I'm up to the challenge."

"Why do I get the feeling I'm not going to like this?"

She wasn't ready to divulge her plan. She needed to talk to Murphy first. "When you call home to retrieve your messages, you'll hear a drawn out explanation as to why I abandoned you in Phoenix."

He raised a brow. "Okay."

She cleared her throat. "Yes, well, I said this thing at the end."

He inched closer. "What thing?"

"It's sappy."

"Let's hear it."

She moved in against him. "Let me preface this by saying, I have issues."

"Don't we all?" He framed her face with his hands. "Spit it out, Marino."

Somehow it had been easier to admit when she'd been speaking into a phone. But then she looked into his eyes, and the words tumbled freely. "I love you, Joe."

He quirked a lopsided grin. "I knew it."

She laughed. "Jesus, you're an arrogant prick."

He winked. "Part of my charm." Then he sobered

and pressed his lips against hers. He melted her bones and confirmed her feelings with a tender, lingering kiss. " love you too, Sofia. It's scary as hell. Disorienting." H stroked his thumb over her cheekbone. "You knocked m on my ass the first time I saw you, and I've been strugglin, to regain my balance ever since. Loving you is the sweetes fucking rush I've ever experienced."

Her throat clogged with emotions. "Wow. I . . . I don' know what to say."

"Say you'll marry me."

Tears pricked at her eyes. "This isn't fair, Joe. Thi isn't the time."

"Whatever those issues are, we'll work through them."

"It could take awhile," she warned.

He grasped her hand and tugged her toward thei family and waiting chopper. "I'm a patient man."

EPILOGUE

Rainbow Ridge, Vermont
Five Months Later

Where the hell is she?

Joe cracked his knuckles. He dragged his hands through his longish hair, adjusted his tie. He sat down on the velvet sofa of Hollyberry Inn's great room. Ten seconds later he stood back up and started to pace.

Outside, on the back lawn, clamored guests of the room and groom. Rudy and Jean-Pierre had opted for an outdoor ceremony, a simple affair featuring gourmet food, live dance band, and tasteful decorations.

Sofia was supposed to be his date. She was twenty

minutes late.

They'd been carrying on a long distance relationship for months. They spoke on the phone almost every day or night. Lengthy discussions about their childhood, their family, their previous careers. They got to know each other very well. Favorite cereal, favorite songs, views on politics and religion. They argued and they laughed. They even had amazing phone sex. But dammit, he hadn't seen her since the day after they'd cleared up the James brothers case. Jesse and Frank were well on their way to murder convictions and life sentences. Mrs. Cavendish would probably receive a lighter sentence, though not by much.

Sofia had surprised and pleased him by announcing that she was retiring from entertainment. Although, considering he was an arrogant prick, she'd informed him she wasn't giving up her theatrical aspirations for him, but because she'd lost her passion, her drive. He could still remember the fire in those sultry, almond eyes when she said she was meant for something bigger.

Unfortunately, she'd elected not to tell him what that bigger something was. All he knew was that she was going back to school. She'd asked him not to press for details and though it was difficult as hell, he'd honored her wishes. As always, she kept him guessing and intrigued.

In the meantime, he'd taken a job with his brother's company, a small company of highly trained professionals who provided executive and personal protection. The handled mostly high profile clients. Politicians, diplomats, celebrities. There was also the occasional hostage extraction and ransom exchange. The danger level ran the gamut. Joe skills were valuable, and as Murphy had been choosing to spend more and more time with his pregnant wife—yeah, boy, that had been a pleasant shock—Joe's workload over the summer had been pretty intense.

He didn't mind. He enjoyed his new job. And as it involved a lot of traveling and supreme concentration, he had less time to miss Sofia. Although, hell, who was he kidding, he missed her every minute of the day.

This weekend he'd flown into Rainbow Ridge for Rudy and Jean-Pierre's civil ceremony. Hence, the monkey suit. Murphy had insisted he wear a frickin' tux. Everyone, he'd said, would be dressed to the nines. Everyone including Jake and Afia, their four-month-old daughter, Hope, Murphy and Lulu—who was six-months along—and the five and seven-year-old siblings they were in the process of adopting. Nona Viv and her husband. Various friends of the happy couple.

And Sofia.

Where the hell is she?

The door swung open and Joe spun around with a big-ass smile. A smile that flattened in a heartbeat. "Oh, it's you."

Murphy knocked back the tails of his tux jacket and slid his hands in his trouser pockets. "That's a hell of a welcome."

"No offense. I was expecting someone a little prettier than you."

"Jean-Pierre?"

"Smartass." Grinning, he moved toward a window and peeked through the curtains. "Speaking of Frenchie, how are he and Rudy holding up?"

"Nervous wreck. Both of them. But, that's mostly because they're worried about everyone having a good time at the reception."

"I don't think they'll have to worry about that." He looked beyond the deck toward the rows of guests and the vine-covered arch. The rolling mountains and cloudless sky provided a stunning backdrop for the festivities. "A lot of people have been waiting a long time to celebrate their union." He turned, brow furrowed. "Speaking of waiting a long time, where the hell's Sofia?"

Murphy smiled. "She'll be along shortly." He cleared his throat. "Listen, I have a question for you. More and more situations are arising where I need a female on the team. How would you feel about working with a woman?"

Joe shrugged. "As long as she's qualified, no problem."

"Oh, the woman I have in mind is more than qualified. Just completed a four-month training course at the Executive Protection Academy. Graduated at the top of her class."

"Great. Bring her on." He glanced at his watch.

Glanced at the door. "Are you sure Sofia's coming? She was supposed to meet me in here twenty-five minutes ago."

"She's running a little behind." Murphy rocked back on his polished heels, looking amused and anxious at the same time. "So, you don't have a problem working with a woman. Great. What about family?"

Joe smirked. "I work with you, don't I?" Then it clicked. "Ah, hell. You're talking about Sofia. When she said she was going to school, I thought, hell, it had to do with martial arts."

Murphy laughed. "Well, that's certainly part of it. So, this isn't going to pose a problem?"

He scraped his hand over his goatee, tried to smother a delirious smile. "Are you fucking kidding? At least I'll get to spend time with her."

"Oh, I think you'll be spending more than enough time with Sofia."

He shook his head. "Never enough time. Christ, I miss her, Murph."

"Yeah, I get that."

"But, personal feelings aside, seriously, I'd welcome her on the team with open arms. She's smart, talented, a kiss-ass fighter, and a master of disguise."

"Knows how to follow directions when person issuing said directions knows more than she does," came a female voice. *Her* voice.

Joe turned, heart hammering like a mother in his

constricted chest. Sofia stood on the threshold wearing a formfitting, white satin dress. A strapless floor-length gown that flowed over her voluptuous curves. White satin and mocha skin, sable hair twisted into an elegant up-do that showcased her long neck and killer cheekbones.

He was toast. "Whoa."

"On that note," Murphy said, "I'll leave you two alone." He glanced over his shoulder on the way out. "Uh, Sofia. Don't take too long. The guests are getting anxious."

Joe waited until he was gone and moved toward the woman of his dreams. "I have to touch you."

She smiled. "Have at it, fuddy-duddy."

He pressed up against her, reveled in her heat and sexy scent. Pulse racing, he slid his hands down her back and cupped that bodacious ass. He smiled when she did the same exact thing to him.

"You let your hair grow, Bogart. Very Renaissance. Very you." Brown eyes twinkling, she stroked her fingertips over his bearded face. "Nice goatee."

He winked. "Chicks dig this thing."

She raised a brow. "Especially this chick. Sexy."

"I was thinking the same thing about you. Sexy and smart. Why didn't you tell me about the Academy, babe?"

She smoothed her hands down his lapel, adjusted his tie. "I wanted to prove to myself that I could stick with it. I didn't want the added pressure of disappointing you or trying to impress you. I just wanted to do it. I'm good, Joe."

He skimmed his lips over her jaw, nipped her ear. "I know."

She laughed softly. "No, I mean at the protection game."

"That's what I meant."

"Liar."

He kissed her, then. Sweetly. Deeply. He savored. When at last he eased away, he gazed into those beautiful eyes and smiled. "Sofia, I have great faith in you. Like Murph said, you're a natural. I look forward to working with you. I won't lie. I might get a little tense if I think you're in danger, but, hey, goes with the territory."

She let out a sigh of relief, dropped her forehead to his. "Okay. Good. Great. So, I wonder if we're still on the same page regarding that other thing you asked me about."

He traced his thumb over those million-dollar cheekbones. "What other thing?"

"The marriage thing."

His racing heart bumped up to his throat. "Are you serious? You're ready?"

She smiled. "More than ready."

He eased away, palmed his forehead. "Shit. Okay. Great. When?"

"I was hoping . . . now."

"Now?"

"We're dressed for it. Murphy took care of the paperwork. Rudy and Jean-Pierre are looking forward to a double ceremony. Oh, and your parents are out there with the other guests."

"My mom and dad are here?" He angled his head, laughed. "You were pretty sure that I'd be up for this, huh, Marino?"

"Thanks to those long phone discussions, I know you pretty well." She held out her hand.

He clasped it and tugged her toward their future. "Sofia?"

"Yeah?"

"You're going to pay for that fuddy-duddy crack."

She interlaced her fingers with his as they walked toward their friends and family and that vine-covered arch. "With pleasure."

Be sure to look for Beth Ciotta's other book from
Medallion Press:

Jinxed
by Beth Ciotta

Chapter One

"Declined."

"Excuse me?" Afia blinked at the quasi-Euro sales associate, a black-rimmed spectacled, chic-suited man who three minutes before had been all smiles and pleasantries.

"Your privileges have been revoked, Ms. St. John."

The woman standing behind her in line snickered. Afia blushed. Exclusive shops such as *Bernard's* treated their patrons like royalty. So why did she suddenly feel like the rabble? "There must be some mistake."

The associate retained a deadpan expression. "Perhaps you'd like to try another card."

Her business manger, Henry Glick (a financial wizard according to her mother), had asked her to make all of her purchases on one specific credit card until further notice. Something to do with interest rates and consolidation. So seven months ago she'd handed over the bulk of her cards to Mr. Glick, except for the American Express that she'd tucked away for emergencies. As her dignity was at stake just now, she considered this a genuine crisis. Fishing her Gucci wallet out of her matching handbag, Afia handed the sales associate her backup card. He slid her platinum plastic through the gizmo next to the cash register, starting the process all over again, leaving her to ponder the mystery of her "declined" Visa. Obviously, the card was defective. As soon as she got home she'd call Mr. Glick and have him order her a replacement.

The clerk glanced up, with one haughty eyebrow raised, and a trace of a smirk playing at his glossed lips.

Afia's stomach clenched. *Stop looking at me like that. I haven't done anything wrong.* Funny how many times she'd wanted to scream that sentiment in her cursed life. But as always she kept her feelings inside.

Calm. Dignified.

The associate sidled over to the phone and placed a call.

Afia tucked silky strands of poker-straight hair behind her diamond-studded ears and willed her pulse steady. *I haven't done anything wrong.*

Casting her a sidelong glance, the associate mumbled a cryptic "uh-huh" and "I see," and then hung up. He returned and passed Afia her American Express. "Declined."

Bernard's four other patrons—plump-lipped, tight-skinned women who looked as though they frequented the same plastic surgeon—conversed in hushed tones. Afia hated being the center of gossip. Mortified, she leaned over the counter and crooked a finger at—she glanced at his nametag—"Douglas. There must be something wrong with your credit card device."

"Our Zon is functioning properly. I'm afraid it's your credit that's in question. Perhaps you'd like to write a check."

"I don't have my checkbook." Mr. Glick oversaw her bank account and paid her bills. She'd been relying on cash and her Visa for months. She'd yet to have a problem. Until now. "Please try again." Panic fluttered in her chest as she re-offered Douglas her Glick-approved Visa. Those strapless, wedge-heeled Chanels sat on the counter waiting to be bagged. The perfect mates to the silk shantung dress she'd just purchased at Saks.

Two minutes later, Douglas re-shelved the wedge-heeled Chanels. On the verge of hyperventilating, Afia fled *Bernard's*. The shoe fiasco had dashed the last of her tremulous composure as she navigated the bustling city sidewalk. She'd survived two high profile weddings and three funerals in seven years. Not to mention the unflattering media surrounding her bizarre personal dramas. Being labeled "The Black Widow" by an unfeeling gossip columnist had been the cruelest blow. Anyone who knew her, knew the insinuation was absurd. Still, her second husband's sudden death had earned her a fair share of suspicious double takes. Her small circle of friends had dwindled to one. She'd managed to cope and found shopping a temporary cure-all for her ever-increasing bouts of depression. But surely, *surely* she hadn't shopped herself into the poorhouse. Each of her husbands had left her a fortune.

Her mind racing with one horrible possibility, she quickened her spike-heeled steps and avoided walking under a workman's ladder only to step on a crack in the pavement. Out of habit she clutched her left wrist and stroked the charm bracelet her dad had given her to counteract ill luck. That's when she felt it. The gap. She quickly fingered the charms, ticking them off in her mind—horseshoe, wishbone, four-leaf clover—stumbling twice in her haste to make it to the car. The third time she went down. Face down on the crowded sidewalks of Fifth Avenue.

Rudy came to her rescue. The muscle-bound chauffeur whisked her up and carried her to his double-parked limousine. "Animal," he said of a snickering passerby and then opened the door and helped her into the back seat.

"I'm all right," she said.

"You're crying," Rudy said. "And you've got a run in your hose."

Afia glanced at her left shin and cried harder. "Darn!"

"I knew this wasn't a good idea. I should've taken

you shopping somewhere cheerful and sunny. Like Miami." Rudy slammed her door, took his place behind the wheel, and revved the engine. "What happened in there?"

"They declined me."

"What?"

"Never mind." *Sniffle*. "I just want to go home." Again, she glanced at her charms. Twelve. She counted only twelve. There were supposed to be thirteen, unlucky thirteen acting as reversed bad luck. She was missing her gold moneybag marked with the dollar sign. The charm that represented "wealth." She could have lost it in any one of several stores. Or on the street. Down a grate, in the gutter. *Gone*, her rational mind whispered. It was the only thing that kept her from going back and searching every square inch of Manhattan. This bracelet had been a gift from her dad, her champion, the good-humored buffer between her and her superstitious mother. Losing a charm was like losing a piece of her hero. It also smacked of a bad omen. Hands trembling, she pushed aside a day's worth of shopping bags and searched her leather satchel for tissues and her cellular.

She punched in her business manager's number while Rudy eased his way into the bumper-to-bumper traffic. "Be home, Mr. Glick. Please be home."

Rrrring. Rrrring. "I'm sorry. The number you have dialed has been disconnected. Please—"

She hung up and speed dialed his cell number.

Rrrring. Rrrring. "I'm sorry. The number you have dialed—"

"Henry, how could you!" She strangled the phone wishing it were Henry Glick's skinny, double-crossing neck, and then dropped the cell in her lap. Mental note: Strike Glick off of my Christmas list! Stroking her wounded bracelet, she glanced out the tinted side window, tears blurring her vision and distorting her view of Manhattan. In her hypersensitive state, the skyscrapers tilted, threatening to crumble and crush her. The relentless traffic melded, threatening to run her over. She missed her Dad. Randy, and Frank. The men in her life who made everything all right. She knew that made her unfashionably dependent. Yet how did one fight one's nature? She'd been trying to cope, struggling to maintain proper grace. Losing that lucky charm, a charm she'd had since she was thirteen years old, had been the final straw. "I can't breathe," she squeaked, suddenly and horribly overwhelmed.

Rudy blared the limo's horn, jerking the wheel left as a taxi veered too close. "Idiot."

Afia sobbed into a handful of tissues.

"Not you, honey. The cabbie." He edged over into the far lane behind an exhaust-belching bus. "What's going on, Afia?"

She blew her nose and then glanced up, meeting Rudy's concerned blue gaze in the rearview mirror. Dear, sweet Rudy. Her chauffeur. Her best friend. Her only link to sanity this past emotionally charged year. "I'm not sure."

"Just remember, honey, everything happens for a reason. No matter how bad it seems, it could always be worse."

Rudy had been spouting new-age assurances for three weeks now. Ever since he'd discovered the self-help section of Amazon.com. She wished he'd stop. The more he tried to lift her spirits, the more she drifted toward despair. Self-help suggested helping one's self. Relying on one's own judgment. Trusting one's instincts. As her mother was fond of pointing out to Afia, following her instincts generally led her to disaster. Sick to her stomach, she picked up the phone and dialed her no-nonsense godfather.

He answered on the third ring. "Hello?"

"Harmon?"

"Afia? I'm in the middle of a golf game, Peanut. What is it?"

"Oh, Harmon." She hiccupped twice before regaining control. "My credit cards. They . . . they . . ."

"What?"

"Mr. Glick. He . . . he . . ."

"What? What did Henry do? Where are you?"

"Manhattan. Oh, Harmon they . . . they . . ."

"They who? They what? Afia stop sobbing and tell me what's going on."

"They were so cute, the strapless Chanels, and I . . . I couldn't buy them. I was . . ." *hiccup, sniffle,* "declined."

Harmon groaned. "Go ahead," he said to someone else. "I'll meet you at the clubhouse. Afia."

"What?"

"Where are you exactly?"

"In the limo."

"With Rudy?"

She nodded.

"Peanut, I have the feeling you're nodding. That doesn't help."

"Rudy's driving," she croaked.

"Put him on."

She leaned forward, handed the phone to Rudy, and then rooted through her bag for more tissues.

"Yes, sir, Mr. Reece." The metro bus stopped short. Rudy jammed on his brakes.

Afia flew forward, landing on the carpeted floor on all fours. "Darn!"

Rudy glanced over his big shoulder. "Are you hurt?"

She climbed back up into her seat and inspected her right knee. "Another run."

He sighed and then focused back on the traffic. Putting the phone back to his ear, he answered, "She's fine." Again he glanced over his shoulder. "Mr. Reece said buckle up."

She nodded and waved him off, contemplating her stockings. Ruined. Much like her life.

"To get home?" Rudy shrugged. "Two to three hours. I'm gridlocked. Yes, sir. As soon as possible."

He passed the phone back to Afia. "Harmon?" She kicked off her three-hundred-dollar Prada pumps and peeled off her pricey sheer to waist hosiery. "Tell me I'm imagining the worst."

"I have to make some calls. Did Rudy stock the mini-fridge?"

She pried open the door with her big toe. "Laurent Perrier `76."

"Drink up, Peanut. Kick back and don't worry. Rudy will have you home in no time. I'll meet you there."

"You're suggesting I tie one on at two in the afternoon, Harmon. That doesn't coincide with *don't worry*."

"Then don't think about it." *Chirp.*

Chirp. She tossed the phone into her bag, cracked open the Laurent Perrier, and proceeded not to think about it.

For three hours and twenty-five minutes.

By the time they reached South Jersey, she was feeling no pain.

Rudy pulled into the circular drive of her second husband's summer home. Odd, Frank had been gone for almost a year, and she still thought of the sprawling three-story stucco as his home. She'd never warmed to the ultra-modern design. In recent months she'd filled the stark, spacious rooms with nineteenth-century art and antique furniture. Anything old to offset the cold contemporary feel.

But for all the clutter the house remained hollow and lonely.

Like her.

She glared through the limo's window at the offending architectural monstrosity, tensing when she saw Harmon waiting on the doorstep.

Rudy opened the car door. Refusing his help, she climbed out with four shopping bags looped over her toned, creamy arms, and, on shaky legs, wove her way to the polo-shirted lawyer's side. "Give it to me straight, Harmie. I can take it." She'd spent the last few hours bolstering herself with vintage champagne and Rudy's guru advice. The more she drank, the more he sounded like the Dalai Lama. Who wouldn't take heart under the Dalai Lama's guidance?

Everything happens for a reason. No matter how bad it seems, it could always be worse. "How much did Glick embezzle?"

Grim-faced, Harmon pulled her into his arms and whispered in her ear.

Rudy was wrong. It couldn't be worse.

"I'll fix this, Peanut."

Afia dropped her bags and clutched her chest, her alcohol-induced bravado obliterated. "I'm *broke*."

"Financially challenged," Harmon countered. "A temporary inconvenience. Wait until your mother hears about this. Henry better pray that it's me who tracks him down."

"Mother's somewhere in Tahiti," she said, half dazed. "On her honeymoon. She left specific instructions not to be disturbed." Weary of widowhood, Giselle had married Bartholomew Tate, a pompous bonbon baron who seemed intent on widening the already canyon-sized gap between mother and daughter. Could Harmon fix that, too?

"She'd want to know."

"She's already put out with me. Absolutely not."

"All right then. You'll stay with Viv and me while

we figure this out."

"Thank you, but no." She turned her back on both men. Stepping onto the manicured lawn, she circled the rose bed in a liquor-fogged daze. "I'm poor." She'd been born into money. Married money. Now she couldn't afford a bubble bath let alone a day at the spa.

"You're staying with me," Harmon insisted.

She was tempted. Harmon would take care of her. Somehow, some way, he'd make everything all right. Rudy's self-help preaching rang in her ears. *The sooner you stop looking to others to fix your problems, the sooner your problems will disappear.* "I couldn't impose," she heard herself saying.

"I'm your godfather."

"I'm in between roommates," Rudy said.

"You need someone to share the rent," Afia said, still circling. "I can't do that. I don't have any money. Or credit." She swept aside her blunt-cut bangs to massage a dull throb at the center of her forehead. "What about my charities?"

Harmon spread his hands wide. "If you're that concerned—"

"Of course, I'm concerned!"

"You could donate your time instead of money," Rudy suggested.

"She already donates her time," Harmon said, clearly annoyed.

Intoxicated as she was, Afia knew what Rudy meant. Serving on a committee was all well and good but there were other ways to help. Still, the thought of not being able to make her usual monetary contributions made her nauseous. Thanks to Henry Glick she was not only unable to provide for others but she was also unable to provide for herself. "How am I going to pay off my shopping debts?" The furniture, the paintings, the *clothes*.

Rudy shrugged. "You could get a job."

Harmon snorted. "That's just crazy."

Afia frowned, rebellion rumbling in her belly. Or maybe it was the champagne. She threw back her shoulders and on second try successfully crossed her arms over her insignificant chest. "Why is that crazy?" She freed one hand and smacked Rudy's impressive pecs. "That's an excellent idea. I'll get a job." Definitely the champagne.

Harmon gawked. "You haven't worked a day i
your life. What would you do?"

Afia nudged Rudy, and together they collected he
designer shopping bags. "I have skills," she informe
her godfather. "Now come inside and help me figur
out what they are. You too, Rudy."

"This could take all night," the older man mum
bled, reaching out to steady her as she staggered towar
the mansion's front door.

She shrugged off Harmon's help along with th
hurt of his lack of faith. Something had snappe
inside of her on the tense ride home. She'd spent he
entire life being sheltered and maneuvered. Being tol
that others knew what was best for her. She'd believe
them, too. Right up until today. When a man she'
trusted implicitly because her mother had told her to
stole her every cent.

Her life was out of control because she had n
control in her life. At least that's what Rudy had sai
midway down the Garden State Parkway. "I'm goin
to track down Henry Glick and get my money back,
she declared as she struggled to punch the securit
code into the keypad. "Starting tomorrow I'm takin

sponsibility for my life."

The door swung open. Miscalculating the foyer
eps, she tripped and tumbled flat out on the polished
alian marble. Heart pounding with determination,
fia pushed herself up on her elbows, blew her bangs
ff of her forehead, and hiccupped. "Tomorrow I'm
etting a job."

ISBN# 0-9743639-4-4

Available Now: $6.99

Jewel Imprint: Ruby

www.bethciotta.com

Also by Beth Ciotta:

Charmed
by Beth Ciotta

The Princess is in danger ...

Beloved storyteller to hundreds of children, Lulu Ro champions non-violence. Just her luck, she's tiara over gla slippers for a man who carries a gun.

Professional bodyguard Colin Murphy is s-e-x-y. To bad he's delusional. Who would want to hurt Prince Charming—a low-profile, goody-two-shoes who perform as a storybook character at children's birthday partie Surely the sexy gifts from a secret admirer are meant f her sister, a bombshell wannabe action-star. Or are they?

Murphy is determined to protect Lulu ... whether sh likes it or not. Perpetually cheerful and absurdly trustin the locally famous kiddy-heroine refuses to believe she in danger.

Tipped off by the FBI, Murphy knows otherwise, bu convincing Lulu that she's the fantasy target of a mobster fixation is like trying to hang shades on the sun. Content ing with a woman who favors bubblegum lip gloss and pink poodle purse becomes an exercise in fascinatic and frustration for the world-weary protection specialis almost as frustrating as resisting her whimsical charm.

ISBN# 1-932815-04-X
Available Now: $6.99
Jewel Imprint: Ruby